'An impressive array of voices conjured up by the author. One is left wondering *which* truly belongs to Ini? Who represents her the most?'

Helen Taylor

'A religious, yet life-affirming mix of seduction, sin and strange adventures. And the character, Iman, is especially flamboyant in a rich, melodic way.'

Sarah Adamu

THINKWELL BOOKS

WHISPERS IN THE WAKE

Ini Ikpe-Etim was born in Kaduna, Nigeria. She graduated in 2000 from Lagos State University (LASU) with a degree in Ancient History and International Relations, worked with autistic children as a teaching assistant and then attended Anglia Ruskin University 2011-14 where she qualified as a theatre practitioner. She is the second child of a banker and teacher (one of six siblings) and the author of one romantic, fictional novel (*Whispers in the Wake*) and one children's book (*I Am Enough To Be Me: A self-belief guide for children*). Her love of short stories and African literature led her to Madingley Hall, Cambridge (Institute of Continuing Education) where she gained a certificate in Creative Writing.

'Dreamy, delightful and daring. There is a simple elegance to *Whispers in the Wake* that I can hardly describe – an ethereal quality, a lightness, which offers both hope and forgiveness. It feels, at times, like you've fallen into a frank, fantastical, yet somehow always *caring* world.'

Jeff Weston

'I'm not sure what impresses me the most – the subtle humour throughout, the bits of history which provide a beautiful lustre to the work, or the multitude of characters who shine and sing. Written in a deceptively simple, colloquial language, the novel grips you without warning, pulls you along and entrances you with darkness and light.'

Vanessa Huxley

'An inspiring, descriptive novel – beautifully written. Refreshing to lose oneself in the characters, especially the protagonist Romilly whose life is shaped by death and abandonment.'

Lilly Hernandez

'Feels like a collection of short stories, but in amongst the disparity and fractures of the novel lies an important message – one which asks "*Who are we really?*" because pain has a habit of killing pretence.'

Susan Thornborrow-Jones

Ini Ikpe-Etim

WHISPERS

IN

THE

WAKE

THINKWELL BOOKS

Edited by Jeff Weston.
Proofread by T Dally & A Lowe.
Interior formatting by Rachel Bostwick.
Published by Thinkwell Books, U.K.
First printing edition 2022.

For my late father Patrick,
for telling me it's okay
to open my mind and follow my path

"People will forget what you said, people will forget what you did, but people will never forget how you made them feel"

- Maya Angelou

Prologue

Abdallah Tukur was in a whore house, drunk, aroused and sandwiched between Togolese twins.

All six legs entwined in a bed that could barely accommodate one person comfortably, but somehow, as if by an unforeseen miraculous resolve, all three occupants snored loudly in what one might call a rustic shack of some kind. If there ever was a heaven, Abdallah thought, this was most definitely it. Life had, after all, thrown him enough bad luck, and if he spent this week's wages on alcohol and prostitutes, then this was him giving life back the silent, but aggressive middle finger.

The devil was always after him.

Abdallah believed everything that didn't work out the way he wanted it to was the unforeseen work of the devil. That devil that lurked in every corner of every turn that Abdallah ever took, waiting for him to slip a little, and then pounce with all his strength at the susceptible and pitiful Hausa man. He was, after all, small in stature and so he couldn't understand why the devil had refused to pick on someone his own size. Surely that would be fair game?

As he contemplated his fate and how affected he was by the devil's antics, Madam Makossa, the owner of the brothel, banged her fists heavily on the door, bringing the already bitter man slowly and swiftly to full consciousness.

"Who be you?" Abdallah screamed silently in response, his speech slurred. He gently moved his head towards the twins, taking a good look at their nakedness as they lay still like vegetables, oblivious to the noise being made by their madam. He felt like his head would explode into tiny little pieces, shattering the empty barrel of wine that sat dispassionately in the corner of the room. Madam Makossa had to do something about her taste in decorating, Abdallah mused amid the disruption.

The voice of Madam Makossa barked back at him: "Abdallah, come quickly, it is your wife." The big, round woman flung open the door without any invitation and walked in, totally ignoring the sight of the people lying unclothed on the mat.

"Fuck my wife, I no come, I dey tired." Abdallah flung his head back in the pillow and pretended to snore.

"You did, and she's in labour."

"I no pay for the twins if I leave na, I never finish," he protested.

"Come now, I look after these two, you don't pay anyway. You still owe me from last week." Her plump hands descended on the twins energetically to wake them up. This must have worked, for they suddenly jerked their eyes open, stumbled and covered their nakedness, frowning and wondering what the commotion was all about; trying their hardest and easily succeeding in ignoring Abdallah's lecherous gaze. The twins looked at him in disgust. He could hardly fuck them properly last night. Perhaps looking was all he was good at.

Abdallah begrudgingly dressed, as the sight of the naked prostitutes stimulated him. Knowing that the madam would not permit him to stay any longer, he drunkenly made his way back home (if one could call that empty and dusty place a home). The only home he knew was saddled between the thighs of the twins after a few sips of Irish whiskey. That dim wife of his always had to find a way of ruining things. Fatima was a nuisance, getting pregnant just like that. If she believed in her wildest dreams that he would give up his drinking and whoring ways just because of a child, and an unwanted one at that, then she was wildly mistaken.

The devil had started again, tormenting him with all of his troubles.

Abdallah Tukur was a once-handsome man whose bodily features had, over the years, depleted to reflect his chosen lifestyle. He appeared to be in his mid-sixties, but he was thirty two years old, jobless, lazy and extremely dull. He had no skills and was regarded by the people of his community as indolent - addicted to a life of drinking and sex. His beautiful wife Fatima, on the other hand, had accepted a life of silence, adapting to ignorance and public humiliation.

For the past five years, Abdallah and Fatima had divided the house bills and chores. Fatima did the cleaning, the working, the farming and the cooking, whilst Abdallah did the spending, the drinking and the whoring.

Abdallah was a vexed man, who delighted in and savoured his own bitterness. He was a failure in every sense of the word and believed that everyone else, along with the devil, was to blame for his misfortunes. Marrying Fatima was the best and only thing he ever did that made his life worthwhile. Due to his wife, he had, however, come to fall in love with his loafing, his bitterness and lack of self-worth. He almost enjoyed playing the victim to his failures and over the years had come to feel like a martyr because of them.

Hell was a very comfortable home.

This chosen way of life had not been his childhood dream. When Abdallah was a boy, he wanted to be a farmer, tending to the cows and the sheep just like his father before him. He always felt lonely in the world as he did not have any siblings. Abdallah had been the apple of his parents' eye until that hideous, religious war raised its ugly head again, just as Abdallah had finished celebrating his twenty-first birthday. This time, the attack had happened in the small mosque by the market place on a Friday afternoon, just when the local Muslims had gone in for their afternoon Salat. Abdallah, although not able to attend the mosque, did not miss his daily ritual.

Taking his plastic kettle with him, his body moved slowly towards the outdoor tap in the fields, and all Abdallah could hear in the quiet afternoon was the sand beneath his feet as he walked. The town was quiet, as it always was every Friday afternoon when the Muslims gathered in the mosque for the Salat al-Jumu'ah. Abdallah had stayed back to tend to the animals - a job he enjoyed immensely. Filling his kettle up, he proceeded to perform the sacred act of Wudu. The word "Bismilahi" escaped from under his breath just as his parents and religion had taught him, careful in his words and actions to do this properly, as the act of Wudu was done to wash away one's sins. The cold water flowed freely from his kettle, washing his hands with a coolness that was welcome in the heat. Three times he counted, then he put the cold water to his lips another three times as he rinsed and gargled the water in his mouth, then his nose, his face, his arms, his head, ears, feet, ankles and toes. Satisfied with the completion of his ablutions, sins washed away from his skin, the prayer that was the custom automatically consumed his spirit.

"Dua-Ash-hadu'an laa'ilaaha'illallaahu wahdahu laa shareeka lah, wa'ashhadu'anna Muhammadan'abduhu was Rasooluh."

"I bear witness that none has the right to be worshipped but Allah alone, Who has no partner; and I bear witness that Muhammad is His slave and His messenger."

The sound of the explosion was completely unexpected - knocking him off his feet, disturbing the water in the kettle, the dust that surrounded him, and the cattle which sat peacefully. In a terrible flash, it was as if the heart of the sun had been uprooted, and all that was left was dust and death. Seconds prior, the voices of children playing and begging the merchants for money had filled the air, the whispers of prostitutes roaming the streets a welcome distraction, and the music from the drums and beats of the ukulele reminded the ears of what God would sound like. Now, all that remained in the city was the smell of blood, the crumbling of walls and the cries and wails of the survivors who would have preferred to be amongst the dead.

The bomb had been planted by Christians, which Abdallah later learned was a vengeful act that occurred due to the Christmas bombing in a church just a couple of months prior.

Abdallah's parents had died instantly, along with over four hundred other Muslims. He had never fully recovered from this incident.

Abdallah had lost all his cattle and become a beggar - an occupation he intended to keep for the rest of his life. That was until he met Fatima five years ago in the village market. She was selling bread and eggs, but she also made the best tea. He knew that if he charmed her, he would never be hungry again.

And so Abdallah had married for food.

And now, how very typical that the source of his livelihood had decided to go and get pregnant.

The fact that he had gotten Fatima pregnant in the first place never occurred to him.

As he stumbled unsteadily into his depressing hut, he felt the bile rise up in his throat, but quickly swallowed as he tried to smile at Doctor Mhona in his bare and dusty living room.

"Docta, how is my madam?" Abdallah asked, trying to keep a straight and pious face but finding it increasingly difficult.

"I'm sorry, Mr. Tukur - we did everything we could. We tried to save her, but she lost way too much blood. She died a few minutes ago. You should have taken her to the hospital." The disappointment in the doctor's eyes did not go unnoticed by Abdallah.

Abdallah stopped smiling as the reality of the doctor's words began to take shape in his mind, albeit very slowly.

"What! Fatima dead? God forbid such bad thing, chaiiii! It's the devil," he hissed, rolling his shoulders and shaking his head vigorously.

"The what?" Dr. Mhona asked.

The midwife, eager to show the new father his baby, hurried towards the two men with the bundle in her arms. "Look, Abdallah, you have a girl. She is verreee pretty. See?"

Abdallah looked at the baby in disgust. How could Fatima manage to annoy him even more in her death?

A girl? What the hell would he do with a girl? Maybe she would die too and then no one would laugh at the fact that he had sired a girl. Who did he kill in his past life? Couldn't Allah at least have beaten the devil this time and given him a boy?

The baby's big grey eyes pierced deep into her father's, and although he felt a bit of emotion towards the infant, he quickly brushed this feeling aside. He had to focus on the best thing to do, and loving this kid would not be part of the plan.

Most of the neighbouring villagers stumbled into the small hut and marvelled at how beautiful she was, and said she looked like Fatima. Of course she was beautiful, Abdallah thought - all Fulanis were. Even though their ancestors had settled in the northern part of Nigeria as poor nomads and goat herders, they were still the aboriginals of the Judaeo Syrian, the first Ethiopians, the black Jews. They were a blessed people, a beautiful people, the true followers of Muhammad, and today he would show the devil who was boss.

First of all, he had to figure out a way to get rid of all the annoying villagers that had gathered at the front of his hut. Some of them had even let themselves in and he hardly recognised them. The only person he knew was Dr. Mhona, because the kind doctor had helped him in the past with all his devil-inflicted ailments; maladies that all happened to be of a sexual nature.

The doctor could stay, but the other strange people had to go. What were they hoping for? Did they think he had palm wine to share? The rudeness of his people was something he could barely put up with.

"What shall we call her?" The midwife's voice suddenly interrupted his thoughts as she glanced at Abdallah with an expectant smile. He looked at her, wondering what the hell she was hanging around his hut for. She needed to take her big fat arse, roundish face and plump fingers off his child and out the door.

Whatever you fucking want.

"I no get time for visitors right now," he exclaimed, changing the topic and waving both hands in the air. "Make una go and come back later. Can you not see that my wife don die?" he screamed in a high-pitched voice, more out of frustration than anything else.

"I need to think, please."

Abdallah had plans for this baby and he was going to execute those plans before life got too expensive. Doctor Mhona was still hovering and the villagers were salivating. Nothing brought troops to a man's hut like a wedding, a birth or a funeral. Allah had today blessed the community with two out of three.

Abdallah was getting impatient with the doctor and the midwife. All he wanted was to be left alone to carry out the plans that had slowly begun to form in his mind; plans that would free him from responsibilities and unwanted fatherhood; plans that would enable him to carry on with his life without any financial difficulties.

"Mr. Tukur." The doctor's voice cut through Abdallah's thoughts, interrupting his plans yet again. "I must insist that the midwife stays behind as you might not be able to look after this baby on your own. Babies need feeding, changing, cuddling. I don't know if you are up to the responsibility at the present time. And of course, you still have the body of your dead wife to deal with. You might want to contact her family."

"Fatima no get family" Abdallah screamed. "I be her only family. Why you dey poke ya nose in my business? You kill Fatima, now please go."

"I did no such thing, Mr. Tukur. Your wife died because you didn't take her to the hospital when you ought to have done. My main concern now is the baby. What are your plans?"

"Hahaha, Docta," Abdallah laughed dryly. "You think say old man like me no fit look after my own pikin?" He swayed, but tried to steady his feet. "You doctas think you know it all abi? Please do not insult me in my own hut. I am com....pee...pee...." Abdallah was blinking his eyes as he tried to figure out the word.

"Competent? Of course you are. The midwife stays, or your daughter will be taken away." Looking at the doctor's stern face, Abdallah was convinced that Dr. Mhona was clearly in no mood for any arguments.

"Okay, Docta, do as you like. Midwife can stay here and look after the pikin." Abdallah took a quick glance at Fatima's covered and still body.

Don't worry Fati, I go bury you soon, then I go deal with the situation. This time, I will beat the devil.

"What plans do you have for your wife's burial?" Dr. Mhona asked as an afterthought just as he was about to leave the gloomy hut.

The doctor was impossible - so many questions, too little time.

"Kai, Docta, abeg no remind me." Abdallah folded his hands, shook his head in grief and bit down hard on his lower lip.

The crazy bitch only had to go and get herself dead. How would he feed himself now? Who would cook his meals? Who would sell fried yams and plantains to the market workers now so he could get his daily income for palm wine and the twins? Wallahi Fatima, if you were not dead, I would kill you myself.

These thoughts followed Abdallah as he ushered the doctor outside, explaining that he needed to think things through. The midwife remained, cuddling and feeding the baby some goat milk.

Abdallah could not bear to hear the noises that the villagers were making as soon as the door opened, so he shut it quickly and retreated back into his hut, locking the door firmly behind him. The problem with his neighbours was that they had no respect for people's privacy. And at that moment all Abdallah wanted was to be left alone. The sound of the new baby was not a joy to his ears. Maybe a baby boy would have made sense, but a girl was just a waste of his time. Girls were only good for household chores and keeping their men happy. Apart from that, they were completely useless.

He longed for the comforting hands of the twins as he tore the baby out of the arms of the midwife and placed her in bed beside her lifeless mother, with the midwife watching him in horror.

"Feed ya pikin, Fatima - feed her. You cannot die. Do I have breast milk? Feed her or else she will join you in the land of the dead you stupid woman."

The midwife shook her head in disgust and picked up the baby again, consoling her.

Abdallah's eyes glanced around his cold, lonely hut. It looked dusty and empty. The stony and grubby floor was bare, but for the scruffy and worn out fake blanket in the middle of the room. Fatima had brought the blanket from her parents' house as they couldn't afford a rug. Abdallah remembered the way the hut looked when they first moved in five years ago. It looked exactly the same now as they never had any money to buy anything. Abdallah's eyes slowly drifted to the green, sunken double sofa in the right corner of the room - the cover material almost ripped to pieces. On the unpainted wall hung a grandfather clock ticking away at nothing. The battery must have surely died a while ago, he thought. On the rocking chair to the left sat the midwife and the new baby who was now asleep. And to the right, on the small double bed, lay the body of his dead wife. Abdallah shook his head in self-pity.

He suddenly had an idea - one that would get rid of the burden once and for all. If plan A did not work, then the only other option would be to sell the child. Allah would help him beat the devil so that plan A would work, at least for the sake of his dead wife. She deserved this.

First of all, he had to figure out a way to calm the villagers, and to charm the midwife, albeit begrudgingly, for he could no longer tolerate the smiling face of that old crone.

"Madam, how is the baby?" Abdallah asked the woman that was carrying his baby on her lap. He tried to smile at her, but failed effortlessly. He couldn't understand why he was struggling so hard to keep his focus. He was tired and he needed more sleep, or maybe some more wine. He wasn't sure which.

"Shhhh, we don't want to wake her up," the midwife replied, not taking her eyes off the baby.

"Please, madam, I need to go buy food and clothes for my pikin. I also need to go plan for the burial of Fatima. Abeg help me stay with my pikin make I go?" he whispered.

The midwife nodded, still not caring to take her eyes off the baby.

That was easier than he'd hoped, Abdallah thought. The difficult task would be to try and get the increasingly large number of villagers out of his front door.

He opened the door and in one swift second shut it behind him to face the villagers. They were all looking at him. He recognised a few of the faces - some of them he had seen in Madam Makossa's brothel. They stood here now with their wives and children as if butter wouldn't melt. All deceitful, good-for-nothing men, just like him. And yet, now they didn't even care that he had just been given a girl by the devil in exchange for his wife.

"My friends, please come back in two days' time. I need to arrange for Fatima's body to go to the mortuary. Please give me two days at least, to arrange everything. I will then get meat and drinks for everybody. My wife don die, but my pikin is alive. So we give thanks to Allah."

Even Abdallah himself was impressed at how he had handled the villagers, for they all agreed with him and returned to their individual homes and activities. Some even whispered that it was the right decision, leaving him to carry on with the day planning ahead. Abdallah smiled to himself; so far he had managed to conquer the midwife and the villagers - things were beginning to move in his direction. Perhaps the devil was beginning to give up on him, and it would be a good day after all.

~~~

The sisters at St. Benedict's convent did not know what to make of the man that stood in front of their door. They knew him as the village tippler. His English was very poor and he smelt of stale cigarette smoke and lingering, cheap alcohol. He also looked as if he needed a shave and long-awaited wash. He seemed unsteady on his feet, but no one could be turned away, no matter what their sins. They needed an interpreter, however.

There was a cleaner who came in frequently to assist them with their chores. She was a local and her English was better than most. Her name was Hadiza - one of the few Catholics in the village. Hadiza attended Mass regularly and worked in the convent diligently. She also stole from the sisters whenever she could, taking no prisoners in her quest for survival.

They hurriedly ushered her in from the kitchen, to help explain to them what the man wanted.
~~~

After a lot of talking and questioning with the man, she finally turned to face them.

"I think we need Reverend Mother here too. That way I can explain to her as well," Hadiza informed the confused-looking sisters.

Reverend Mother Mary Thérése was in her late thirties. She was way too young to have assumed such an important role. She was even younger than some of her colleagues back home in England, but her position was the church's decision and she saw it as the will of God. It was a position that came hand in hand with the missionary work that had brought the nuns to the Jos Plateau.

The reverend sister at the time had done her research on the country to which she was about to be sent. Apparently, Nigeria was very safe - not that it mattered. It boasted of rich, natural resources of oil, but like other Third World oil-rich nations, such money was not evenly distributed. This meant that a few Nigerians enjoyed immense wealth, becoming billionaires, whilst the majority of the population lived in extreme poverty.

The church believed that the country just needed time to mature, and that it would help for the sisters of the church to go and work for the poor, especially in educating the children. This decision was made in the summer of 1983, when the sisters first arrived in Jos. However, they had lived a year now in Nigeria and the revenues from oil had suddenly dropped significantly due to a worldwide over-supply, leading to a critical decline in the economic situation of the country. A coup d'état had also ensued, and the result was the overthrow of the president, Mallam Shehu Shagari, replacing him with a new military head of state, Muhammadu Buhari.

The sisters had been told to go back home to England, so that they would be safe. They were to leave in a week's time and so Reverend Mother Mary Thérése was packing her items. She only hoped that the others were doing the same.

She would miss the children. They all loved to hang around in the convent and the reverend mother had indulged them all the time with sweet treats.

The knock on her door was unexpected.

"Come in," she answered. It was Hadiza, the lady that worked here. She didn't trust her very much, for each time Hadiza cleaned her room, something always seemed to go missing. It started with the little chocolate boxes that she kept by her bedside. One truffle would disappear, and then two; sometimes, a scarf, or even her shoes. She even stole her pink bra and Mother Mary Thérése could not understand it. She had not been completely sure of the culprit who was stealing her things until she saw her silver necklace dangling unsteadily across the lady's neck. Even then, the reverend mother had said nothing. There was really nothing to say, for Mary Thérése did not care much for material things. Part of her religious vow was to renounce all earthly pleasures and wealth.

"I'm sorry to disturb you, Mother, but there is a man outside who wishes to speak with you."

"Me? Who is he?" It was a very small village and everyone knew everyone.

Hadiza wanted to say something like: "It's the rascal Abdallah, the drunken old fool." But she knew such language would not be tolerated by the young reverend mother. So instead, she said: "It's Abdallah. He said he needs your help with his daughter. His wife died this morning giving birth to a baby. He said he can't look after the baby. He needs you and the sisters to take the baby."

Mary Thérése tried very hard to hide the confusion that was welling up inside her from appearing on her face, but Hadiza's smile was proof that she had failed.

"But we can't do that. We are leaving in a week's time and the Nigerian government won't allow us to just simply walk away with a random child. Not to mention the British government."

"I don't know, Mother, but maybe you should come and talk to him? I will interpret. His English is not too good." Mary Thérése still flinched when she was addressed as Mother. It came with the position, mainly out of respect. She was given the title by the bishop before embarking on her trip to Africa. She expected to be used to it by now, but she was wrong.

The reverend mother was thinking that she did not have the time to listen to Abdallah. He was mostly intoxicated, and all the inhabitants of the village were aware of this. However, she did not want to believe that Fatima had died. That wife of Abdallah was too kind, so quiet and hard working. That poor woman ought to have been a nun.

She quietly followed Hadiza down the stairs, wanting so badly to get the forthcoming conversation over and done with.

Standing in the hallway, awaiting the unknown, were all the other nuns - looking up to her and also looking at Abdallah with curiosity.

"It's okay, Hadiza. I can understand Abdallah. You can go back to what you were doing." Mary Thérése had been in Jos for a year now and during that time she had mixed with all the locals, so she understood them perfectly. She was even beginning to learn a little Hausa.

"Yes, Abdallah. I just heard about Fatima. I'm truly sorry."

"Hmmm, what can we do? Allah gives life and Allah takes away."

"How can I help you?" the mother asked, after a lengthy silence.

"The Catholic Church dey do charity? Please help me. I no get any money. I need to bury Fatima and I need to let go of my baby. I no fit look after her."

Mary Thérése knew that if she gave Abdallah the money, he would go straight to the brothel where he spent most of his time.

"Let me see what I can do about Fatima's body. I will arrange for her body to be taken to the mortuary, and I will pay for the burial from the charity funds. But we can't take the baby. We are going back to England."

"What? Why? Please stay, no go, please." His plea looked sincere, even though he was struggling to stand up straight.

"It's not up to me, Abdallah. I wish I could stay. I have so much packing now to do and so little time. Come back tomorrow evening, and we can discuss the baby." And, as an afterthought, without really knowing why, she added: "Bring the baby with you."

A few hours later, when Mary Thérése had arranged for Fatima's funeral, paid the undertakers their fees, and settled in her bedroom for a nice cup of tea, a knock sounded on her door.

"Come in," she said quietly, hoping that the person behind the door would have missed her invitation and therefore retreated. Her wishes were ignored and in walked Hadiza.

"Reverend Mother, I'm so sorry to disturb you." Mary Thérése reminded herself that it was the way Hadiza always started her sentences. She was very polite on the surface, but rude to one's belongings.

"Yes, Hadiza. Is everything okay?"

"Well, I was thinking that I could carry on working for you after you go back to England." The young nun sat up straight, confusion enveloping her mind and face.

"It's about the baby. I can look after the baby and you can pay me until the child is old enough, then you won't have to pay me anymore."

"But the child is not my responsibility." Mary Thérése knew that her kind-heartedness was being taken advantage of, but she did not know how to turn people away.

"The child might die. I want to look after the child, but as you know, I have no income. I can't do it on my own. And Abdallah will not do it."

"I'm sorry, Hadiza. But like I said, the child is not my responsibility. Please, you can leave now, if you don't mind."

That night the young nun could not sleep. She tossed and turned in bed, begging the good Lord to show her what to do. She didn't trust Abdallah, but she didn't trust Hadiza either. If she was to keep the child, then she would have to adopt her, not legally of course.

The following evening, when Abdallah turned up at her doorstep, she took one look at the baby, reached out and held her in her arms. She knew instantly that nothing else mattered apart from keeping this vulnerable soul alive.

Abdallah, sensing the weakness in the young nun, jumped at his opportunity. "You can keep the pikin. I no fit keep her, but if you keep her, you go pay me something?" He began to laugh to ease the ridiculous request presented to the reverend mother.

"As long as you walk away and let me raise her in England, without any further interference. Not as a Muslim, but as a Catholic." (The nun's eyes never leaving the infant, as she cradled her.)

As far as Mary Thérése was concerned, Hadiza was not an option. There were no child protection rules in Jos at that time, and the government did not care what happened to children like this one; after all, Mary Thérése had seen so many children beg on the streets. If she could save this one, then she could live in peace.

She gave Abdallah some money and he disappeared without looking back, thinking to himself how cleverly he had managed to defeat the devil this time, touching his pocket full of notes and smiling to himself as he walked away into oblivion.

The young nun gave the girl her own birth surname.

In a hurried, Catholic Church baptism before the nuns left for England, the little girl was baptised as Iman Evangeline Williamson. Iman was a Hausa name which, when translated into English, meant faith and belief. This was mainly because the nun did not want the infant to ever forget her roots.

She stayed back in Jos for another three months attempting to process the documents needed for the child. The documents could not be processed, however, and she was summoned back to England. She had no choice but to leave the child with Hadiza against her better judgement.

This child surely would need all the faith in the world, thought the kind reverend. And even in that thought lay the greatest understatement.

Chapter 1

Ciara

The truth of the matter is I can have any man that I want.

I am bold, confident and sassy. I could have any man *or* woman for that matter, whenever it took my fancy. I have always been this way and I do not apologise for it. Every single man is ready for me as soon as I walk into a room. I see it in their eyes as swiftly as I smell it in the air. They crave my attention, my lips, my eyes, my hips, my bum, my body. It all begins with a smile and I can draw them all in. It doesn't matter if they are committed to someone or not. They forget who they are with as soon as I clap my eyes on them and show them a tiny bit of attention. They could be married, single, widowed, divorced, gay, straight, old, young, desperate, rich, horny or sexed.

They all belonged to me.

It didn't always happen like magic. I knew what they wanted - that is the trick. When you know what someone wants in any given situation, and you know exactly how to deliver, then the world can be yours. Knowing is one thing, delivering.....now....that is the magic.

I always knew how to draw them in and excite them. I was the queen of the art of seduction – a wild vixen one moment and a docile puppy the next. They could never have enough of me, and they got addicted to the feeling of the mixed emotions I induced in them. No man wanted a good girl. Life was boring already. Every man wanted me.

My father was a newspaper salesman with the face and body of an overweight drunk. He fucked everything in a skirt, including my mother of course. He tried it on with my equally big, fat, older sister Gloria and I swear she let him. When he decided to try it on with me, I knocked him unconscious with his own gin bottle. Alcohol was cheap in Rome; he could always buy another. As a child I watched as my father brought different kinds of women to our family home when my mother was out selling takeaway pizzas at her stall. He would fuck them all rather loudly as well. And they enjoyed it. He gave them coins from my mother's cookie jar.

"Buy yourself some dinner and I'll see you next week," was what he said to every one of them, and see them the following week he did.

My mother was a short, rounded, handsome woman from Milan. She was definitely Gloria's mother as I couldn't tell the difference between them. However, I often wondered if I was adopted, for I did not look like any of them. Not my father, not my mother and definitely not my sister. When my mother did not smell of pizzas, she was accusing my dad of stealing her money. There was never a moment of peace in our home, but there was also never a moment of boredom.

We lived in an apartment in Esquilino, one of the most dangerous places in Rome, and the poorest. Gloria and I were partly home-schooled by a nanny that was somehow related to my mum. The nanny got paid in pizzas. She got fucked by my father too. In fact, my father said she was grateful for it.

"The old cow probably never saw a dick in her life before I came along. I am rendering her a service."

My parents didn't have much time for us and so we were left to make decisions for ourselves. Gloria met Pedro when she was sixteen, got knocked up by him as soon as she turned eighteen and escaped into marital life. He worked as an apprentice chef at Vatican City. As far as Gloria was concerned, he was a goldmine and getting knocked up was her ingenious plan. Away from Hell. Away from poverty. And away from my family. She had three children in quick succession. Perhaps she was scared that she would lose Pedro if she didn't have kids speedily. I couldn't blame her; my parents were not exactly what one would like to come home to.

I was determined to have a different life. I didn't need anyone to tell me that I wasn't like the rest of my family. I knew how beautiful I was. If I didn't know it, then people took the liberty to alert me all the time.

"Hello, beautiful - can I buy you a drink?" was a sentence I was accustomed to.

When Gloria left, I was truly alone. Instead of occupying my mind with hobbies or helping my mum with her pizzas, I figured that joining the neighbourhood girl gang would be far more interesting, so that was what I did. That was where I learnt how to use my beauty to its full potential.

I mastered manipulating any man to get what I wanted. I truly was, I suppose, my father's daughter. He was happy to have me out of the house, and that way, at least I didn't have to listen to his sexual escapades any longer. To tell you the truth, I was grateful. I went out and got back home when I pleased. My parents were too tired to ask any questions. After all, I was no longer a child; I was seventeen and growing very fast with each passing day.

My father noticed that I was dressing quite expensively. I was making money from numerous, rich boyfriends and he wanted his share.

"Pagaci o parti," he screamed at me one day. I didn't think twice. I had three young men that I was juggling. I chose the richest one and moved in with him. He was only too happy to have me. I'd rather live with Antonio than pay my useless father a dime.

The good thing about Antonio was that he didn't care that I was seeing other men. However, he did expect me to cook for him, clean his apartment, and fuck him whenever his dick got hard. In return, I got a free boarding pass. As far as I was concerned, it was a win-win situation.

We'd been together for three years and I thought I loved him. In fact, I was willing to give up my wandering ways for him. Who are we kidding? I *did* give up all the other guys for him. The mistake I made was in thinking that he had given up every other woman for me as well. He told me he loved me and I believed him. I told him I loved him too. I think I almost believed my own deception. Until of course, that fateful day, when he told me he was getting married, and needed me out as soon as possible.

I moved in with Gloria.

"I promise it will only be a few weeks. I have nowhere else to go."

I lived with them for a while and I cried every night for six months.

My life after that was a party. I never gave my heart, never got involved. I met some rich men, attended high-profile parties and saved up a lot of money as a down payment for my café in Venice. The rest I borrowed from the bank. It was easy for me. All the men fell at my feet one way or another, and sooner or later they always gave me what I wanted. I realised that the less I cared, the more they wanted me. Men were such babies.

Marriage was not for me. Building a family was not part of my plan. I had been doing just fine for so many years. I would not change my single status for a billion Euros. I would not get married and tie myself to one man for the rest of my life, even if the Pope had requested it.

And then one day everything changed - on the day of *la festa di san pietro e san paolo*. My heart leapt in a way that was unusual to me. Never before had any man had such an effect on me, so that I thought if I didn't have him I would lose every sense of self and meaning.

The problem was that he was never going to be mine. I knew this from day one, but I had to try. When I slipped that note into his pocket at his birthday dinner, I had no idea what the outcome would be. I was just being my very bold self. My motto was if I didn't ask, then I wouldn't know the possibilities.

The sex was the best I had ever had - my legs often in the air, moaning and groaning. With him, I was one horny, sexy bitch. He was simply delicious. And I would have given my life for him. There was a big problem standing between me and my dreams though. It was not his priesthood – no, that would have been too easy.

I realised a bit too late that his heart was a tiny bit too big - his philanthropic, giving, selfless heart.

All he wanted to do was volunteer in poor communities. This need haunted him, tormented him and tore us apart. That was all he cared about. What about me? What about us? What about sex?

Life had stopped for me and the only thing that existed was him. When we were together, we wined and dined and ate ice cream. He paid for everything. Not once did he let me pay for a drink, or dinner, or even an espresso. We danced and made love and all was perfect in my world, until he decided to go travelling to Africa and India.

Even then, I refused to give up hope. I wrote to him. I waited for him. I did not let any other man touch me. I knew, in my heart, that I belonged to him and only him. I knew he belonged to me too. How could he not? How could this deep connection not be mutual? Even when he refused to reply to my letters, I made excuses for him. I knew there was a good reason. I would wait forever if that is what it took.

And then, after what seemed like eternity, on one of my trips to visit Gloria and her family, I found out that he was ill in India and that they were all praying for him. They didn't think he would survive. I fasted and prayed. I said my Rosary ceaselessly for him. I forgot to eat most days.

I returned to Venice a few weeks later and moved around like a zombie. Not once did I forget to pray for him. Not once did I give up hope that I would see him again. Oh, how I loved him. "Dear God, please keep him alive," I prayed. "If you do, I promise to leave him alone for you." That was the extent of my love for him.

A few months later, I received a letter from my sister and a picture. She said that he had fully recovered and was now reassigned to England for a few months. I looked at the picture. It was of the parishioners in England. He had taken a group photo and sent it to his uncle, the cardinal, and Pedro too.

"I know how worried you were about our friend," my sister wrote, "so to reassure you, I borrowed this picture from Pedro to send to you."

I looked at the picture and immediately my heart was overjoyed. The more I looked, the more I noticed that he appeared different, leaner and even more handsome if that were possible. There was also a glow about him that travelled to his eyes. They were looking into the eyes of the nun who stood at the far end of the picture. She was pretty, in an innocent sort of way, almost saint-like. I felt my heart begin to panic, to sink into sadness, into a dark place that did not feel so good. I did not want to feel this way. I did not want to notice these things, but my instincts never lied.

That was when I decided to be sure, beyond every reasonable doubt, that I had not wasted my years waiting for a man who would never be mine. I decided to hire a private detective. He wasn't cheap, but he was worth every penny.

It took a couple of months to hear back from my detective. He didn't have any proof, he said, but he was sure that there was something romantic going on between the priest and the nun. He saw him go to her quarters a couple of nights, and that wasn't right. He also noticed the way they always seemed to navigate towards each other whenever there was a gathering of some sort.

That was enough information for me. Although I still found it hard to move on as the detective had not actually got any proof for me other than his own judgement.

Every day I prayed to God to help me forget him. Perhaps I was being punished for seducing him. Was I supposed to suffer forever? I needed to be free of him. I needed to forget about him. It was obvious that he didn't feel the same way about me. It was evident that he'd never been in love with me, at least not in the way that I had been in love with him - so deeply, so passionately and soundly. I loved him too much; one must never love any man too much.

And so, I didn't believe it when I heard the bell on my counter that late morning. I didn't expect to see him standing there, tall, dark and handsome. So very lean, he had grown more desirable with age. And that glow was still there. It was like an invisible halo that illuminated all around him, making him stand out like a star amongst us mere mortals.

All my feelings came rushing back as I flung myself at him. Oh, please say you love me again, I thought, and I will always be a slave at your feet.

He didn't say any of that. He couldn't even look me in the eyes. He hadn't come to see me because he loved me. No, he had come to pay me off - to ease his guilt. The bastard wanted to get rid of me quietly. I hated him. Oh, how I hated him. It was true what they said about the thin line between love and hate.

He didn't even deny his relationship with the angelic nun. Could he not have lied? Even for me? Did he not know how badly I ached for him? How could he not think of my feelings, even as he broke my heart?

I could not recall *when* I picked up the sharp knife. I could not recall *when* I stabbed him, for my rage was too severe - taking over me like a demon that was about to be slaughtered. It happened too quickly, and in less than a second I realised what I had done. All I wanted to do afterwards was fade away…into oblivion…where no one would ever find me and my evil heart again.

Well, now I had my chance.

He was rushed by the paramedics to the hospital, but he had lost so much blood that I didn't think he would make it. The police would, inevitably, come looking for me, as my prints were all over the knife.

I did not want to live in a world where he did not exist. Ever since I met him, I had lived only for him. Maybe I might be given another chance to love where I was going, or maybe I would meet him there?

~~~

The trip from Venice to Rome was a peaceful one. I paid for my ticket in cash. That way I would not be traced.

On the train, I scribbled a little note to my sister.

Dear Gloria,

I am sorry that I have not been the sister I should have been to you. I think I have failed myself in so many ways. I have also failed you and failed God. I will be going away as I do not think I can bear it.

Please do not look for me - know that I am safe and okay. Maybe, someday, we will meet again, either in this life or the next. It doesn't matter, but we will certainly see each other again someday.
~~~

The café is yours. You can sell it or do whatever you want with it. It doesn't matter.

I love you and Pedro and the children.

Please, I did not mean to cause you pain.

Love always

Ciara

My train travelled past Bologna and Florence, and in just under four hours I arrived at the Roma Termini station.

I left the station very carefully and was grateful that there were no *Carabinieri* in sight. I flagged a taxi down and jumped in rather swiftly, trying to feign calmness so as not to raise suspicion.

"Citta del Vaticano."

"Va bene."

There was hardly any traffic from the station to Vatican City. It was as if the universe had made the way clear for me.

It was one of those hot days that exhibited no humidity and no unnecessary tourists wandering amongst an already-heavy crowd. The sun was streaming down amidst the clouds in the sky which produced a mixture of bright blue and white rays. It looked like the sky was in love, in harmony with the world. Rome must have looked like this before the murder of Julius Caesar.

I asked the driver to drop me in front of the post office. How else would my sister receive her letter? I could not risk going to her place. My time was limited. By now, the *polizia* would have had time to look at the street cameras. They might even know my exact location. I had to move fast if I was ever to make it out of here.

"Quanto?" I asked, a little bit impatiently - my hands shaking as I struggled to unzip my wallet, failing and yet trying again. If he noticed my troubled disposition, he said nothing. My arm pits were also beginning to feel damp and my forehead felt quite wet.

"Trenta euro," he replied, looking at me through his front mirror.

I paid him the money and stepped out of his cab.

"Gratzie."

"Prego," he shouted back, looking at me with uncertainty in his eyes before driving off.

After I put the letter through the post box, I began to run.

My heels knew where they were taking me. It was a place where he and I had kissed many times. It was important to be there one last time. I knew that it was unlikely he'd still be alive, as the blood that gushed out from his skin was all I could see.

I kept running. I saw nothing, heard no one - just the sound of my shoes beating against the asphalt. I was running from all the pain I had caused, the regret, the anguish. I was running from my father and my mother, from my sister's perfect marital life, from my loneliness, from a failed love. I was running from Antonio, from the heartbreak that he caused me years ago - a pain I carried with me through to my adult years, a pain that had suddenly and swiftly faded away when I set my eyes on the young priest. I was running from the sweet-looking nun in England, who would never be a nun. I was running from law enforcement agents who I knew would catch up with me soon if I didn't run faster. I was running from death on earth. I was running *to* death on earth.

And faster I ran. I did not even stop at the traffic lights when the symbol turned red. Opposite me stood the Castel Sant'Angelo and in front of this beautiful castle stood the Ponte Sant'Angelo with its medieval bridge that rained down its regal head over the River Tiber. It was befitting that I intended to end everything on the most beautiful bridge in the world.

I stopped before the bridge to catch my breath. I took a swift look around. There was no one looking at me suspiciously - just the usual looks of admiration that I had become accustomed to. My eyes took in the ten statues (stood on tall plinths) - full of potential movement and lightness, looking so serene, so pure, so holy. These marbles of angels held in their hands instruments of passion. For me, it was a preview of Heaven's gate. A *Via Crucis* of my heart was imminent, as I needed all the graces in this life and the next. I walked to the base of the bridge and looked at the statue of Saint Peter holding the keys of Heaven and to Saint Paul holding the sword. This bridge was symbolic of the Passion of Christ. May Christ see my heart and not judge me too harshly.

My heels stepped upon the travertine marble that held the bridge. I carried on walking until I came to the middle, barely touching the Angel With Nails. I stepped onto the almost-sacred pavement and at that moment heard a loud noise. I turned around for a second only and noticed that the *polizia* had located me, about four or five of them, running towards me, attracting the attention of passersby.

It was now or never.

Without another thought, I placed my Gucci handbag on the floor beside me; someone would make good use of that. Where I was going, I didn't think I would need it. My Prada shoes, however, would come with me - I loved them too much.

A small tap on my shoulder silenced my thoughts, but not so much my plan.

"What are you doing, my dear?"

It was an old man with a walking stick. He couldn't have been less than ninety. "Please don't do this. There are other ways."

His English was flawless, almost American-sounding - perhaps an American who had found himself unable to leave Rome.

I started to shake my head as the tears flowed freely and wildly down my cheeks.

"There is no hope for me. All is lost...all is gone," I whispered, grateful for his kind face, his gentle smile, his human touch.

The movement of the polizia was clearer now. They were closing in. I either moved now or spent the rest of my life in jail. Jail was not for me - death was better than any confinement.

I felt nothing. I heard nothing. Not the sound of the cars that screeched to a halt, not the tourists screaming wildly for me to stop, not the locals knocking over their espressos (failing to get to me in time).

Even now, all I could think of, all I could dream of, all I could wish for....was him.

Chapter 2

Iman

I am married to Christ, and one might think that that is a lonely relationship, but it isn't. Okay...*who are we kidding?* I am sometimes lonely, but being a nun has its perks - like not being confined to the walls of a psychiatric unit because, quite clearly, I am mad. So, being a nun means I can hide my insanity under the umbrella of a convent....and get away with it by wearing the mask of a Rosary.

This way, I sometimes feel safe and protected; a divine kind of umbrella, shielding me from the impurities of this world. I could easily equate this feeling to that of someone restricted by the walls of a prison cell. Deep within my heart, I was also completely and profoundly *fascinated* with the outside world. I was taught that I could never have both, because the way of the world was sinful and dark, an incontestable road to perpetual fire, denunciation and damnation. The way to Heaven, on the other hand, was a life stripped of noise and devoid of premarital sex – the complete non-existence of worldly and sinful music, provocative short skirts, night clubs, and most definitely the inability to think for oneself and make up one's own rules. This pious route would, in return, give me perpetual peace of mind, a flowing river of endless joy in my heart and the elimination of every potential darkness and depression that could possibly befall my world as I knew it.

If this was the case, then why was I still tormented by a great emptiness? Why was I constantly haunted by suicidal thoughts?

There was a strong hunger in me that yearned so badly for a world I could not have. Due to this desire, I despised *being* me, I did not want to live *in* me, I did not like my life one bit and I did not feel the need to remember my past. So I was all that I did not want, and this disposition was killing me slowly from inside. When the night came and surrounded me, with its cold winds and shiny blue romantic sky, I would pick up that little overused blunt razor and press the blade deep into my skin…until I heard it slice so quietly and yet, rather loudly too.

These days, I needed a new blade.

The sting was, thankfully, still a welcome pleasure, never disappointing, always creating in me a new exhilaration through the trickling and the coldness of the thick fluid that sent me into a world of pure, oblivious bliss.

Then, out of unpolluted and proverbial Catholic guilt, I would kneel down by my bed and pray, asking for forgiveness, knowing that He could hear, believing that one day my freedom would come, but never truly knowing how or by what means.

I also did not know what I was praying for. That was the height of my mystification.

My problem was deeper and darker than I could face or mention in prayer – however, it was *there* nonetheless, haunting me and whipping my soul to nothingness.

I felt trapped, wounded, dirty and condemned. I was definitely going to rot in Hell, for no matter how much I prayed I could never wipe away the image of the past. No matter how much I scrubbed my skin in the shower, I could never clean away the dirt of the sinful acts that I had committed.

The God in me saw everything.

One only had to look at the people who had incurred God's fury in the Old Testament.

Sodom and Gomorrah did not even come close. Moses, after only one disobedient act, was not allowed to enter the promised land of Canaan. The God of the Old Testament was one who took no prisoners, and so I was constantly reminded of the phrase: "The fear of God is the beginning of wisdom."

My penance was devoting my whole life to Him - my marriage to Christ in becoming a nun, and the sacrificing of the world that I loved so much for the huge walls of the sister's convent.

Yes, I loved the world and all the sinfulness that I was told it embodied.

Before coming to live in the convent at the age of eighteen, I had been to a few parties, kissed two or three handsome frogs and had sex countless times from the moment I hit the ripe old age of fourteen. I managed to speak falsely and be in denial about sex during my interview. Lying had never been easy. For me, at that moment, it was survival, however.

I remember that day as if it were yesterday.

"Miss Iman Williamson - please do sit down. You look quite nervous." The reverend mother had said this without a smile on her face, as her eyes sunk into my very soul, inducing vulnerability so deep that I failed to feel my bottom slide against the hard wooden chair. She was not the disappointment I had imagined in my bedroom that morning; rather, she was every bit as scary as I had feared.

My fake mother told me that she was my benefactor - that she was the one responsible for feeding me from birth.

I did not like the reverend mother. She looked too stern, too composed, too strict - middle-aged, white and *very* upper class.

My fake mother had informed me that if I played by her rules, I would get to live a very comfortable life in England. According to Hadiza, the reverend mother promised that she would come back for me when I turned eighteen and, true to her word, she had shown up.

The rules Mother Hadiza laid out were not too difficult to follow.

"You must tell her you want to become a nun. She will then get your papers arranged for you to go back to England with her. When you get there, you must remember who looked after you all this time, and send me money every month for my old age. That way, we both win. You win, I win. Or you can stay here and be poor and unfortunate like your late mother and drunken father."

My fake mother always looked for a reason to remind me of my desolate roots. And I did not want to be like my underprivileged parents. I did not want to carry on living this life. I wanted something different.

The hidden books and reading had exposed me to a world outside my current reality - a world seemingly beyond my reach, a universe that *perhaps* I could be part of if I played according to the rules.

"So tell me, Iman…" The reverend mother's voice brought me back to the present. "Is it true that you would like to become a nun? Or is this just a way out for you from here?" Her hands spread out like the wings of a hummingbird to elaborate what 'here' meant.

I remained silent as I contemplated what my reply would be. Did she have no idea at all of the world that I had been subjected to with my fake mother?

There was a smile that my mother Hadiza always reserved for such special people. It was so sweet and innocent. It was hard to believe that this perfect being with the adorable smile did not embody the traditional sense of motherhood in the way a child would have hoped. Every time I looked at my mother, all I could see were eyes that betrayed me and refused to care.

"She is the kindest of souls, Reverend Mother. She is so innocent, so pure, so gentle, so….."

The reverend mother put her hands up to gently silence my theatrical mother. Then she looked at me, rather sternly as before and asked, without any warning whatsoever, "Do you have a boyfriend?"

I was caught slightly off guard and had to think for a second before my reply. It had to be perfect. And I was to be *very* convincing; not without reminiscing of course. It was a habit of mine. I clarified the truth in my mind so that I could filter it out completely. And the result? A well made-up lie. I was, after all, my father's daughter.

My first boyfriend was Oti. He was overweight and cute. We kissed once and he tried to slide his fingers up my skirt. I slapped him and ran off. I never saw him again. I was twelve years old. My second boyfriend was worse. He didn't even try to kiss me. His hands were in my pants before I even agreed to a date.

I do tend to fall in and out of love every week from one man to the next. Quite randomly.

"No, Reverend Mother." I was surprised at the calmness of my own voice.

"Have you ever had sex?" This next question was equally unexpected, but I had come prepared and groomed by my fake mother. Hadiza explained that I was supposed to be a virgin, pure and ready to be married to Christ. The Catholic Church was against any premarital sex whatsoever, and so if I ever confessed to my sins, all chances would be lost.

Oh yes, lots of times - at home, on the sofa in the living room, behind the garden shed. Well, if you count giving a blow job to the old neighbour for a few bucks.

My fake mother would be well qualified to answer this question - after all, she was and is my pimp. I sleep with men for her financial gain. She provides the men and the condoms, of course. Thank God for those, otherwise I'd be dead by now from one disease or another. Or maybe, just maybe, I would have been a mother to a few hungry children of my own.

"No, Reverend Mother. I'm a virgin." I wasn't sure if she believed me. She did hesitate for a while before asking me the next question. It was either that she found my previous answer to be a complete lie or she was bracing herself for my next reply.

"Do you see your father often?" This question made me want to laugh out loud.

"No, Reverend Mother." At least that part of the interview was true.

"So tell me, Iman - why do you want to become a nun?"

Very interesting question, Reverend Mother. Where do I start?

I could tell you a part truth - that I have been brought here by my fake mother to tell you these lies. Or, I could tell you the full truth – that, although I am adhering to the wishes of Hadiza, I do feel a strong need to wash my sins away. I do not want to be a nun, but I must pay my penance and be married to Christ. To be honest, being locked away in the walls of a convent sounds pretty good to me.

"Iman?" The white woman's voice reminded me that she was still waiting for an answer.

Whilst indulging in my thoughts, I had forgotten what my fake mother had instructed me to say in reply to this particular question, so I just looked at the reverend mother without uttering a word. It was safer to be silent than to voice the wrong thing, my fake mother would pronounce.

"Answer the reverend, darling." My mother was smiling when I looked up at her, but her eyes told me she would eat me for dinner on this occasion if I said the wrong thing or nothing at all. Suddenly, I knew I had to improvise. Anything would be better than nothing.

"I have always wanted to be a nun. That's all I ever think about. I hope you can help me turn this life-long dream into a reality. I have kept my body pure for Christ and I hope that He will accept me just as I am." Wow, I definitely deserved an Oscar for that performance.

The reverend mother smiled at me for the first time that morning.

"He is gracious to all, my daughter - both the clean and unclean."

You're saying this because you have no idea how unclean I am; but don't worry, I attend Mass every Sunday and say my Rosary. Mother Hadiza says it's important to pretend and manipulate people.

I watched in silent horror as the nun got up and walked towards me. What did she want?

"Don't look so frightened, my dear. Would it be possible to give you an embrace?" Her question astonished me, but her eyes revealed a kindness I had never known. I got up from the chair to let her hug me. I did not hug her back, not because I didn't want to, but because I was too bewildered by her warmth and kindness…for I could not remember ever being held in a loving embrace by anyone.

She promised to arrange all my travel documents so that I could go and live with her in England. I thought she was lying. I knew it was an impossible dream. Why would she want to help *me*? *Who* or *what* was I to her?

A nobody. A Hausa church rat. A prostitute.

I joined the sister's convent in England exactly six months later in September, in the year of 2002.

My journey had been an exciting one, albeit filled with fear as I had never been on a plane before. I prayed throughout the whole flight, asking not to die. Life had not been particularly kind to me so far, but I wasn't about to leave the stage just yet.

When my plane finally landed at Heathrow airport, I couldn't wait to scramble out of it, but I noticed that people waited in line respectfully. In Jos, nobody waited in line, so this was new to me. Everything was different. The air smelled different. The people spoke and looked different; it was all a very *good* different, and all I wanted to do was stand still and take it all in. I couldn't, however. I had to keep moving.

I went through the airport security after answering a few questions and after standing in a very long line.

Reverend Mother was waiting for me, along with a middle-aged white man. She introduced him to me as the parish priest from Ireland. His name was Father Charles McCormack. They both hugged me like a long-lost daughter and, for the first time in my life, at eighteen years of age, I felt a sense of self-worth. I felt loved.

"Where is your luggage?" Father McCormack asked - his glasses dangling over his eyes, almost touching his beard in a theatrical manner. He never stopped smiling. He reminded me of the silent calm in the midst of an Indian monsoon.

"Oh, all I have is in my rucksack," I replied. "I'm sorry. I don't have much."

"Don't be sorry, my dear," the priest replied. I looked at Reverend Mother for approval. I hoped she wasn't disappointed in me for not having more items. Back home, one was only respected when one had lots of material goods.

Her smile said it all - that same kindness that I could not forget.

I wanted to cry, for I felt grateful for this profound reception. Right there and then, overwhelmed by this astounding acceptance, I vowed that I would do everything in my power to make her proud of me. I would repay her kindness with nothing but kindness.

The journey took us almost three hours, and I was thankful for the silence that ensued in the car. I did not speak much for I was quite diffident, so the less people spoke to me the better. I think both reverends must have picked up on that. Father McCormack tried to talk to me, but gave up rather quickly, for I didn't give him much to work with.

When we arrived at the church, I didn't know why we were there, as it was already so dark and the clock in the car read 22:02. Did they say Mass this late in England? I almost let out a heavy sigh of relief when I realised that the church entrance and the convent entrance were one and the same.

Reverend Mother delivered me to my room, after an endless walk along many corridors, through numerous wooden doors. The room was small, with a single bed, a wardrobe and a modest desk and reading lamp. I was grateful for the lamp, for I could never go to sleep without drowning my thoughts in a good book. There was another door, and this led to my shower cubicle, a toilet and a humble bath.

"This will be your room for as long as you are here."

"Can I stay here forever?" I asked.

"If you want to, my darling." She was smiling at me. "There are clean, fresh towels in your wardrobe and some toiletries. Let me know if you need anything else and I will try to provide them for you."

"I don't need anything else. You have given me too much. Thank you from my heart."

"Good night, Iman. Tomorrow we will talk some more and you can meet the other sisters. They are all older than you, so you will be pretty spoilt, I think."

"Good night, Reverend Mother, and thank you again." She nodded and closed the door behind her. I realised then that loving her would be the easiest thing in the world to do.

The shame of lying to her was eating me up inside. However, 1 reminded myself that I was merely surviving, and that if she knew the truth about me, I probably wouldn't be here.

The following day I discovered there was a lady a similar age to me – perhaps about two years older and from the Philippines. Reverend Mother introduced her as Maria De Leon. We became very good friends. We had something in common: we were *both* new and nervous.

Maria lived for the life of the convent. She excitedly told me that all her life she had wanted to be a nun, and now her dream was about to come true. She prayed all the time and was never without her Rosary. I emulated all that she did. And, for the first time in my life when I prayed, I meant every word. She thought I was a saint. She said I reminded her of a quiet angel, always willing to help others with a kind face.

I knew I was a fraud, a cheat that gave kindness in order to pay for my penance. I said 'Yes' to everyone - whatever it was that they wanted my help with. I eliminated the word 'No' from my mind.

I was comfortable with being a doormat. I had been a doormat all my life. I would continue to be a doormat. In England, I was just a different kind of doormat. Being a doormat was my constant normal, my default place in the world.

We began our training together at the convent, in our small church in a tiny, beautiful village called Broadway. Father McCormack kindly gave us a tour of the village, explaining that we ought to familiarise ourselves with the place so as not to get lost. He showed us around, describing it as the heart of the Cotswolds. We walked up the high street, delighting in its charming, petite, independent shops, museums and art galleries. The horse-chestnut trees and stone cottages filled my inner world with bewilderment. Nothing in the books I had read about England prepared me for such astounding beauty. Father McCormack said people visited the village all year round to gaze at its exquisiteness, especially American tourists. He said people liked to walk the hills and enjoy the surrounding countryside.

"Where I come from, walking is for the poor people who do not have cars," I blurted out, without thinking, provoking giggles from Maria and a broad smile from the priest.

"I bet the poor live longer than the rich?" He smiled at me. I wasn't sure if this was another joke, but I found it impossible to laugh at. Back home the poor died like rats, no matter how hard they worked or exercised.

It took me a while to understand the jokes that the British told. And the sarcasm in almost every sentence. Or the way they said 'Yes', when they actually meant 'No'. Or the emphasis in the word *lovely* when they admired something. Everyone smiled at me when I walked past them. Initially, I refused to smile back. Perhaps there was something wrong with them? Why smile for no reason?

After living in England for a few months, I too began to smile, and it felt good. It felt so good inside smiling at strangers. I was learning to love others. It was a strange emotion, but it felt...wonderful. In Jos, people loved, but they were normal people with normal families. I only had Hadiza and that relationship was definitely the opposite of love.

Maria and I were given a trial period of six months. In those six months we studied the life of the sisterly order. We immersed ourselves in the study of the liturgy and we trained and studied the Catholic prayers. I worked really hard and tried to be the best that I could be for the reverend mother. I passed. I was successful for the first time in my life and was allowed to advance into the official training to become a nun.

This lasted for three years. At the end of the three years, I was ordained as Reverend Sister Iman of the Sisters of Broadway. I was to be a new person. Out with the old and in with the new. I worked really hard to prove my worth. I did what was required of me. I prayed, I did penance, I went for confession, I cleaned and cleaned, and I was quiet in solemnity. I was also loved by the kind women around me. These women had always wanted to be here. They were happy here. I didn't know if I was happy. I didn't know if this was God's plan for me. But one thing I was sure of was that I would never go back to my fake mother's home again. I was done with that life. This was a new chapter - a fresh start, a new day.

I found it hard, however, to erase the past from my memory. It haunted me every day. I felt like a fraud amongst Saints. They thought I was a virgin like them, that I had lived a pure and untainted life. The truth was that I could *never* confess my sins for fear that I would be judged and put back on a plane to northern Nigeria. If that happened, it would be the death of me.

It was the most difficult when we sat around the table and discussed our past. The stories they told were filled with laughter and promise and holiness - lovely families with supportive siblings.

When it was my turn to speak, or when I was suddenly thrown a question like "Did you like to go on holidays when you were young?" I'd reply that we never had any money growing up. That was always a good answer. It was also somewhat true.

When they asked what sort of toys I liked as a child, I chose the most popular - Barbie. Everyone knew Barbie. I liked Barbie, but they didn't have to know that I never had my *own* Barbie. So, again, that wasn't a complete lie. When they asked if I missed my home and my mother, now that was when the lies came pouring out.

"Oh yes, I miss her sooo much - our long walks together, her lovely hot milk before bed time, her cooking, her hugs and kisses, and the way she always made me feel safe."

Reverend Mother would look at me without revealing anything. I always felt everybody in the room believed me apart from her, but she was the one I wanted to please the most. If only they or she knew what I had grown up with.

Life at home with my fake mother was never an easy ride. She screamed if I didn't sweep the floor properly. She looked for the tiniest spot to remind me of my inability to sweep up. She fed me once a day, but if she was particularly happy I also got a snack. She hated me even when she was happy, and I felt her wrath when she was feeling depressed, which was frequently. Whenever she was unhappy, I was always there to pay the price.

"I hate you, Iman Williamson.

"I wish I could kill you. You think you're pretty, but you have big eyes like an idiot and you wander around the house like a fool.

"You belong in an asylum, never to be touched by a man, never to be loved. For that is all you deserve, you dirty piece of shit."

I have lived in England now for twelve years and, in all that time, I have struggled with her voice.

I have tried to block it out, but have consistently failed.

I am on a different continent far away from her, yet unable to forget her.

I found solace in isolation and prayer, rosaries and novenas, midnight Masses and daily conventions, charity work and volunteering my services to the poor and ill-fated (ignoring the sadness in my heart, as well as the feeling of emptiness and dissatisfaction that slowly crept up within me every morning and every night). I knew there was something missing, but I wasn't sure what it was. I had just turned thirty, and with age came an evolved sense of clarity - a wanting and need so deep it scared me.

As if I wasn't weighed down enough already! I was dealing with my past and now I had to deal with my present. All of a sudden though, the hell of my past didn't feel like Hell at all.

Chapter 3

Young Romilly

I am Romilly Kurt Vanderbelt and my life belongs to my family and not to me. I was born in Berlin in January 1984 to a German father, Hansen Friedrich Vanderbelt and a French mother, Marie-Ange Saint Rose Vanderbelt. I am the last of three children and the second male child.

Before I was born my future had already been decided for me like a raving time bomb with a constant, warning tick. I was groomed from the day I learnt how to understand the mannerisms of men, from the moment I knew how to think for myself and from the second the toddler in me took form.

This tradition was one that had survived in my family for many generations. It had always been this way for the last son in every Vanderbelt line. It was not something that was questioned or debated. One simply submitted to one's responsibilities for the family. It was my job to adhere to my father's wishes. My innermost desires were to be buried and forgotten.

I was, one day, to become a cardinal in Rome.

That was the rationale for my birth. That was my destiny. My family expected it and the church sanctified it; a silent arrangement, if you will.

I was never asked what it was that I wanted. I was never permitted to choose. It had been that way for centuries amongst the Vanderbelt families. Every last son was handed over to the Catholic Church as a contribution to priesthood and, in return, the connection to the church would act like a habitual pathway to the golden gates of Heaven. My father strongly believed that the only road to eternal bliss was through the Roman Catholic Church, and so if this was the case then what better duty than to donate one's own son to the services of the church? It was a *huge* sacrifice, but one that was definitely worth making.

The Pope never failed us. Every member of our family made Cardinal.

Hansen Friedrich Vanderbelt was a powerful and rich international banker. He travelled the world and owned properties in France, London and Austria, plus the house in Berlin where I was born. However, tradition meant a lot more to him than riches, position and religion. And although he was well-travelled and highly-educated, he was first and foremost a Vanderbelt. My father was a millionaire, but my father was also a slave – a slave to his beliefs.

I remember when I dared to ask him about this great sacrifice. I was nine years old. This was the age I began to doubt my calling. I knew then that maybe priesthood wasn't for me.

"Why me, Papa? Why not Alfred?"

Alfred was my older brother - a scoundrel who bullied anybody that crossed his path. He believed that he was better than everyone. Surely he would benefit more from the priesthood life than myself? Did he not need to atone for all his sins?

"Alfred is to take over the family business. Alfred is bold and strong."

"But I'm also strong."

"No, my dear - you are too shy, too timid and sickly. You will make a fine priest."

"But what if I don't want to be a priest? Isn't priesthood a calling?"

I wished I could have taken those questions back as soon as I asked them, for the look on my father's face said it all as he grabbed me by the arm and slapped my face so violently that I thought I would die. Then he tossed me brutally across the room. My body landed in one of the far corners - my head slamming against the brick wall. I might have passed out for a second or two, or not at all. I simply can't remember. But one thing I recall is the blood that trickled down my face – the result of a tiny scar that followed me into adulthood; a scar that reminded me to be obedient to my father.

My mama was not home at the time. He would never have grappled with me in her presence. Not that he feared her reaction, but mainly to avoid her inevitable, high-pitched screams. Mama always said, repeatedly, that Hansen misinterpreted the Bible and did not know God at all.

But to my father, anger, every action he took, was the right one, or so the Bible 'said'.

"Spare the rod and spoil the child."

So he was very quick with his fists when trying to teach me or my siblings a lesson.

"The man is the head of the home and his wife must be submissive to him."

And so he flogged his wife into submission. She was, however, mostly stubborn and refused to submit to his will.

"Pray without ceasing."

We had a praying altar at home where Mass was said every morning by the local village priest, and the Rosary was recited every evening after dinner, before bedtime. No matter what was happening in the world, no matter if someone had dropped dead, my father believed that this routine should not be broken.

"We must never offend God," was his motto, but my mother would argue with him, for she was not as traditionally-minded as he was. She laughed at him behind his back with her French friends and mocked him in his absence.

"J'en ai marre de ses régles."

"I'm fed up with his rules."

"Il pense qu'il sait tout."

"He thinks he knows everything."

"Dieu ce, Dieu qui."

"God this, God that."

"Meme Dieu n'est pas intolerable"

"Even God is not this intolerable."

This boisterous behaviour always had a way of reaching the ears of my father and he would give her a good beating for her disloyalty.

A man must put a woman in her place, he always said. It was the way God wanted it.

I know all this, because as the youngest child, I was very close to my mother. I clung to her as a nomad would cling to his water bottle in a dry desert. My mother was life. She was beauty. And the kind voice of reassurance. Her kisses in the morning and at night were the most comforting and her scent was the best in the world. I enjoyed the time I spent with my mama and hated the way my father treated her. I could never see any wrongdoing in Mama. She was lovely, beautiful and kind to everyone around her - sometimes even Papa.

Whenever my father brought out his belt to flog his wife, he didn't care who was around. He was, after all, the king of his own jungle and he ruled on his throne with an iron fist. He called it a form of Christian Domestic Discipline. When Mama threatened to leave him, he swore that she would never see the children. She cared for all three of us, but I think she loved me a little bit too much for my father's comfort. So he took out his frustrations on me and whipped her when she denied him his way. I think Mama only stayed with him because of me. I know that might sound conceited, as I have other siblings, but I truly believe it.

I was a comfort to my mother and I was always there for hugs and cuddles and to wipe away her tears when Papa hurt her. But I was also a growing boy who, at the age of twelve, confused my height for a man's physical strength.

Papa had just returned home from one of his business trips. He had been gone for two weeks and during that time had rung the house every day to confirm that Mass was being said and that we were all reciting our rosaries in the evening. My mother's voice sweetly told him everything he wanted to hear.

It was the same routine each time my father went away. He would take one last look at us – his family - as we stood in the hallway to bid him farewell.

"Marie-Ange," Father would call his wife sternly, as if she was nothing more than the hired help. One found it hard to believe that he was actually talking to his wife.

"Yes, my darling," my mother would purr rather sweetly in her thick French accent. Sometimes I thought it easier to understand my mother when she spoke in French than when she spoke in English. English was only spoken in our home because Mama could not understand Dutch.

"Please make sure that the children attend Mass each morning. Remember that Romilly is to be a priest. We must do our bit as parents." As far as I was concerned, my two older siblings were not exactly children. Anjelika had just recently celebrated her twenty-first birthday and Alfred was almost nineteen. Dad insisted that they were to remain at home whilst attending university. He threatened to disinherit anyone who dared go against his wishes.

"I promise, my love," Mama would reply, and then she'd bid him farewell. As soon as she closed the door behind him, however, she would mutter "*Homme fou.*" Crazy man.

And then she would do the exact opposite. She would take me by the hand and walk two miles to the priest's home, leaving my older siblings to party as they liked.

That was my mama. She was flexible and as fun as a barrel of monkeys and wine.

"Ha, Marie-Ange - I think I know why you are here." Father Vissar would look at Mother sternly and smile down at me. "Do you think this is wise? Going against Hansen like this?"

"Please take the two weeks off, Father. I'm taking my son on some lovely days out. We will go to the beach and we will have ice cream. We might even take a train to London and see a show." Unlikely, but my mama was dramatic like that.

Then she would look at me and mutter *"Papa a de l'argent, permet de depenser de l'argent."*

I wasn't quite sure that I shared her enthusiasm for spending Papa's money. I suppose I knew what the outcome would be and I feared for her. I did, however, enjoy the times we spent together. It meant that I had *all* of her attention and didn't have to share her affection with the rest of my family, my father included.

And we *did* spend Papa's money – in the crazy and free fashion that my mother enjoyed. She knew her husband would hear about it. It was almost as if she wanted him to know. Why else would she tell Father Vissar of her plans - the village gossip who delighted in spreading not only the word, but everyone's business too?

This was the way things carried on at home. And it became a righteous circle…until that fateful day during one of Mama's trips.

"It is a beautiful day to enjoy the city of Berlin," she screamed in delight.

And so, we visited the American Memorial Library and sat down together reading funny books. I particularly enjoyed the *Archie* comics and I think Mama enjoyed them just as much, because we read and laughed like two teenagers.

I noticed a few of the other kids in the library with their parents. One particular family that caught my eye was a young dad and his daughter. It was the way he chased her around, full of laughter and giggles. The father was not afraid to show his affection towards his little girl and at one point lifted her so high and planted a kiss on her forehead.

I had never been kissed by my father, or even hugged by him. The most affection I ever received from him was a pat on the head. All the love and affection I experienced, I got from my mother.

"Please can we buy a comic book?" I asked for the umpteenth time, even though I knew the answer.

"No, my darling - your papa doesn't like you reading comics." And, as an afterthought, she added "He wants you to start reading the *Biiible*."

It was a private joke at my father's expense and I laughed not only to indulge her which was an easy exercise for me, but because she was so naturally funny. It was the way she said things, the way she dragged her vowels coupled with her hand gestures. I could laugh with Mama all day and never be bored. She was like an adult with a child's sense of fun - a complete mismatch for my father.

The story of how they met always fascinated me. It was hard - almost impossible - to visualise my father ever being remotely romantic. There were, of course, two very different versions of the story though - one from Papa, and one from Mama. I will start with Mama's version.

I discovered this account a few months ago when Mama came into my room to tell me a bedtime story. She always invented stories off the top of her head - stories that sent me into barrels of laughter, stories that she never finished, stories that she forgot the very next day so that I had to remind her where we were up to. I was finally growing out of her stories, however.

"I do not want a bedtime story anymore, Mama. I am a big boy now." She tried to hide the sadness in her face.

"Okay, Romillyyyyyy."

"Mama, stop it."

She pouted as she sat on my bed right beside my skinny legs. "I will miss our stories. I can't believe it's over."

I felt slightly sorry for her, so I tried to indulge her. "Oh, I have an idea," I almost screamed.

"What is it? Tell me?"

I swear I was the adult and Mama the child. "Why don't you tell me about how you and Papa met?"

She looked at me strangely, coughed a few times and then shuffled into my bed, before beginning her story.

"Your papa and I met in Paris. I was a waitress and he was a 'high-flying' student in his final year at university. He came into my café all the time and all the ladies wanted to be noticed by him because he was so handsome."

"Papa? Handsome?" I started to laugh.

"Your papa is a fine man, Romilly. He would be even more attractive if he smiled a little."

"Did he smile then?"

"Yes. A lot. Do you want me to carry on with my story?"

"Sorry, Mama." I stifled a yawn. I didn't want to be rude - not that she would ever mind. Everything I did was accepted by her.

"Well, as I was saying, all the ladies wanted Papa, but he only had eyes for me. He only ever wanted me to wait on him. He would come in and ask for me all the time, and if I wasn't there, he would not have his coffee, I was told. He asked me out to the movies very boldly after about two months of coming to the café. I can still remember our first date. We went to see a romantic movie called *The Earrings of Madame de...*" She paused and smiled dreamily, looking into space.

"Mama!" I shook her gently, urging her to return to our conversation.

"Oh sorry, yes, your papa was very charming. And then after just six months, he asked me to marry him. He said he would like me to move back home with him to Berlin. My parents were very poor and your papa was and is from a very rich and powerful family. My parents wanted a better life for me, so they encouraged our union. The rest is history."

"Ha, a whirlwind romance," I said teasingly.

"What is this? What is this whirlwind?"

I was reminded again of the occasional gaps in Mama's English vocabulary. "*Romance tourbillon,*" I replied to her in French.

"Aha, yes, whirlwind romance. *Romance rapide.*" She nodded in acceptance.

"Do you still love Papa?" I couldn't help but ask. I couldn't imagine anyone being in love with my father, let alone someone as beautiful as Mama. And I couldn't imagine all the ladies at the restaurant Mama used to work in only having eyes for Papa. He was not bad looking, for sure, but he frowned a lot and was frightening when he barked orders at us. I thought ladies liked men who could make them laugh, not the ones that frowned all the time.

"Of course, *mon fils*. I love your papa very much...sometimes."

This comment made me giggle and, on cue, Mama began to chuckle too.

My father's version of this story was slightly different. It was almost a week after Mama told me her version.

I was working in the garden with Papa when he decided that we should rest and drink the cool lemonade that Anjelika had made.

"I wonder where your mama is. She should be helping us in the garden, but I presume she prefers the company of her good-for-nothing friends."

My parents saw no wrong in complaining about each other in our presence, especially my papa. I can't remember a day that passed by without a word of criticism coming out of his lips. If it wasn't about his workers, it was one of us irritating him. If it wasn't the cook's horrendous dinner, it was the handyman's inefficiency in getting things done. If it wasn't the laziness of the housekeeper, then it was the small stain on his made-to-measure trousers. If it wasn't my mother speaking French in a household where only English was allowed, then it was her equally-unwanted French friends.

Papa, to me, was simply insufferable.

"I think she is volunteering at the church today," I replied. I did not like to hear him complain about my mother. Marie-Ange could point a gun at the head of my siblings and I would still view her favourably.

"I don't trust her. She has changed," he barked silently.

"She told me how you two met. I thought it was rather romantic," I said, before I could stop myself, trying to change the topic to a happier one.

"Ha - what did she tell you?" he asked, looking interested.

I proceeded to repeat everything that Mama had relayed to me. When I had finished speaking, I noticed that he was deep in thought.

"Papa - what is the matter?"

"Well, what you were told is not exactly true."

"Did I miss anything out?" I was suddenly eager to hear his side of the story.

"She tricked me. She got pregnant with your sister and so I had no choice but to marry her. A mistake I have to live with." With that, he got up and walked back into the house, leaving me to finish the work in the garden.

My papa, indeed, was an impossible man.

"Can you see what I'm seeing?"

Mama's voice brought me back to the library as we strolled out of it just as enthusiastically as we had walked in. Only this time, we were going to a nearby cake and ice cream stand. Our sweet treats accompanied us to the Reichstag Building situated just north of the Brandenburg Gate. Mama explained to me that the dome was the seat of the Weimar Republic government until it was seized by the Nazis in 1933 - when it was severely damaged after being set on fire under mysterious circumstances. It was later partially refurbished in the 1960s, and was completed about ten years later.

My mother liked to give me history lessons whenever we embarked on these journeys. I didn't understand most of the lecture, but I loved heights, so it was fun looking at the whole of the city from the top of the dome. We ended the day by walking to the park and feeding the ducks in the river.

"Mama." I felt this was the time to speak my mind to my mother. We were very close and I felt that I could trust her with what had been bothering me since I turned ten, two years ago. I had never mentioned what I was about to say to her with anyone.

"Oui, mon coeur?"

"I have been painting quite a lot of pictures and I think you might like some of them."

"Oh? Have I got a mini-Monet on my hands?" She was smiling at me and yet I knew she was also teasing.

"Stop it, Mama. I'm serious." I feigned a frown which created the opposite effect, for she fell into peals of laughter.

"OK, Romilly - why don't you show me these paintings of yours when we get home?"

"You know Papa is coming back today, right?"

"Yeah, I know." It sounded as if my news had conjured up a dark storm on an otherwise sunny day.

"What do you paint anyway? And why haven't you mentioned this to me before?"

"I don't know. I didn't want Papa to get cross."

"Ha, but it's only a few paintings. Why would that upset him? He'd be proud of you - really." She held me close and planted a kiss on my wavy auburn hair.

"Don't do that, Mama. We are in public and I'm a big boy now," I protested. Reminding my mother that

I was growing up seemed to be an anthem of mine in all or most of our conversations. Either she chose to ignore that fact or she simply did not see it.

"Oh, I'm sorry, big man," she giggled. "We better hurry back home before your father gets in, and remember, young priest, we prayed every single day." She wagged her finger at me in warning.

"Now, that's what I was thinking of discussing with you. Can one be an artist, as well as a priest?"

"Well, I suppose priests are allowed to have hobbies."

The problem with her statement was that I did not want my painting to be a hobby. I knew, at the tender age of twelve, that I wanted it to be my *life*.

We walked back home together in silence, each of us in our own little world; the quiet space between us feeling both ominous and refreshing. I had so many things that I wanted to say, but I lacked the courage to say them. My mother did not ask any questions, maybe because she was scared of the answers. The look on her face suggested just that. She looked worried and kept stealing glances at me. I ignored her and pretended not to notice.

Her next words were unexpected but sweet to my ears.

"Je t'aime, mon bébé."

"I love you back, *ma douce maman*."

Papa's Jaguar was outside the house and with that realisation came an expected fear in my heart. This fear was fuelled by the fact that my mother was no longer supposed to take me out on childish journeys. The trip was forbidden as far as my father was concerned. Also, my father always visited Father

Vissar's parish when he came back from a trip. It was important for him to hear an account of our religious activities whilst he was away. The priest was one to tell the truth, and sometimes he added a little seasoning to that truth. How else could he persuade my father to donate to the church? His services were always well received and paid for.

All my life I had felt sheltered and protected by my mother. It was now time for me to protect her from my father.

"Don't worry, Mama. I won't let him hurt you."

My words must have been like an unexpected earthquake that suddenly jolted Mother back to the land of the living, for she immediately grabbed my shoulders and turned me around to face her; her eyes piercing into mine rather fiercely and forcefully (such a visual connection easy to accomplish, as I was already as tall as my mother who stood at five feet six).

"You will do no such thing, *mon coeur*. You will go to your room and keep out of it. Please, Romilly - promise me, promise me you will not be rude to your father." Her voice was reprimanding, but her eyes were pleading with me - her accent a little thicker than usual.

"Yes, I promise," I whispered back, more to soothe her agitation than anything else. I could not deny my mother this request, even though I felt like a coward. However, I had no intention of going upstairs and keeping out of it, hearing her scream while my father's belt tore against her flesh.

I'm sorry, Mama, but you are asking me to do the impossible. I will, however, pretend to oblige you, but this will be the last day that Papa ever hits you.

If I had known that my wish would be granted, perhaps I would not have wished it.

Chapter 4

Iman

Her husband was almost looking, but not quite looking. There wasn't a flicker of recognition, or even a smile between them, but it was the satisfactory way in which they glanced at each other so subtly, even though they were both engaged in conversations with other families. There was a silent understanding that they were together, that they looked out for each other, and that they would rather die than let any harm come to the other. '

I wanted that, but perhaps I would never have it with another human being. I had it with Christ though, and they say that when one has Christ, one has everything. However, they also say that one always wants what one cannot have, and so I have found myself in the latter dilemma.

I had to be good at something, but in reality, I had very few skills. So, in order to build up my self-esteem, I pretended to be good at a few small things - like weeding the garden, helping in the kitchen and volunteering at any institution that required help.

Deep down, however, I was convinced that I was practically useless. And, in addition to this, so far as my looks went, I was rather plain in comparison to most women.

When I looked in the tall mirror that stood by the wall in my tiny bedroom, all I saw was a skinny, ordinary-looking nun, who was not even allowed to wear a little lipstick or eye shadow to enhance her features. God knew I needed it. When I wore a dress, it hung upon my shapeless, scrawny frame like I was a mannequin. When I walked, it was with zero confidence, as my face looked to the ground hiding my unusual, grey eyes; eyes that illuminated through my dark skin - the skin that was blacker than the night, the skin that housed an archipelago of tiny moles around my face and neck. Perhaps I was somewhat pretty, but in an odd sort of way, and whenever I spoke, it was without thinking, for my words came directly from my heart and were not filtered through my brain.

Maria, on the other hand, along with some of the other nuns, received what I liked to call a ton of admiring glances from the opposite sex. I saw the way the men in the parish looked at her - even the married ones. I saw the way men looked at the other nuns when they were not in uniform. No one ever looked at me like that. I could easily have been invisible.

They spoke to me, and they were polite, but they never actually saw me in the way I wanted to be seen. I was, I think, the only nun on the planet that craved this male attention. Of course, it was utterly inappropriate for me to want a life that I'd sworn I would resist, but with each day came a desire which burned with increasing ferocity; a yearning so strong, it strained at the very essence of my being.

And so, not only was I carrying with me the burden of the past - soon I added to it a burgeoning collection of problems; an undying infatuation, so alarming, and so regretfully wanted and unwanted by my soul.

And if I thought for one moment that my problems were severe, I couldn't have been more wrong. I didn't know what emotional uproar was until that day at the garden party, when I first laid my eyes on the man that would take over everything that belonged to me - including my soul.

Rev. Father Romilly Vanderbelt was, of course, French German and excitingly tall. Six feet four was my guess, with an endearing Dutch accent, plus a French twang which made him seem sexy when he said my name - or anybody's name for that matter.

I watched as he walked and greeted people with a quietly confident demeanour that drove me into an unexpected frenzy. I tried to control it, to stay calm, but never in my life had I been affected so much by another human being. The more I remained in the same breathing space as him, the more I found it incredibly difficult to tear my eyes away from the beauty of the man. And I wasn't the only one he captivated. He had the same effect on all the nuns - even Reverend Mother giggled like a schoolgirl when he spoke to her. And she was in her sixties! Oh yes, prim and proper Mother Thérése had a *huge* crush.

His exact age was a mystery, but he definitely had to be in his thirties - slightly older than me, I thought. In my head I had to give him a name. This wasn't hard, as he reminded me so much of Michiel Huisman in *The Age of Adeline*. So, for now, I would call him Michiel.

Two months had passed since he came to our parish from Rome or India - I wasn't sure which. There were rumours. Some said his base was in Rome, but that he had undertaken voluntary work in Africa and India. Everyone spoke about him, but I was yet to meet him. I could not avoid the dreamy look in the eyes of my colleagues when they mentioned his name. It was then that I recognised they were all human beneath the veil. Perhaps I was not the only one who yearned for a tiny bit more than what we had.

After each stolen glance at Michiel, the sinful feeling of lust within me slowly intensified; a feeling that I knew I would be wise to bury; a feeling that was slowly creeping up on me like a scorpion in a desert, without warning, but nonetheless there.

I watched, silently intrigued, as the nuns fell over themselves, trying to chat with him, smile with him, laugh with him. What was the point? I thought. It would go nowhere. We were not allowed to be romantically involved with each other and we were not allowed to daydream about *ordinary* men, let alone men who had given up their carnal desires to pursue Christ.

"The party is thrown by the workers of the church," Reverend Mother had explained to me when I was much younger during my very first summer in England. "They spend months planning it, organising and collecting money. Then they leave a list after every Mass for people to put their names down if they are interested in attending."

"Who does the cooking?" I asked, scared that she would say the nuns. I was a terrible cook. My fake mother, Hadiza, told me that all the time.

"Volunteers. Church members. The meal is the same each year." She continued: "Vegetable quiche, jacket potatoes, salads and cheese. There is always a barbecue and cold meats as well for the meat lovers. It is a lovely time to meet with the other parishioners, and to mingle with old friends, and also to make new ones."

At that time I wasn't familiar with English food and struggled to enjoy it, but one had to eat, and not long after I couldn't eat anything else.

The party was always the same. I had come to expect this sort of church gathering twice a year - once in the summer and once at Christmas.

As I walked around the church garden, I could hear the whispering grass beneath my feet, reminding me where I was and to focus on acceptable thoughts only. Our church garden, in the midst of summer festivities, was awash with a golden glow as the late morning dew slowly disappeared. As if on cue, the birds in the sky fluttered between the trees - their beautiful chorus lingering in my ears, lilting an age-old melody. Bobbing robins and buzzing bees surfed through open spaces, from flower to flower, from person to person. I expected the bees preferred the pollen that floated in the air, like pixie dust in the blustering wind.

My eyes suddenly caught sight of the fountain in the middle of the walled garden - a symbol for the fountain of life which wouldn't be the same without the statue of the Virgin Mother. Walking through here always left me feeling peaceful and at one with the splendour of nature. It was, after all, the *Hortus conclusus*. And the enclosed garden housed the tall cedar known as *cedrus exalta*, the well of living waters (the *peteus aquarium viventium*), the olive tree (*olive speciosa*) and the *plantation rosae*, which was the rose garden. Beneath the Virgin Mother were the words that transfixed me:

Hortus conclusos soror mea, sponsa, hortus conclucus, fons signatus.

A garden enclosed is my sister, my spouse; a garden enclosed, a fountain sealed up.

The frogspawn, glistening like earthly stars in the pond that washed the Virgin's feet, was a welcome diversion as I luxuriated in nature. The frogspawn's enhanced spots suggested they were alienated and old and that they knew more about this place than I could possibly imagine. They seemed to remind me that it was time to join the others and embrace the occasion. The gate to my right, as I walked past it, took a path that led to a long, garden wall covered in thick-growing ivy, creating a lush delight for my eyes. The atmosphere was humid - reminiscent of a rain forest.

As I strolled towards the party to try and mingle, my legs re-directed me towards a grove of mulberry and maple trees that cowered beneath the church, bluebells with their cerulean gongs, and apple trees situated in the centre of the garden casting clawed shadows onto the grass. Adjacent to one of the apple trees, which was weighed down by its ripe, swollen red fruits, was the back of a fence that failed to restrain the riot of brambles encroaching onto the bed of green, sweet-smelling grass.

It was here that families sat on picnic blankets - husbands, wives and children, laughing, loving and smiling at one another. I couldn't help but notice that under the apple tree stood a very long bench, laid out beautifully with jugs of sangria and summer cocktails, and an ice-bucket of cold beer and cola. Chips, cold quiche, strawberries, crisps and mini sausage rolls adorned a table, with jugs of squash and water. And in the middle of it all stood a red, flaming barbecue roasting different types of meat: beef, chicken drumsticks, burgers and hot dogs.

The heat of the smoky barbecue amid the fragrance of the flowers was my little Heaven on earth. For a brief moment I soaked it all in and forgot my inner troubles. However, when I looked at the way the men held their wives and gazed into their eyes – and even the children and their grandparents, people in the local community and members of the clergy - I knew in my heart I wanted that for myself. It was a familiar longing for a world beyond my reach and it interrupted any feeling of bliss that I might have previously felt.

Everyone looked beautiful and summery and gay; even the priests looked smart in their casual clothes. The nuns, however, had to dress in tunics and veils, with no makeup whatsoever.

I tried to mingle in with the locals, but ended up playing with the children. I was naturally shy at such gatherings, so it was only normal that I would hide away with the kids - that is, until a shadow hovered over me and introduced itself. The deep, masculine voice had a strange accent and intonation, but with a beautiful sound nonetheless. It was one I had heard before.

"Hello, I'm Romilly. I've been sent here on assignment for a few months. I don't believe we've met."

My eyes shifted from the sandcastle I was building with the children and swept across his face, settling briefly on his green eyes, lingering for a few seconds on their captivating beauty. I held onto his gaze as he held onto mine. It was then, in that moment, I think I ceased to exist, and a new me began; a new me who was completely different to the old one. Shamelessly, I could not help but stare at his firm lips and the auburn curls that cascaded around his head. I started to wonder why God would create such a perfectly beautiful creature and keep him all to Himself.

The little boy I was playing with tugged at my skirt to get my attention back.

"I think, at this point, he needs you more than I do. I'll come back later."

My eyes followed his broad, yet lithe frame and muscled, toned legs that refused to hide beneath faded, black skinny jeans.

I turned my attention back to the little boy and the sandcastle we were making. I smiled when he spoke to me and answered his questions with feigned enthusiasm. I even entertained his other friends when they joined us - digging and playing, and burying our bodies in the sand.

However, one thing remained clear: my mind and thoughts were elsewhere...with the handsome priest who had just introduced himself. And I think we had begun to play a little game of our own. Each time I tried to look his way, I caught his eyes on me - piercing, questioning, flirting, laughing. I would hold his gaze for a second or two, then break free and turn my attention back to the kids.

At the back of my mind was a stern, but fading voice - a voice I had no desire to obey.

"You cannot encourage him."

"He is a priest and you are a nun."

"The church will not tolerate it."

"Where will you go?"

"Where will you live?"

"You have no skills."

The voice did not matter. Nothing mattered but his green eyes. I had seen those eyes before in my dreams. And now they had seemingly found me. But how could I be sure?

It was about two years ago. I vividly remember my thoughts before falling into a deep sleep. I had wondered out loud at my soul's purpose, as I was a hundred and one percent certain that this wasn't it. What was I doing in the convent pretending to be a nun? Surely death was better than a life that wasn't mine. I asked for guidance. I asked for romance. In all the questions that I posed, there was no doubt I also harboured feelings of guilt for not wanting to be here. Life was a lot better than it would have been in Jos, but that did not lessen my concern.

I hated my life, my job as a nun, my black tunic and veil. It had all become so stale and routine that the whole reason for coming here in the first place no longer mattered. Then that night, after questioning my maker, I had a dream. It involved a lovely man with green eyes. He had been on one knee with a ring, begging me to marry him. I had said yes as he whisked me into his arms and kissed me passionately. The kiss had stirred an intense heat in my body that caused me to awaken with a jolt.

I thought about that dream a lot, and I wondered what it meant. Would I really meet a man with green eyes? Would I ever be allowed to live the life that I wanted so badly? Would I fall in love and be happy? Maybe even get married?

Perhaps I didn't deserve such bliss.

That night everything came back to haunt me. My obnoxious father who, I heard, had never really wanted me, my real mother who had passed away so that I could be born, my evil guardian who was still waiting for me to send money to her in Africa, and of course the self-inflicted scars on my skin, resulting from the insurmountable torment of my soul. My thoughts drifted back to the man in the dream. He was so striking and looked so kind. He seemed to represent everything good, and I wanted to feel the same way he made me feel in my dream. But I didn't. I was alone in the world with the family of Christ. Only sometimes, I think that Christ did not hear the suffering that persisted within me.

I looked up again at Romilly and this time he was talking to Reverend Mother and she was giggling like a schoolgirl (yet again). Even the Catholic Church could not erase human attraction, or the natural need to be flirtatious. My eyes drifted back to him – watched him listening to what she was saying. Then he turned and caught my stare. He smiled at me, but shifted his attention back to the reverend mother. I exhaled, for I wasn't sure how embarrassed I was. I tried one more time to steal another glance and, indeed, he looked at me again.

Then, I just knew.

I knew that the end of all my pain was in the hands of this man, for I was completely consumed and besotted by him.

I also knew that those were the eyes from my dream.

I could sense it.

I could feel it.

Like a hunch or intuition. But it was there nevertheless.

"Hello, Iman. Here is a hot dog. You've been playing so much with the kids you've forgotten to eat." Maria, my dearest friend, had suddenly come to find me, and I was grateful for her company.

"Thank you. Hope you're enjoying yourself and mixing with the locals." I smiled at her as I said this; it was a habit of mine. I could hardly speak to people without smiling, as I subconsciously felt that a smile automatically made every conversation easier.

She pulled me up, off the ground, and away from the children, who were so engrossed in their game that they didn't miss me at all.

"Will you be coming for the dinner tonight?"

"What dinner? I never know about anything around here," I joked.

Maria looked at me fondly and replied: "Father McCormack is throwing a formal dinner for Father Vanderbelt, to welcome him into the Broadway family."

"Who is Father Vanderbelt?" I asked, bewildered.

"You know. *Him*," she signalled - her eyes sliding to where he was standing.

"Oh, Romilly Vanderbelt," I whispered, as his identity suddenly made sense. *My* Michiel.

At the mention of his name, I could feel my cheeks heating up and I was thankful that my darker shade of skin hid my obvious admiration. I looked casually at the spot where he had been talking to the reverend mother, but now he was chatting and laughing with one of the young mothers. I couldn't control the pang of jealousy that suddenly sprung up in me.

Easy, Iman - you're better than that, surely.

"Well?" asked Maria. "Will you be attending? I couldn't possibly go on my own. And we don't usually get to attend fancy dinners."

I looked at my friend and knew that nothing mattered but being in close proximity to Romilly, but I was also scared that the world would immediately see - in my eyes - how I felt about the new addition to our family.

The fear I was feeling took precedence.

"I'm sorry, Maria, but I'm so tired and I have to wake up really early in the morning."

"We all have to wake up really early. Think about how rude it would be if you didn't show up."

"I don't think anybody would notice. I'm not that important."

"When you smile like that, I don't know if you're being serious or joking. Come and have a bit of fun."

She took one look at Romilly and continued: "He is so gorgeous though. If I wasn't a nun, God help me. Iman...he's looking at you."

"Don't be silly. He's looking at everyone - trying to get to know everybody."

At this point my back was to the priest, so I could not turn around, and it would have made things too obvious anyway. Maria, on the other hand, was facing him directly and she suddenly started blushing.

"Oh, my goodness, Iman - he's walking towards us. Please don't turn around...please don't...oh dear, you have."

I couldn't help myself. I had to watch him coming towards us.

"Hello again." He wasn't smiling, but I was - rather nervously. He didn't wait for a reply and instead looked at Maria. "Hello, Sister - I'm Romilly. Nice to meet you." He held out his hands and took hers. She was laughing for no reason, grinning and introducing herself all at the same time.

"It's really nice to meet you, Father. I hope you're enjoying yourself. We are so happy to have you here. I'm Maria, and this is Iman." She said this in one breath and was laughing the whole time.

"Hi, Maria." He smiled for the first time. Then his face turned towards mine. "Iman - that's a lovely name. Where is the name from?"

"Nigeria - the northern part." Green eyes filled my dark grey ones.

"What does it mean?" he asked.

"Faith and belief. Where is your name from and what does it mean?" I blurted out, before I could stop myself.

"It's French. It means citizen of Rome. It's funny - I was in Nigeria about nine months ago, the eastern part. Cross River?"

"Oh, yes. What were you doing there?" I had no fond memories of home. Of all the places in the world, what were the chances? I could not stop looking into his eyes and thinking of the dream that haunted me. Those eyes!

He stared back at me - his eyes never leaving my face, searching for *what* I did not know.

"Perhaps I'll tell you someday. I was hoping that you'd both come to the dinner tonight at the parish home?" He took one glance at Maria and then turned his attention back to me.

"Yes, of course, Father," Maria replied.

"You don't need to be so formal. You can call me Romilly." It was as if he suddenly remembered that she was there, and decided to be polite.

"If I did, I think Reverend Mother would send me back to the Philippines."

They both started laughing and I joined in, even though I didn't see what was funny. I couldn't breathe. This was all a bit too much.

"Come with me, Father Vanderbelt. There is someone I'd like you to meet." It was one of the church elders, dragging Romilly by the arm away from us. He smiled at Maria and nodded at me.

"See you soon," he whispered to both of us, before being whisked off.

Maria could not stop giggling, as she too had fallen under the spell of the charming German priest. I, on the other hand, desperately needed to retire to the confining calm of my bedroom.

My prayer was answered more quickly than I anticipated, as the party suddenly came to a close and people said their long goodbyes. I helped the other nuns and parishioners clean up, and I was grateful for the distraction. It didn't take us long to return the garden back to its original state.

I snuck out quietly with an easy lie to Reverend Mother that the sun had given me a headache. The truth was that the familiar feeling of sadness was slowly creeping up on me and I just wanted to be on my own for a while - to fight it the only way I knew how.

"Are you okay, Iman? I was hoping you'd attend the dinner this evening."

"I'm so sorry, Reverend Mother. I don't think that I can." She looked disappointed, but remained quiet and accepting of my decision. I was grateful to her for not insisting.

My relationship with her over the years had been one of mother and daughter. Everyone called me her adopted child. She looked after me and cared about my feelings in the same way only a real mother would. And, although I do not think I deserved it, I knew that in the whole world she was all that I really had. And Maria, of course.

As I walked towards the convent and the safety of my room, the thought of what was about to come quickened my pace. I was almost running. The feeling was near. I could not wait to close the door behind me and settle into my solace. The wind around me had begun to die down and the newly-minted moon was beginning to appear, replacing the yellowy sun with its silver, melodic light. Yapping fox cubs could be heard in the distance and the forlorn hoot of an owl made me think of a lost phantom in the early evening darkness.

When Maria visited me early that evening to try and persuade me to go to the dinner, I used the same lie that I had previously told the reverend mother - that I had a bad headache, brought on by being in the sun for too long.

I had been in such a hurry to begin my personal therapy that I'd forgotten to lock my door.

The knock was sudden and unexpected, but gave me just enough time to hide my activities before the door was flung open without my say-so.

"I don't believe you. I think you're feeling low again," Maria responded, hopping in, as jolly and happy as ever.

"No, I'm not," I lied. "I'm just tired. I really would just like to take some pain relief and go to bed."

Her eyes slowly drifted to the red, stained razor blade by my bedside table, and slowly she peeled the sheets off my arm.

The blood was still dripping and most of the hidden, soaked tissues dropped to the floor. I was full of indignity. I never realised that she had her suspicions about what I did behind closed doors. I thought my secret was safe.

"Is this what you've been doing? Is this why you won't come to the dinner?"

"You have no right!" I almost screamed. "How dare you barge in here! You have no idea what I have been through. You run around feeling happy and content with your perfect life. Well, take a good long look." I spread out my arms without any care in the world, exposing rows of marks from previous cuts. My blood was now dripping onto the floor from the fresh wound, without any tissues to suppress it. "This is my perfect life."

"I wasn't judging you, Iman. I'm just trying to understand."

"Please leave me in peace. I hope you enjoy the dinner." My feet carried my tired body to the bathroom. I needed a warm shower.

Before the sound of the water hit my ears, I heard my door open and close. I shut my eyes as the warm water cascaded against my skin, breathing a sigh of relief at Maria's departure.

When I returned to my room, I noticed that the floor was clean, and that the bloodied tissues had been thrown in the bin.

Chapter 5

Iman

It was always so easy for me to escape the walls of the convent, unhindered, in the summer.

"I am going for a walk, Reverend Mother."

"I am tending to the garden today, Reverend Mother."

"I am visiting the school children, Reverend Mother."

Such statements were received with a joyful smile and a cheerful nod. She knew that I needed to be alone. She suspected that I was troubled and had tried to help me a few times.

"Should you, maybe, talk to someone?" she asked me once, the very first time she saw my scars. We were in her office. I was helping her with some paperwork. The day was sunny and very hot, and a yellow, flowery dress was sufficient in that heat. The problem was…it exposed my arms.

"What do you mean?" I asked. "I don't understand."

She walked up to me and gently brushed her fingers across my left hand. "This," she said benignly, looking at me - her eyes begging me to trust her and talk to her.

I could not. I was ashamed.

"Oh," was all I could say in return, as the embarrassment of the situation washed over me like a warm shadow of despair.

"We can refer you to the local general practitioner and you can discuss whatever is bothering you?"

If only she knew what was bothering me. If only she knew the truth, she would never look at me in the same way again.

"Please, let's not bother about that. I'm fine. I promise. I don't do it anymore. These are old scars."

She looked at me disbelievingly, but decided to drop the matter for my sake. She was thoughtful like that.

I didn't particularly mind visiting the children, working in the garden, or going for long walks. It was, however, the only way I could escape haunting thoughts of frustration, and it provided an immediate, but temporary diversion from loneliness.

These days, the past didn't haunt me as much, but in its place was the torment of my emotional attraction towards a man I could not have. Such an unanswered feeling was new to me - more painful than all my memories put together.

It had been almost a month since the garden party and I had not seen him. Someone had mentioned that he was volunteering in another parish and would be back soon. I didn't know *how* soon. Not seeing him hadn't diminished my feelings for him. I longed for him day and night. His eyes haunted me. He constantly occupied my mind - controlling my every step, my every breath. I knew the reason. It was because I had never been in love before. I wasn't even sure if it was love; perhaps it was an obsession. It would pass. It had to. The convent was all I had, and besides, how could any man love me when I could not even love myself? My beaten, abused, self-destructive self.

Today, when I woke up, it was with a feeling of loving and wanting darkness. I did not want sunshine. I did not want to hear voices. I did not want food or water. I wanted to stay in bed and cut my flesh so deep that the running of hot blood would release my soul into oblivion.

The church bell had begun ringing. It was five in the morning. It rang five times and I had to get up and prepare for my daily routine.

Brush, check.

Shower, check.

Wash hair, check.

Blow dry hair, check.

Tie hair into a bun, check.

Put on tunic, black shoes, sister veil, wristwatch. Check, check, check, check.

Pick Rosary up and slip into pocket while letting the cross dangle outside my tunic. Pick prayer book up off bedside table. Say morning prayer. Bow my head. Walk to the corridor in silence. Walk into the church and get ready for Mass at six in the morning...

Check!

Being a nun, I was expected to set a good example and sit on the front row, and so I took my place there, abolishing every other thought, surrendering myself to the presence to God.

My head remained bowed in prayer as the choir began to sing. I stood up along with the rest of the congregation, for the *ad ostium* of the priest and his entourage. My head remained solemnly bowed in humility as the angelic voices of the choir filled my ears with the most beautiful *a cappella*.

"Sweet sacrament divine, hid in thine earthly home, lo, round thy lowly shrine, with suppliant hearts we come. Jesus to you our voice we raise, in songs of love and heartfelt praise, sweet sacrament divine, sweet sacrament divine.

"Sweet sacrament of peace, dear home for every heart, where restless yearnings cease, and sorrows all depart. There in thine ear all trustfully, we tell our tale of misery, sweet sacrament of peace, sweet sacrament of peace."

I joined in and sang quietly so that only I could hear the sound of my voice. At the end of the hymn the church became so completely silent that I could hear the breath of the man standing next to me.

I continued to bow my head so I would not have to look at anyone, smile at anyone, or talk to anyone.

The voice of the priest penetrated the silent air of the ancient building, in celebration of the morning Latin Mass.

In nomine Patris, et Filii, et Spiritus Sancti. Amen.

Even in Latin, I could not fail to detect that German/French accent. My heart stopped as I looked up - eyes transfixed by his in that exact moment.

He smiled.

His eyes shifted almost too soon back to the congregation.

I was still looking at him.

I couldn't stop.

I couldn't look away.

I was mesmerised.

He must have felt it.

He looked at me again.

This time he gazed deeply and piercingly even as he celebrated early morning Mass - his eyes hardly leaving my face.

He spoke about kindness, giving to the poor, charity. He stated that nothing else mattered apart from our service to others. He said it was a gift to be able to give. He said it was not always about money, but maybe a kind smile to an old neighbour, or a helping hand to carry their heavy bags, or a gentle good morning when we walked past others on the street. He said that as we departed to carry out our daily activities for the day, we ought to pose one question: "How will I be kind today?"

His voice drifted through the old building like a gentle melody. Everything about him was beautiful.

As I listened to his voice my heart filled with peaceful exuberance. My initial nervousness - heart pumping, legs shaking, sweating profusely – upon first hearing him greet the congregation could conveniently be blamed on the hot weather.

As we mentally waltzed through the *Kyrie*, the *Gloria* and the *Credo*, it was unlike me to *not* think about the words or relax my soul into the songs. For that was truly the *only* thing I loved about Mass. It was the only way to show God how much I loved Him. From my spirit to His spirit. This morning, however, my soul had been captured by a mortal man.

A priest.

A man of God.

When the time of offering arrived, I was grateful that I was not one of the ushers as I wouldn't know how to cope.

I noticed that he had begun to play cat and mouse again, and I religiously obliged him. I looked, he looked away. He looked, I looked away.

After the offering, he continued with the communion rites. A kaleidoscope of emotions ran through my mind. He would give me Holy Communion. He would place it on my tongue. I didn't want to participate, but then I was a nun. I was expected to go for communion. I was scared. He would see right through my feelings for him. He might judge me. He might be disgusted at my sinfulness. Oh God, help me please. Please help me today as I walk up that aisle. I promise not to cut myself this week. I promise to eliminate all sinful thoughts. Please don't let him see right through me.

The communion hymn brought the building alive even as we stood and lined up for the body of Christ.

Be thou my vision, oh Lord of my heart

Nought be all else to me, save that thou art

Thou my best thought, by day or by night

Waking or sleeping, thy presence my light.

The beautiful hymn rose up through the old, eighteenth-century building and lifted me off my seat as I joined the queue to receive the body and blood of Christ.

The closer I floated towards him, the nearer to dying I felt. And all too soon, I was stood right in front of him. I had a choice. I could spread out my palms to receive the communion, or I could open my mouth and let the priest place it on my tongue. I wanted to give my hands but they were shaking uncontrollably. I looked at him. He smiled at me. "Body of Christ."

"Amen," I replied.

He placed the communion gently on my tongue - all the while looking deep into my soul.

I gave silent thanks to God for preventing me from crumbling and falling flat on my face. I gave thanks as I walked back to my seat. I also gave thanks as I knelt down by my seat. And the whole time, the only thing I could think about were his eyes. This was too much. This was too crazy. This was too confusing. This would get me into serious trouble. I was slowly becoming an undeniable catastrophe.

At the end of Mass, lots of people navigated towards him to bless their items, or to have him place his hands on their prayer books or rosaries or whatever new items they had brought with them that morning. Some merely wanted to thank him for the lovely service. He was gracious and polite to them all. I watched him even as I helped tidy up the church (putting the hymn books away). He didn't look at me again. He was too busy with members of the congregation. He spoke to people as if only they mattered in the whole world. He gave them his full attention, looking into their eyes, smiling at them, making them laugh with witty comments.

It was my turn to clean the church today. I was grateful for the quiet and stillness that surrounded me once everybody had left. He, however, was nowhere to be seen and the silence of the church filled my heart with a familiar sense of tranquillity. Perhaps it was the smell of the incense floating around freely. Perhaps it was the church candles burning quietly in their little corners, seeing everything, saying nothing.

I carried my cleaning bucket from the laundry room into the church. I liked to clean the altar first. It freed up the stage for anyone who wanted to come in and pray.

"Hi."

I felt my back stiffen as I turned around. He had changed from his priestly robe and in its place he wore the same pair of black, skinny jeans that I think adorned his legs at the garden party a month ago. But this time he complemented them with a grey jumper and tiny designer emblem. His lean frame, slim muscular arms and chest, which could be seen through it, were proof that he exercised now and again. His legs were proof that he exercised a lot.

"Hi. I'm sorry, Father. I did not hear you come in."

"I'm sorry. I did not mean to startle you."

So many *sorrys,* I thought.

We both fell silent, standing there looking at each other rather awkwardly, and then I felt I had to say something to fill the space that was slowly expanding; maybe help him out a little bit.

"It's nice to have you back, Father. Mass this morning was very enjoyable."

"Thank you, Iman. I'm so glad that you came." He remembered my name. I wondered if he remembered everybody's name, or perhaps he was just naturally good at it.

His eyes never left mine. He stood there, his eyes searching through me for an answer, an epiphany, a way in or out of this emotional mess.

"I'm not allowed to miss Mass unless I'm ill or away, and today I'm glad of that rule." I was playing along. I didn't quite know how long this game could carry on though. I wasn't oblivious to the crucifix behind me, judging me, filling my soul with treacherous guilt. Our next moment took our acquaintance into a whole new dimension.

I can't remember how long I was away for, he appeared to be thinking, taking me by surprise. "Three weeks and two days," I blurted out in my usual manner before I could stop myself. And only then did I realise that he already knew and was testing me to see if I had kept count.

There was no room for embarrassment. I couldn't undo what I had already revealed - that I'd missed seeing him so terribly that it hurt me to my very soul; that, at this moment, nothing else mattered.

He was smiling like the cat that got the creamiest soufflé.

"I missed seeing you too, Iman. I thought about you a lot. You were strangely on my mind."

"Really? Why?"

"I don't know why." A beat of silence. A nervous twitch. "Did you think about me too?"

"I did think about you, a little bit, but there is simply no point."

"Why do you say that?" He was staring at me very intensely. I was struggling to control my breathing. Before I could answer, he went on to say, "I was sad when you didn't turn up for the dinner party. I was so looking forward to talking with you that evening, and then you didn't show. Why didn't you come, Iman?"

"I was afraid, and poorly, and confused maybe," I whispered.

"Confused about what?" he whispered back, mirroring my ways.

"Your eyes." I could not tell him about the dream. I could not tell him that his eyes haunted both my sleep and waking moments. I could not tell him that maybe in another life, in another place, in another time, I might have belonged to him. I could not tell him about the electricity I felt when I was with him, and also, when I was not with him.

"My eyes? Hmmmm," was all he said in return, as he carried on watching my face most intently.

"Look, Father....."

"Please. *Romilly*." He put his hands in the air. The pain in his face suggested that I'd just slapped him. "Don't ever call me Father - except, of course, when we are in the presence of others." I couldn't, at that time, understand why he disliked his well-deserved title so much.

"OK, Romilly. I need to carry on with the cleaning now."

"Can I help? Can I help with anything?"

"No, thank you. Reverend Mother would be upset with me if I let you help. You did your job this morning. Now, I must do mine."

I turned my back and started cleaning. I could feel his eyes on me, and I would give anything to know what he was thinking.

"Come with me," he whispered, whilst taking my arm.

"To where?"

"Just come," he said.

I dropped my cleaning mop in the bucket and followed him. I was too weak to resist. I didn't know where he was taking me. I simply followed his lead effortlessly and easily. Although I tried to stay calm, inside I felt a burning so deep I thought I might die from the excitement.

We walked through an ill-lit, narrow corridor, past the church offices. The darkness blinded me as we made our way down the empty hallway with only his footsteps to guide us. Without his strong grip on my hand, I would have felt barren and dead on the endless, seamless road that seemingly led nowhere. I was secretly hoping that no one would come out and see the way we were hurriedly striding past - his hand on mine leading the way. It would bequeath an interesting scene - one for gossip no doubt.

He didn't seem to care though.

We ended up in a small office at the end of the corridor and I breathed a sigh of relief as he opened the door and ushered our bodies in. Without looking, I heard the door shut and the turning of the lock. There was no going back, no retribution - only the empty pit of my stomach and the stormy beat of my heart.

"This is my office for the period that I'm here."

"And how long is that?" I couldn't help but ask. I needed to know.

He didn't reply. He just looked at me tenderly.

He slipped his hands over my head and gently took off my veil. His fingers found their way into my hair and undid the knots so that my curly locks came dancing down around my shoulders. I was thankful that I had washed my hair the night before; even I could smell the sweet mixture of lemon and cardamom as my strands of hair wafted through the air around us.

He drew me close and pressed his face into my hair so that I felt his chest on my face. He then brought his face so close to mine that I could smell the sweet fragrance of coffee that he must have drunk that morning. Then his tongue was in my mouth. It happened quite unexpectedly but as assuredly as I knew that it would. Before I could find enough time to recognise what was happening, his hands were around me, as sure and as hard as the wall that he suddenly pushed my back against, gently but forcefully. I felt helpless as the yielding and weakness of a slow warmth arose in my body that I could never before have imagined feeling. His insistent mouth covered mine, probing, tugging, drawing and sucking, sending my body into a wild frenzy of multiple sensations. And just as I thought that there was no religious feeling that could ever compare to what was happening to me right now, I realised - and without any shame - that my fingers were tangled in his hair, and that I was kissing him back vigorously.

When I knew I could no longer breathe, I slowly moved my mouth away in order to compose myself. I was drunk with him.

"I'm sorry," he said.

"No. It's okay," I replied - my breathing slightly heavy, my self-control failing slightly.

"Are you okay?" he asked, as he held me tenderly in a protective way.

"Yes, that was really nice."

"Well, I'd like to do that again."

This time, both his hands cupped my face and drew my lips to his, touching tenderly at first, savouring the outline of my mouth, caressing my lips with his - slowly, passionately and demanding. His tongue eased into my mouth, creating in me a desire so strong that there and then I would have given myself to him without thinking.

We suddenly heard footsteps outside the door and so we stopped, fear gripping us like thieves about to be caught.

Then the footsteps lingered for a second, but drifted away.

"I think you'd better go." Those might have been his words, but in his eyes I could see him begging me to stay.

I didn't want to leave him now, but common sense told me that he was right.

"You're shaking." He was looking at me with those lovely eyes.

"I can't help it." I didn't know what else to say. I was struggling to think, to remain calm, to breathe. He drew me close to him and held me in a silent embrace.

I thought then that he would let me return to my cleaning, but I guess he wasn't finished with me...yet. This time he pulled my whole body towards his and ran his hands up and down my back, my hips, my thighs, my breasts. His lips captured mine again, this time like a hungry lion with no intention of letting go of its prey. I was completely helpless as my body sank into his strong arms, dancing along to the rhythm that he had created.

Then we both stopped in unison, like we could read each other's minds.

He pushed me away from him gently.

"I need you to leave now."

"But...." I began to protest. My body was yearning and wanting him. How could he ask me to leave now?

"Shhh. Not today. Today, I want you to think of me. I want thoughts of me to exist in your very awareness, just as you will exist in mine."

"This is crazy," I whispered back, feeling hurt.

It was like he could read my mind. "I want you with such urgency that it drives me insane, but we can't do this like this. There is so much at stake here. I have to think."

"Romilly. Please." I was shameless.

"Stop. Don't do that. There is so much I want to say, but I can't. Things will work themselves out. They always do. But like I said, I really do need to think."

He reached out and opened the door for me, signalling to me that it was time to leave.

The church was quiet. I looked at the time on my little digital wristwatch. It was 09:09. I had to expel inconceivable sexual thoughts and concentrate solely on the cleaning of God's house.

As I walked down the corridor, I felt that I was being followed. I felt it even before I heard the footsteps - the clicking of high-heel shoes.

I felt someone's eyes on me. I wanted to run and hide. I wanted to cry and scream. I wanted to die. I would deny everything that might have been heard. I would lie to protect Romilly, for I cared not for myself.

I turned around slowly to face my judgement.

She stopped. Standing in front of me was Evangeline Dimitri, a wife of one of the top workers in the church. Her disapproving eyes told me that she'd heard everything, and all I could do was wait and listen.

Deaconess Evangeline Dimitri was Greek with the mannerisms of an upper-class English woman. She spoke with a polished, Greek accent infused with the dignity and staunchness of the British. She had lived in England for thirty years and she was nearing her fiftieth birthday. If she deleted from her past the part where she got married and had children, one would think of her as a very dignified reverend and holy mother; immersing herself in everything Catholic and deciding of her own accord - to anyone that would care to listen - that Catholicism was the one and only true religion.

The rock of Christ - the church that Saint Peter built.

Everything else was a joke - an abomination of the human mind, a false pretence of togetherness.

She was the foundation of the church and the mother of priests. She cooked for them. She cooked for us. She filled our fridges with fruit and vegetables and drinks. And she knew how to throw a good party. She also knew every interpretation of each name in the Bible.

I had overheard her a few times at some of the children's christenings.

"So, what have you decided to name him?"

"Jacob," the new parent would reply proudly.

"Aha - Jacob. Do you know what the Bible says about that name?" Then she would proceed to tell a very long story about the origin of the name as well as the symbolism.

"Noah."

"Aha - do you know about the greatness of Noah?"

"Elizabeth"

"Aha - the mother of John the Baptist."

She knew it all and I smiled each time, thinking what a waste of one's life.

When I turned around and saw her, I wished that it was anybody but her.

"Hello, Deaconess," I smiled fearfully. "I didn't see you there."

She walked up to me and put a hand on my shoulder.

"What's going on with Father Vanderbelt? He seemed to be in such a hurry."

I wasn't sure if her eyes were accusing me of something. It would have been far easier to communicate with her if I knew what was in her head. She had always been a friend to me, and a sensible voice of reason.

"I don't know. He said he has a meeting to attend to."

"With you? He seemed to drag you rather swiftly into his office."

"Oh, that. We were discussing something that he needed to show me. I'm afraid I can't tell you what it was about. It's rather private."

"Oh, okay. I mustn't pry. As long as you know what you're doing. Everyone fancies him you know. He's rather dashing, wouldn't you say?" She was searching my eyes for answers. I looked away.

"I wouldn't know about such things. He also wanted to know if I needed any help with the cleaning. He is so kind."

"Oh, that is kind. So, will he be helping you clean?"

"No, no, no, no, no……" I shook my head in nervous laughter, with perhaps too many nos. "Reverend Mother would be so cross if I were to let dear Father Vanderbelt do the cleaning."

"Okay, darling. I'm off work today. Can we perhaps have tea together later and maybe you can help me with the sitting arrangements for my dinner party."

"Oh, will you be throwing another one?"

"In a few weeks. For all of you, as a thank you for your kindness and hard work in the church."

"I would love that very much."

The truth was I was grateful for so many things at that particular moment - the fact that she didn't suspect anything and the fact that I would be able to occupy my mind with other, less boring events.

I watched her walk away and only then did I let out a big sigh of relief. But then she started to walk back with a look of confusion on her face.

"Just one more thing, Sister Iman."

"Yes?" I was smiling at her now, relieved that her mind had drifted away from Romilly and I.

"You know I walked past his office just now and heard no sound? No sound at all. I could have sworn neither of you were talking."

I felt the colour drain from my face. I had no words. No excuse. I said nothing as I felt the sting of tears and humiliation embrace my face.

"Do be careful, honey."

She turned around with a smile and scurried off.

I did not attend the afternoon tea. I did not think that I could face her so soon after my humiliation. I sent her a quick text message instead explaining that I was needed at the children's hospice. She replied fondly. It was okay, she said - maybe next time.

That night, I cried. I don't know why. Perhaps I was too confused about everything that was happening. Perhaps I knew I would end up hurt.

Please, dear Father, give me the strength to fall out of love with him. My whole life has been one of emotional turmoil. From the woman you gave me to be my mother, to the abusive way she treated me and traded me among her friends. I was not only her slave, but I was an instrument for all her material and sexual desires. I am trying to forget, but the scars simply won't heal. I thought this life would help me heal, but how can I heal when I am constantly judged by You and Your children...Your followers? Romilly has awakened a joy in me that I never knew existed. How can that be so wrong?

I picked up the razor by my bedside more out of habit than pain, stained with blood from a few nights ago. I walked to the bathroom and ran the hot tap over it so that it would be clean again, able to be used. The metal felt wet and rustic. I sat on my bed and very gently placed it next to my skin.

I looked for a spot that was free from scars. Such a blemish-free area didn't exist apart from a small section between my elbow and wrist. I felt the smooth part of my skin amidst the crowded, scar-laden rough.

I sliced.

The drops of blood allowed me a much-needed escape to a tranquil void.

Later, after I cleaned up the blood, I sank into bed and smiled, remembering the kiss. I was troubled - yes. I had scars – yes. But I was slowly finding happiness, and that alone was worth everything.

Chapter 6

Young Romilly

"Where have you two been?"

My father's voice stung like a dangerous viper, laden with anger, fuelled with poisonous venom.

Mama turned to me and fearfully instructed me to go to my room immediately.

"No, he will stand here because he is no longer a child. He will witness all that will happen here today. I am the head of this family and Romilly will only go to his room if and when I deem it okay."

"Perhaps you should have told me you were Hitler. Maybe I would have thought long and hard before marrying you." Even through her fearful anger, I could hear the sarcastic humour in her voice.

"Don't you dare!" Papa exclaimed.

"Oh yes, I *do* dare. You act like a bully and then you bury it all under the pretence of Christianity. Maybe I do not like this God of yours. A God that commands you to batter your wife at every opportunity. What type of God is this? Oh wait, God never commands that." Her arms were outstretched in confused wonder.

"If you blaspheme, things will only get worse for you."

Mama thought Papa's last statement was very funny indeed. She began to laugh in a way I had never heard her laugh before. It was a toxic laughter, filled with derision. Papa and I looked at her in confusion; I, more with fear, as I looked at Papa whose determination to teach his unruly wife a lesson had grown greater.

"You mean things will get worse than they are already?" she chuckled. "Don't make me laugh, *mon amour*. You do kill me with your ways. We should be making love and dancing, but no. I must be punished for enjoying a day out with my son. Only promise me one thing…"

Papa sighed regretfully and asked her what she wanted.

"Kill me this time, for I am done spending my life with you. If you do not kill me, then alas, I must take my own life."

"Mama!" I screamed. I ran to her and wrapped my tiny but strong arms around her waist. I began to cry. I couldn't lose my mother. She was everything to me. She was going to look at my paintings and tell me to focus on being an artist. She was going to take me far away from Papa so that I would never become a Catholic priest.

"Please don't leave me, Mama. Please, I will do anything you ask. Please don't die."

My mother took me in her hands and embraced me in a warm hug. "Never mind your mama, Romilly. I am too dramatic. Of course, I will not die. I was simply upset. I love you." She then kissed my hair, a habit of hers. Just as I was cuddling up to my mother and enjoying the comfort and reassurance she gave me, I felt my father's strong arms pull me roughly away from her embrace. I was too confused to come to terms with the situation as my body was flung to the other end of the room. I must have passed out for a few seconds, for when I came to all I could hear were my mother's screams as my father's belt dug into her.

This was like no other time. There was blood everywhere and I feared for my mother. He would kill her if I did nothing, so I ran towards him to beg him to stop but he simply directed the belt at me and carried on beating my mother. Mama had stopped moving and I didn't know what to do. There was one thing I was sure of: I had to stop my father.

I screamed out for my siblings - calling their names, but they were clearly not in the house. Either that or they had chosen to remain out of sight. It was the unspoken tradition in our family - when Papa hit Mama, everyone stayed away. Well, not me. Not this time.

I looked around the grand hallway and all I noticed, in one brief second, was the coat stand, with numerous coats hanging from it, and the chrome candelabra, with unlit candles. I picked the latter up and brought it straight down onto my father's head - the church candles flitting far and wide.

He stopped. My hands refused to give up the candelabra - still gripping it with vigour and vengefulness.

Papa turned around and looked at me in a state of utter shock and confusion. He fell to his knees - his eyes never leaving mine; a look of fear and wonder at his gentle, quiet son.

I was the child who protected the spider that everyone else wanted to kill.

I looked at my mother's body and, fuelled with anger and disdain for my father, I launched the candelabra once more onto my confused father's head. He fell to the ground and lay motionless on the floor. I didn't care or think about his welfare as I ran towards my mother.

"Mama, Mama." There was no movement from her - her face covered in blood. I ran towards the phone and called the ambulance.

"Hallo," I screamed down the phone.

"Hoe kan ik u helpen?" How may I help you? The female voice replied rather calmly in contrast to the panic I was feeling.

"Meine mutter stirbt." My mother is dying.

I was holding back tears, and was very surprised that the lady on the other end of the phone could hear me properly. Her voice remained calm and reassuring. She asked for my address and I gave it to her in one breath. She confirmed she knew where I was. Everyone in Berlin knew the Vanderbelt estate. I proceeded to go back to my mama.

I looked where Papa's body had been lying, but I was shocked to find that he was no longer there. I was suddenly filled with dread and relief. Relief that I hadn't killed my father after all, and dread at what he would do to me now that he was still alive. I really didn't care. All I cared about in that moment was to find a way to help my mother. She was all I had - my only ally in this big, cold house.

"Who were you talking to on the phone?"

My papa's voice was like a thunderous knife that sliced a little fear into my soul. I had never been more scared of the unknown.

"The ambulance." I did not look up at him. I could not face him now after what I had done. I did not regret it - on the contrary, I'd do it again if such a situation arose. As a matter of fact, I wished with all my heart that *he* was the one lying lifeless in my arms instead of my mother.

"Good call," came his response.

I was taken aback at his calmness. I was expecting him to drag me from my mother's body, tear my trousers down and give me the whipping of a lifetime - the way he had whipped my brother when he was expelled from school.

I looked up slowly at my father. I wanted to be convinced that he wasn't mad at me.

He had a bandage tied over his head. His expression was without any emotion. I was confused. I was doubtful.

"Is Mama dead?"

"I think so. But you must work with me. We cannot tell them what happened here. They will put me in prison and they will send you to a madhouse for doing this to me." He pointed at his head.

"You deserve to go to prison if you killed Mama." I was becoming hysterical. "You deserve to die a thousand deaths!"

"Quiet, boy! People will hear you. And you - do you *want* to go to a madhouse?" My father's face was a mixture of authority and fear. I think he was confused over what emotion he preferred to convey at this particular time.

The thought of going to a madhouse filled me with dread. I had heard about madhouses and psychiatric hospitals. They were horrible places filled with horrible stories. No one in our family had ever been to a madhouse, so I would be the first. But I did not care really - a madhouse would be better than living with Papa, in this house, with my siblings whom I never got on with. And life would be hell without Mama.

The ambulance siren could be heard in the distance, and the noise prompted me to look at Mama.

I saw her fingers move. And then her hands, rising up, signalling for help.

I attended to her - calling her, screaming, wanting her to open her eyes.

"Mama, I'm here. You will be okay. Mama, can you hear me? Please stay with us, please Mama." Tears and snot streamed down my face uncontrollably. Only this morning we had been laughing at books and comics in the library and enjoying ice cream afterwards, feeding the ducks by the river and making the most of the sunshine. How could everything be so different so soon? Why was life so cruel?

She opened her eyes, slowly at first. Then her soft, manicured hands touched my face gently. She struggled to smile between a mask of blood. It must have been difficult, yet she persevered.

I continued to cry. My dear mama was in so much pain, yet I could do nothing to help her.

"The ambulance is on its way. They will be here soon. Can you hear it? They are coming to help you." I hardly recognised my own voice. All I wanted was for her to be reassured.

She nodded gently and smiled. My mama was always smiling, even now, in the face of pain.

"I am truly sorry, Marie-Ange. I never meant for things to get this bad. I lost control. Please forgive me, my love." My father was crying. I wondered why he was crying now. He certainly didn't cry before when he thought that she had died.

I heard the ambulance park outside.

"Let me do the talking. You are to say nothing. I will handle this. Please go to your room."

"I want to stay with Mama," I wanted to scream. I looked at my mother and saw a new, raw fear envelop her face. She shook her head vigorously in a way that was louder than any words.

"No, I will not leave Mama," was all I could muster amidst the confusion.

"Then I will tell them that you did all this. You hit me and almost killed your mother. I will cook up a story that will have you in the madhouse this very instant."

"I will deny it," I responded - the sudden realisation of the monster my father was affecting me deeply.

"Who do you think they will believe?"

I looked at my mother on the floor. She was looking at me, but not saying a word.

"I'm sorry, Mama," I whispered, as I walked meekly to my room; an act I would live to regret for the rest of my life. I was a coward indeed. I should have ignored my father and stayed with my mother. I should have held her hand when she needed me the most. But no, I let my fear of the madhouse overrule the thing I ought to have done. I hated myself at that moment in a way I never thought possible.

I could hear my father let the paramedics in. I could hear them trying to talk to my mother. But as I closed the door to my bedroom, I could hear nothing.

I stood facing the loneliness in my room. The room had been designed by Mother - from the French tapestry curtains, to the boyish, funny pictures on the wall. All designed to reflect my interests; my love of tennis, horses and my inquisitiveness regarding space. They were all here, somehow, in this room. My mother was thoughtful in that way and I completely trusted her judgement. My room was a mixture of light blue and white colours. It was the way my mother wanted it. She said the colours were calming and they would help me feel happy if I was ever sad. I loved it because she loved it. It was my cosy, warm and safe place. It was my little haven.

My room was certainly lived in. There was the faint scent of sweat and unwashed socks, because I hardly ever opened the windows. That only happened when Mama complained about the smell.

Beside my bed was a small table made of old, white German wood. On top of the table was a framed picture of my whole family: my brother, my sister, my parents and me. Beside the picture stood my air humidifier which helped me sleep at night by letting out a cool or warm steam depending on the weather.

In the middle of all this was my Rosary.

I picked up the big, brown beads that were given to me by my late grandfather as a christening present, and got on my knees by my bedside.

I started to pray the Hail Mary.

I wanted my mother to be safe, because I didn't know how to live in a world where she didn't exist.

I blocked out everything and focused on my Rosary.

A shadow appeared at the door of my room. It then moved towards the wall near my bed, stopping in front of me. It was the shape of a woman wearing a veil - her hands clasped together as if in prayer. The Virgin Mary, I thought, had come to visit me.

Or an angel.

Or an ancestor.

I was scared. Fear rose from my feet like a feather slowly crawling to my heart. I wanted to run, but there was nowhere to run *to*. I had to stay in my room, or my father would ensure that I ended up in the madhouse. My fingers gripped the beads of the Rosary until they hurt me and made dimples in my palms.

I closed my eyes tight and willed her to go away.

Then I heard such familiar words - words that changed everything before me.

"I love you, mon fils."

I opened my eyes with a sudden burst of urgency and realised that the shadow on the wall had disappeared.

I was alone in the room once more. My mother - where was she? I had definitely just heard her voice. I got up, sprang out of my room and raced down the corridor, before descending the stairs.

It was then that I heard the ambulance man talking to my father.

"Het spijt me, Mr. Vanderbelt, we hebben alles gedaan wat we konden..."

I'm sorry, Mr. Vanderbelt, we did all we could.

My eyes drifted to the last place I saw Mama on the floor. It was now empty. I approached my father, screaming. I did not care about the madhouse. I did not fear my father's threats or belt. "Where is Mama?" I demanded.

All the grown-ups looked at me, but my papa remained silent. He said nothing. He could not look at me. His face simply stared at the floor.

The ambulance man had kind features. He walked towards me and placed his hand on my shoulder.

"I'm sorry, son. She didn't make it. It must have been terrible for both your parents, being attacked by bandits like that."

He then walked out of the house and drove away with his crew and my mother's perished body.

I was whisked off to France that night. My papa did not wish to take any chances. We made a pact: I was to remain quiet and the madhouse would elude me. I didn't get to attend my mother's funeral. I didn't get to say goodbye. I didn't get to indulge my passion, my painting again. And I didn't even get to say goodbye to my siblings. Not that this last bit mattered very much.

I stayed with my grandparents in Burgundy for five years, and even if Papa had not threatened me I would have said nothing for fear of causing hurt to them. It felt much easier remaining quiet and introverted in my suffering. I was already fluent in French so making friends and integrating into school life was not hard to accomplish. Although I found it a little difficult to make friends, I did not find my studies arduous at all. I had only one dream, one future - the vision that my family had carved out for me: becoming a priest. I let that thought dominate my whole existence - for that was my only light.

And when I turned seventeen, I was sent to a seminary in Rome to carry out my family duties.

Papa congratulated me on my contribution to the family when I qualified. The truth is that I didn't do it for him. I did it for me.

Life was simply waking up every morning and performing my duties. I assumed that my life would remain that way until the day I left this world.

Then I met Ciara, and she taught me about bodily pleasures. And because of her, I knew what I had known all along: that I was never supposed to be a priest, and that I would never make Cardinal.

Chapter 7

Young Iman

I woke up hesitantly, yet with a hopeful sound in my chest, not really knowing what to expect. I did not expect anything extraordinary. As far as I was concerned, it would be like previous birthdays I had had. They were never any different from other days. I did not get presents, or cards or birthday greetings from my mother. On my birthdays, I was usually grateful to my school community though. My teachers and class mates would gather round with a huge card and a small chocolate cake. The Happy Birthday chorus would engulf my ears in a rhythm of joy and, for that moment alone, I would smile.

They would put a crown on my head. They didn't have to go that far - I was content with the fact that someone remembered, because at home no one did.

It was a ritual that happened in school. The difference between me and everybody else was that the other kids' parents provided the cake. With me, my teachers did. It was a day that brought both great and sad expectations; great because I always received presents like pencil cases and journals - presents that I was never allowed to keep because my mother would sell them and inform me that I had no need for them; sad because it was a day that was impregnated with *more* rules, *bigger* changes and *heavier* chores.

When my classmates asked me what I had received at home, I would lie. Every. Single. Year.

"Oh, I received a new television for my bedroom." This was because one of the kids had said the exact same thing a year ago.

And the previous year: "Oh, I received a Barbie Doll house."

And the year prior to that: "Oh, I received a pretty blue dress with ballerina shoes."

When I looked at my teacher, Mrs Pot's face, I got the feeling that she knew I was lying, for her smile wasn't one of genuine delight, but rather profound sadness.

My birthday was never a thing of joy for my mother, but a road to more rules and duties around the house. The older I got, the more chores my mother introduced. So, as I awoke this morning, I anticipated the trouble and screaming of orders that awaited me. I could actually feel the trembling of my body, the quickening of my heartbeat and a small patch of ice beginning to rise from the base of my spine.

I heard footsteps navigating towards my door and it was as if a thunderous storm cloud was closing in before its inevitable pouring of heavy, dark, ominous rain into my heart.

There was a reason why I dreaded birthdays so much. I had learnt from them an anguish that always returned.

From the age of ten, I had been called into my mother's room and informed that I would have to start paying my way in her house. I was, of course, too young to perform certain duties and so she listed for me the chores I was to execute each morning before going to school.

Wake up at 5am without fail. Clean the toilet with the brush and mop the floor. Tidy the dishes left in the sink from the previous evening and sweep the floor. Dust the living room surfaces and sweep the floor. Have bowl of cereal and go to school.

That was when I first developed my check system. For if I forgot any one of my duties, no matter how well I had performed with the others, I was certain to receive a good, sound beating.

I remember once when this happened. Funnily enough, it was on my eleventh birthday. It was also the day I discovered that she was not my real mother.

My classmates wanted me to come out and play with them after school.

"Iman, you never come out to play. It's your birthday - let's go to the park."

I tried to get out of it, for I knew my mother would never let me.

"I'm not feeling too well today. My tummy has been hurting all day." Lying was something that I did very easily. To me, it was survival.

They pushed and pushed, and in the end I agreed to see them that afternoon - a decision I would come to regret.

After school, I thought that if I cleaned the house quickly and did my afternoon chores, then Mother wouldn't mind so much.

My afternoon chores involved changing her sheets and cleaning her bedroom, as well as emptying her bin. You see, Mother had so many customers that came in daily and they all worked in her room with her. It was important that I kept this room clean for her next customer. It was equally important that I emptied the bin, as she said the bin was the most important job of all. I didn't understand why - after all, all I emptied each day were a few tissues.

So, on this day, I changed her sheets, and put the old ones in a bucket of hot water to soak, just like I had been instructed to do. I wiped down the surfaces of the bedside table and chest of drawers, and I swept the floor, but I forgot the most important thing of all: I did not empty the bin. I would have but for the knock on the door; my class mates bellowing for me to join them. They were lucky that Mother was not in. She was never at home in the afternoons. She cleaned other people's houses at that time. It was why cleaning her room was important, as she had more customers in the evening.

Anyway, I forgot to empty the bin and I went out to play. I forgot what time it was as I was having too much fun. I also forgot that I was not allowed to play with other children. But most importantly, I forgot how cruel my mother could be.

"I have something to tell you," she said to me, after I arrived home just before 7pm. Her last customer had this minute left and she was surprisingly very calm.

I remained quiet. I was too scared to speak, too scared to move, too scared to breathe.

"I did not want to tell you this just yet, but your actions have pushed me to it."

Then she waited for a while before carrying on.

"I am not your real mother. Do you know that?" The look on her face was one of disgust and there was no doubt in my mind that she was telling the truth.

"Do you know that?!" She was almost screaming at this point. I felt inclined to answer her, so I shook my head as I could not find any words.

"Your parents never wanted you and so I took you in, but this is how you repay me?" Her voice was rising rapidly and I couldn't stop the words that slowly began to form in my mouth.

"I'm sorry...but...you're *not* my mother?" I was so confused.

"Tonight I will show you that I could *never* be your mother."

In one swift movement, she grabbed me by my arm. I was too much in a daze to understand the speed of what was happening. I was too confused to fight her or struggle.

Then, I felt my body being dragged down the stairs and eventually flung into the basement.

The lock on the door sealed my fate.

The basement was dark and cold, and it had a rusty, wet smell of old wood. I could hear creepy crawlies - maybe mice or cockroaches. I wasn't sure which, but I was certain there was something crawling about looking for food. That certainly did not bother me compared to the darkness. She knew I was scared of the dark and so this was the worst punishment that she could ever have given me.

At first, I thought I would be kept there for a few minutes, or maybe hours. But what I thought would be a few hours turned out to be three days. It was in there that darkness itself, in every form, enveloped me - from the outside into my soul. It was in that basement that I stopped feeling. It was in that basement that I became an adult, and childish things and childlike thoughts left me completely. It was in that basement that the seed of hate was planted; hatred for my *real* parents, hatred for my *fake* mother, hatred for my *friends*, hatred for the *world* and hatred for everything else that came near me.

There was really no love before, but now, there was no love at all - period.

I was locked in there, without food and without water. And the corner of the room was my toilet.

The door to the basement helped me count the days, as well as the noise from our boisterous neighbours. I could see sunbeams illuminated through the door and when it got darker they disappeared.

On my first day I cried and cried - wallowing in self-pity. I was thirsty and hungry, and so all I did was pray. I also needed the toilet very badly, but decided to hold it all in. When I fell asleep, however, and woke in the morning, I realised that I'd wet myself. I stayed in those wet clothes all day until the following afternoon when she came and finally let me out.

"You smelly thing!" she barked, upon finally opening the door. "Clean this place up and go wash yourself and eat some food. Then you must return to your chores."

So today was another birthday and this time I needn't be worried about friends asking me to play, for they had given up on me and my moods long ago.

That morning on my fourteenth birthday, just as my eyes slowly awakened to the ray of sunlight that beamed through my window, the footsteps approaching my room sped up my coming to.

My door was flung open without a courteous knock.

"I thought I told you to get up at 5am every morning and do your chores!" she screamed. "How dare you defy me, you ungrateful wretch. Do you know where you would be if I hadn't taken you in when your useless mother died?" She then stormed right out.

I looked at the clock by my bedside. It was 05:05am. I had overslept by five minutes.

Our home was always noisy at night. It was a wonder I got any sleep at all. Disturbing our neighbours didn't matter, for they too were noisy. They hardly ever went to work during the day, and they listened to music all night, dancing, swearing, cursing and sometimes fighting. This was very normal for me though; the only life I knew.

Because of the noise, I couldn't sleep until they had quietened down themselves. If I was lucky, this was usually around 2am. If I was unlucky, it wouldn't be at all. It was no wonder that my school work suffered.

Mother blamed the school for my bad performance, as well as my laziness. And, in private, she would ram her words down my throat.

"If you ever tell anyone in school about my midnight guests, I will starve you to death. You must remember that that is the only way we have a place to lay our heads. It is the only way I can put food on the table."

Food on my table was twice or sometimes once a day. I was therefore very grateful for school dinners.

I rose to get ready, but was shocked to hear footsteps approaching my room again.

What was the problem now? I wondered.

She walked in this time with a calmer demeanour.

I watched as she shifted her weight nervously from one foot to the other and fluttered her eyelids as if she were on a very windy beach.

"Well, my darling daughter - I need to ask you a question."

I assumed I must have misheard. Darling? Me? Daughter? Wow - what was going on?

My mother never *asked* anything. She simply ordered and I obeyed. How could I not? Also, I did not want a flogging or days in the basement.

She frequently reminded me about my unloving father and my weak mother who died simply giving birth. She, my mother Hadiza, was apparently the kind one, the good one, the one that deserved all my love and respect.

I didn't trust myself to reply, so I just stood there, motionless and looked at her - not knowing what her question would be, not daring to guess. She had called me her darling daughter, so why was I not overjoyed? Why, instead, was my heart filled with dread?

"I have come to talk to you about your future now that you are fourteen. You look older than your age suggests as you have been lucky enough to mature early."

"More chores?" I asked.

She laughed. I had never heard her laugh at me or with me before so I just looked and wondered what it was that she wanted from me which made her so friendly.

"I have very rich friends who come to visit at night. They would like to meet you and get to know you." She paused to see what effect her words had had.

"I will do anything to make your friends happy, Mummy. I want you to be happy and I will be very glad to finally hang out with your friends like you do." If only I knew what I was letting myself in for.

My mother's face was euphoric. My heart danced in that instant with elation, for I wanted so much to please my mother. Maybe things would finally begin to change around here. Maybe the evil treatment would stop or, more realistically, reduce.

"So, that's settled then. Today we shall go out and buy you a lovely dress, as we want you to look your best."

I couldn't believe it. I was to have a brand new dress - not hand-me-downs from the charity shops.

The world, for me, suddenly changed. It appeared to look the same from my bedroom window, but inside me something had changed and I felt happy about it. I vowed in my heart to always please my mother, and to make her friends happy.

We went shopping that day after school, and first wandered through a lingerie stand in the town market.

"Why are we here, Mother? I thought we were buying a dress?" my innocent voice whispered in a confused state.

"Ha, yes we are, but nice lingerie makes our dresses look even nicer. It gives us confidence," she assured me.

So much to learn about becoming a woman.

I didn't care much about nice, lacy undergarments - after all, no one was going to see them. The dress, on the other hand, was a completely different story. I was bursting with excitement; my very first, brand new dress.

After my mother had purchased what I thought to be the most disgusting outfit ever - red lingerie covered in laces that looked too big for me - we started looking at dresses.

I was surprised that she bypassed the children's section and went straight to the ladies department. I said nothing as I did not want to appear disagreeable and ungrateful.

My mother, without asking me, chose a flattering, red short dress that had a wide opening at the chest. It was so short that I would be afraid to pick anything up off the floor for fear of exposing myself.

I hated the dress, but I said nothing.

At this point, I began to feel my initial excitement slowly evaporate - leaving in its place a void, an uncertain loss. I could not understand the basis or reason for buying such clothes. Perhaps it was the way her friends dressed? I had, after all, never met them. I was always in bed by the time they arrived and, under no circumstances whatsoever, was I permitted to leave my room until morning.

Evening didn't come soon enough. Mother advised me not to eat anything so that my stomach would remain flat and skinny. I was starving, but said nothing. I was also tired and wanted to sleep. I had lost all excitement for what was to come.

"They usually come late – any time from 11pm - so please try and stay awake. Or, better still, go and sleep now," she concluded as an afterthought. "I will wake you up when they are on their way."

I was grateful for this bit of kindness bestowed upon me. I knew that sleeping would take away my hunger. Experience had taught me that.

The soft shaking of my body gradually and gently woke me from my deep sleep. I looked at my bedside clock as I always did. It was 11.55pm - almost midnight.

"Iman, wake up, they are here, and they so badly want to see you. Go and wash your face and use some of the mouth wash. I've laid out your clothes. Remember to wear them as I showed you." Her voice was full of kindness, and her eyes danced with love for me.

"But, Mum, I'm so tired. Can I please see your friends tomorrow?"

My mother's sharp hand against my face was sudden and unexpected. It was as if someone had picked up a very heavy book and thrown it against my eye. And it stung like a million stings.

"How dare you negotiate with me, you ungrateful piece of shit! Do you choose to embarrass me in front of my friends? You will get dressed this minute and meet us all downstairs, or I will show you who is boss around here."

My bedroom door shut with a bang following her exit.

I knew at that moment that my mother had never meant to be nice to me at all - that she did not wish to make my life any easier. She had other plans, but I wasn't sure what they were.

I was to do as she desired or else I would get a lot more than the taster session that she had just inflicted on me.

I managed to dress up as she asked, crying as I did so. By the time I walked down the narrow staircase and fearfully crept into the living room, I was a sea of emotion. I could hear them laughing before I walked in, and they did not sound like women. I entered the room and was faced by four bulky men with big bellies and drunken eyes.

I once heard my mother tell one of her friends that the African showed his wealth through the size of his stomach. The bigger it was, the richer he was supposed to be. It meant that he ate well and slept well.

"Come here, my child," one of the men said to me. I looked at my mother's face. She was the only woman present and she nodded at me whilst smiling. The sting on my face still lingered, reminding me of what could happen if I refused to obey.

I walked towards the man and he looked me over.

"How old are you?" he asked.

"Fourteen."

"Seventeen," my mother interjected.

"Well," he smiled, revealing brown teeth, "I can find out for myself if both of you are unsure."

In front of my mother and the other men, he slid his fat fingers across my leg and gently walked them to my underwear. I slapped his hands off me and ran, tears streaming down my face.

So this was what my mother wanted me to do with these men. I had been taught sex education in school and had a feeling that these men did not want me to just sit on their laps and be fed ice cream.

I ran straight to my bedroom and shut the door behind me, locking it so that even my mother would not be able to get in.

I was breathing heavily, waiting, knowing that she would come stomping up the stairs with all the anger in the world for not getting her way.

I did not have to wait long. Even though I was expecting it, the bang still made me jump.

"Iman - open this door at once."

I remained standing where I was. I would not let her use me for sex with those men.

"Iman, if I have to break this door down, you will spend a whole week in the basement, I promise you."

Suddenly sex with those men did not seem so bad compared to the prospect of spending a whole week in the basement reduced to a church rat. I didn't give my mind room for thought or negotiation as I walked towards the door and gently undid the lock.

That night I lost my virginity. I worked for my mother one night a week after that. She supplied me with condoms and new clothes, and I brought the money in when she couldn't.

In my heart I had ceased to exist, for nothing mattered in the world and nothing made sense.

Chapter 8

Romilly

My twenty-seventh birthday happened to fall on the day of *La Festa di San Pietro e Paolo*. All my birthdays fell on this day, but on my twenty seventh, something more interesting happened to me - something that had never happened before.

It was a feast celebrated by all of Rome, and my initial plan was to remain indoors, as usual, within the walls of Vatican City.

I still missed my mother, particularly on special occasions like Christmas, her birthday, Easter and my birthday. So today, missing her was no different. I struggled - even after all these years - to come to terms with the knowledge that my father had murdered my mother, and that I was the only one who knew about it. I remained silent, never having the inner strength to report my father to the authorities; just acting and living as if it had never happened.

I was a true coward.

My father had, I heard, recently died from cancer. When my uncle, the cardinal - who had been my guardian in Rome - informed me, my first response to him was: "Oh, well, the world is now a better place."

Cardinal Hugo instructed me to say ten Hail Marys in confession.

There was not a man on earth who was as righteous as my uncle. He followed the Catholic faith with all his spirit and, as someone possessed of diligence and discipline, I could only admire him. I, alas, knew I would never be like him. I carried too much anguish in my soul, like a heavy burden slowly dragging me down. The more I sought solace and peace, the more troubled I became. There was nothing that could erase the way my dearest mother had died. I simply could not move on from that.

I did, however, perform all the rituals expected of me from the church. I fasted during Lent. And I prayed and studied the Bible - immersing myself, practising the liturgy and engaging diligently in pastoral learning, church history and preaching.

I got a little comfort sometimes, but there remained within me a pain that would not heal. And the truth was, despite all my theological understanding, I knew of no way to heal it, no way to lessen its grip. A darkness hovered over me at night. It was the last feeling I had before I slept and the first feeling I had upon waking.

It was always there - reminding me of my mortality, telling me I was nothing or no one.

One would presume that living in Stato della Città del Vaticano at the seat of the Roman Catholic Church would eradicate such darkness. That is what I thought when we moved from Uncle's parish in Naples to reside permanently inside the headquarters of the church.

As I celebrated my birthday along with the feast of St. Peter and St. Paul, mixing with the locals and rejoicing were delights I opted to forgo. I preferred, instead, to live like an ascetic - relaxing in the comfort of my own bedroom, burying my head in a good or bad book, and dreaming of painting; but not actually being brave enough to buy a canvas.

So today was no different from the way I had celebrated my birthday in all the years I'd been in Rome. I enjoyed attending Mass in the morning, however, as it was celebrated by His Holiness.

The Basilica was not big enough to accommodate the thousands of people that had come not only to be blessed by the Pope, but to rejoice. It was a public holiday - a day surrounded by noisy tourists, enthusiastic locals, under-confident musicians and exuberant thieves.

I could not help but look out of my window in order to feel and sense the life that I had chosen to avoid.

The tall clock tower beckoned all the traffic to the centre of the square, where it inched along the papal enclave. Scooters and mopeds zipped between cars and picturesque little shops, somehow cheating what one thought were inevitable accidents. The shops were many: the *tabaccheria*, with its racks of newspapers and magazines tumbling out of the entrance as if struggling to be set free; the *farmacia*, with its neon green cross; the *salumeria*, serving all manner of hams that dangled in the window, inviting one to step in and savour a piece; and of course the pavement *cafés* where the tables were always - and I mean *always* - taken by the locals.

I frequently wondered how people survived financially if they sat in bars all day - chatting, eating and drinking espressos. All *I* wanted to do was remain in my quiet place.

Thankfully, I did not have any friends to celebrate with. Perhaps people thought me strangely quiet. I was shy and didn't know how to behave in company, or have the first idea of what to say. I was only comfortable in the presence of my uncle, whom I had known since birth and who'd been chosen by my grandfather to become a priest. My uncle, to his credit, always organised a dinner party of some sort for my birthday; a few people close to him invited. Such gatherings, such occasions were held in the evening, so it was surprising to hear a knock at my door. My eyes drifted to the clock. It had only just gone 11am.

I had settled down to read a book that I'd picked up from the market a few Saturdays before. It was written by Leon Uris, a well-known Jewish-American author. *The Haj* was about a Palestinian Arab family, as witnessed by the youngest son, Ishmael. I was just beginning to get into it, so the interruption was not welcome, but, as always, I was civil.

As I opened my door, I was shocked to find my uncle's head chef standing there, smiling at me.

"Buon giorno, Romilly."

"Buon giorno, Pedro," I replied with a grin.

"My family and I would like to invite you to join us at St. Peter's Square for a small picnic to celebrate your birthday."

I couldn't refuse such a kind gesture, and in this case it would be rude to decline. Even though I was looking forward to having some private time with my new book, the thought of enjoying a picnic at the Piazza San Pietro on my birthday with a lovely family didn't sound like such a bad idea at all.

"That's very kind of you, Pedro. I shall get dressed and join you downstairs."

"Okay, we will be in the centre of the square. Just make your way towards the Obelisk - you won't miss us," he said in heavily-accented English, knowing that my Italian was still below par. Pedro was considerate like that - mixing it up a bit when conversing with me.

"*Grazie, Pedro.*"

"*Prego.*"

He rushed off, presumably to join his family.

Speaking of Pedro and his family, from the first day I arrived in Rome, they made me feel at home, and they had been the family that I silently craved. Gloria, his wife, was a very good cook too. I knew this because she always brought treats to my bedroom - Italian sweets and luxurious pastries. Her homemade zabaglione with berries was out of this world, and I would literally kill for her chocolate gelato sandwiches.

I quickly changed into a pair of smart, black jeans and kept my light blue top on.

Leaving my room, I walked obligingly along the corridor, and down the spiral staircase. As I opened the main door, I was greeted by the blazing sun that beamed its golden rays upon the thousands of people roaming the square. Even when crowded, the square did not seem to lose its enchanting lustre.

I couldn't help but take in the heavenly smell of the food on the stalls. Right in front of me stood a booth selling the *chitarra* for pasta making. I was always amazed at how the Italians used the guitar strings to cut off sheets of pasta into a *tonarelli*. This sudden view reminded me of Gloria because she made the best *carbonara* with these square sheets. It was a good thing I went running for two hours each day, otherwise I might have ended up a bit too big.

The smell of spit-roasted *porchetta* and baked rolls inflamed my nostrils from the sidewalk. I was about to ignore the delicious aroma when I was tormented by the *fritti* in a corner, and at every stall stood a justifiably massive queue. There was food literally everywhere, from pizza stalls to *olive ascolane*.

I ignored them all and stumbled through the crowd to where Pedro's family was waiting for me.

I was glad I wasn't stuck in my room when there was so much life out here; enough Italian street food to last for decades.

As I joined Pedro and his family by the Obelisk, I noticed that there was a beautiful addition. She couldn't have been his daughter as she didn't look quite young enough. Pedro had three teenage sons - all as hefty and big as their father. Gloria was equally, very plump, but I suppose she couldn't help it, since she lived in that sweet-smelling kitchen.

The addition, however, had striking looks, beautiful curves and captivating eyes. I tried not to look at women, but I couldn't help myself. Beautiful women made me feel good inside and I never hesitated to indulge myself. I noticed too how women looked at me, and without shame. I had become accustomed to it. I first noticed it when I turned seventeen, and I enjoyed it, but pretended not to.

It was a sin to acknowledge these feelings. I was committed to a life without women, a life without sex and a life married to Christ and the church.

There was only one problem.

I felt like there was a different life for me somewhere else; a life with a beautiful woman, children of my own, and plenty of art galleries filled with my paintings. The only time in the day when I felt happy was whenever I imagined this world. I would sink into my subconscious and enjoy a moment of bliss.

"Hello, Romilly." Gloria grabbed me in an affectionate embrace. She treated me like one of her sons and at the same time maintained a respectful formality when required.

"Thank you so much for this, Gloria. It is wonderful. I can't wait to tuck into your picnic basket." They all found this comment very amusing even though, deep down, I was actually serious.

"Come and meet my younger sister, Ciara. She came to visit us from Venice. She runs a café there. She likes to attend Rome for *La Festa di San Pietro e Paolo*."

"Nice to meet you, Ciara." I leaned towards her and gently grazed her blushed cheek with my lips.

"Hello, Father. It is lovely to meet you too." Her accent was simply beautiful - sexy even. It was the way she spoke, with her eyes never leaving mine. She looked at least ten years older than me, even though she had tried to conceal her age with heavy eye shadow that so perfectly adorned her face. She smiled sweetly, holding my gaze. My eyes drifted around her as I felt slightly uncomfortable. She was beautiful and my admiration for women always ended there, but somehow I had a feeling that Ciara would be bold enough to demand more.

If her extended family noticed, they said nothing and pretended not to look at us. They were just busy laying out the food.

"It is the best, isn't it?" She began to walk towards the Vatican Obelisk that stood over 25 metres tall. It was said to be the oldest Obelisk - brought from Egypt to Rome in 37AD.

"It is definitely very intimidating." My legs followed hers without any thought or reason. All I wanted was to remain in her company.

"Intimidating? The Obelisk or me?" Her eyes sank into mine, dominating my senses. I looked away.

I turned around and noticed in the midst of the crowd that Gloria had set up the picnic, and suddenly I remembered my manners.

"We should get back to your family. I'm rather hungry."

"Ok - we must talk later." Her request sounded more like an order than a polite invitation.

I just simply nodded in obedience. I was not accustomed to such bluntness.

Gloria had laid out red wine, tea, coffee and lemonade on a colourful, chequered, Sicilian picnic blanket.

It was a pleasant surprise to find that most of the food I had passed in the square was in this huge basket of Gloria's; a whole leg of pancetta, with hot rolls, warm pizzas, olives and a fresh bowl of *panzanella*.

"Wow, you must let me contribute something towards the cost of this feast. I couldn't possibly let you pay for all of this!"

"I will hear of no such thing. It is your birthday, so eat up."

This was said with affectionate authority by Pedro and I was overwhelmed with gratitude. Suddenly, I felt like a little boy years ago who would not let his mother kiss him in public. If that child had known what would happen later on to his mother, then perhaps he wouldn't have refused her affection so stubbornly.

I pushed the sad memory of Marie-Ange to the back of my mind, and chose instead to focus on the lovely family before me, Ciara included.

"So, Father - clearly you are not Italian. Your accent is hard to place." Ciara was not giving up on me so easily.

"I'm not. I grew up in Berlin and Burgundy. I came to live in Rome with my uncle when I turned seventeen."

"Ha! I knew I could detect a French accent there," she teased.

"I wouldn't exactly call it that. I still believe my German accent carries more weight in my diction."

"Which is rather sexy, I might say. No?"

I could have heard a pin drop in our little party, even in the midst of the colourful fireworks, the musicians playing the *Inno e Marcia Pontificale*, and the children screaming at the nearby fairground. I could see the embarrassment and anger in the eyes of Pedro and Gloria. Then, I did what came naturally, for bubbling inside my belly was laughter so strong that it could not be beaten down. Without warning, this effervescence of mirth escaped my lips - for I found her comment both witty and audacious. And it must have released the tension for Pedro, Gloria and their three sons as they too joined in the laughter, albeit a little uncomfortably.

"Please forgive my sister-in-law, Romilly. She lives in Venice - a land for dreamers in love."

"There is nothing to forgive, Pedro. I find Ciara rather delightful and a breath of fresh air."

This time I gazed into her eyes and she held my stare. She was clearly more experienced than I was for I quickly discontinued the moment and changed the topic of conversation. And although we talked about the church, our community, the Pope, politics, history and religion, just one thing uncontrollably consumed my mind: Ciara.

I was smitten, and I knew it. I was also not scared of exploring things with her. I did not have the courage to pursue her, but if she came to me I knew I would not turn her away.

I did not know what it was like to be in the arms of a woman, let alone a beautiful and sophisticated woman like Ciara. I had only ever had such encounters in my dreams. Now, however, I had a strong feeling that I wouldn't have to wait long for such splendour to present itself in reality.

My inner battle between good and evil began to torment me, telling me that it was time to leave.

"Thank you so much for this, guys. I must go and get ready for Mass."

"Oh, where are you saying Mass, Father? And at what time?" Gloria asked.

"At the old people's home at four o'clock. They can't enjoy the celebrations, so I promised to visit and say Mass for them."

"You are so kind, Father. Please don't forget your dinner party at eight."

"Oh, yes - that. I don't think I can eat anything else today." My hands rubbed my full stomach.

"I think your uncle would be hurt if you do not attend. Some of the nuns will be attending along with deacons of the church. They are all looking forward to it, as they do each year." Pedro looked like he would burst if I dared cancel my own dinner party. I guess I had no say in the matter.

The nuns frightened me. I was always scared that they could see in me what others couldn't. Perhaps I was just paranoid, but I could never shake that thought away. I simply did not like nuns, and to think that they would be there judging everything I said, looking down their noses at me - the quiet lad that they couldn't figure out.

The deacons, on the other hand, were rich men who fed the church with their money and made up the rules that we all had to follow.

I did not wish to attend this party of mine, but I felt if I didn't then Pedro would be the one with the broken heart.

"I'll see you all at eight then, Pedro." My eyes navigated towards Ciara's. She was looking at me. I could not tell what she was thinking. Were her thoughts the same as mine?

"Will you be attending my birthday dinner, Ciara?" I asked.

"Well, now that you ask, I couldn't possibly refuse." Her smile could not have been wider - eyes still holding mine.

"Great. See you all soon."

I gave the boys a friendly punch each, shook Pedro's hand and kissed Gloria on both cheeks.

Then I looked at Ciara. I couldn't fathom what she expected of me, but I gave her a friendly wave, not trusting myself to get too close.

I thought about her as I said Mass that afternoon, and I thought about her when I walked home. As I had a few hours left before the dinner party, I tried to settle back into *The Haj*.

I couldn't.

In that moment Ciara was all that made sense to me. It was the way she'd looked at me. It was obvious that we both wanted each other. I didn't know how strong that yearning was though, or if I was willing to commit such a grave sin, or whether I was willing to risk everything for one night of passion. I didn't know if she was worth it - or if *I* was worth it.

Later on that evening, just before eight, I attended my birthday dinner. The multitude of voices emerging from the great dining hall indicated that I was probably one of the last to arrive. Perhaps I had the wrong time?

One look at the feast laid out made me want to turn around and run for my life. I couldn't, however, deny the hard work that had been put in - preparing the spread and room decorations, and summoning all the guests.

The huge mahogany table took up most of the room in the great hall. It could easily have seated twenty people, along with the Italian dishes, silver and candelabras that boasted smooth, grey, church candles, silently dripping wax. Hanging above the table, in the centre of the room, was an old, wrought iron chandelier in which several white candles were lit, creating a soothing, serene feeling and almost angelic atmosphere. Perhaps the walls in the great room needed some paint, but that did not dampen its grandeur. It was a fine, medieval room, fit for princes. And floating through the air was the enchanting *Clair De Lune* courtesy of the gentle fingers of Debussy.

The Catholic Church paid for this luxury - my uncle was, after all, a cardinal of not just anywhere, but Rome.

After that delicious lunch earlier, I didn't have much space left in my stomach. Even the four mile walk to and from the nursing home failed to restore my appetite. It was imperative, therefore, that I devise a plan - maybe one with similar mischief to that which I created when I was little. Surprisingly, you see, despite being French, my mother was a very bad cook, and since I would rather die than hurt my dear mama's feelings I'd sit at the table and pretend to eat my food. When she looked away, I discreetly shovelled some into the dog's ever-watering mouth. Unfortunately, there was no dog to help out right here.

"Hello, dear nephew. I'm glad you managed to turn up. I was told you didn't want this dinner," my uncle teased.

The room suddenly became quiet, in anticipation of my reply.

"*Mea culpa*," I whispered to my uncle, placing my hand on my chest in the traditional gesture of humility, plus humorous pleading for forgiveness.

My emotions danced around as I studied the people already seated for dinner.

"*Buonasera*," I said with a smile, appreciative of their attendance but not deceiving myself one bit into thinking that they were here for me. It was obvious that their presence was out of respect for my uncle, Cardinal Hugo.

I noticed that Gloria was struggling to ensure that the preparation of dinner was orderly and unchaotic. I could hear her moving around the adjacent kitchen giving orders to the waiters. Instinctively, I began to get up to give her a hand, but my uncle's frown and shake of the head signalled for me to remain seated. I was still in training as a newly-ordained priest, and so everything I did I executed with his permission.

The meal started with the *antipasti* - sharp blue, Dutch Edam and Havarti cheese in tiny wedges, adorned with Genoa salami, *prosciutto*, *mortadella* and sliced *coppa*. The wonderful smell of the roasted baby peppers tantalised my nostrils, awakening in me an appetite so strong that nibbling on the black olives and sliced cucumber did not seem like the wisest thing to do.

Then, in came the first course - the *primi;* a heavily laden platter of rice, pasta and *polenta*. I filled up my plate with the polenta and a tiny bit of pasta, as the corn would certainly not fill me up ahead of the *secondi*; this dish appearing before us, as if by magic, in the form of a hearty plate of salmon, shoulder of lamb with buttered baby potatoes and roast vegetables.

One would think I couldn't possibly take in any more delicious food, or drink any more wine from my uncle's vineyard but, surprisingly, I fancied a *gelato* for dessert. Besides, it was my birthday and the contents of the table would not eat themselves.

I wanted to burst.

Minutes later, as we were enjoying coffee and I laboured to finish a cake, Father Sylvano - one of the priests at the end of the table who I personally found insufferable - suddenly exclaimed: "I have never been acquainted with such a disparate circle before."

"Please explain what you mean, Father Sylvano," my uncle mused, wondering if his guest was a little intoxicated.

"Well, we've got four wonderful nuns all seated together on my right, Pedro and his three sons on my left, two deacons and their wives opposite me, the great philosophy professor Alessandro, a cardinal (that is *you* of course), a beautiful lady I have never met before, and your nephew. Pretty motley, wouldn't you say?"

At this stage, it was clear that Father Sylvano had consumed too much wine.

"Don't forget yourself, too," the professor added. The remark prompted much laughter. Professor Alessandro was a physicist and a philosopher from the University of Rome. He was very close to my uncle, and I had learnt a great deal from both men ever since I arrived in Rome. My uncle raved about religion and Alessandro contradicted his views with science.

In my mind it was possible for science and religion to co-exist, although I was still trying to discover the road to such a place.

"Well, the real world is filled with diversity, Father Sylvano," my uncle fired back, rather calmly.

"Now, that is what bothers me, Cardinal. They are saying that we are too archaic, that we ought to change the laws. They want our priests to take on wives and families. Very soon women will become priests and even the Pope might one day be a woman. What a hideous world that would be." He shook his head in disgust, as if the mere thought of that had already given him palpitations. My eyes naturally drifted to the women at the table, feeling sorry for them already. The nuns were obviously in agreement with the traditionally-minded priest though.

"The Catholic Church has lasted thus far due to its traditions. *Nunc et usque in aeternum et ultra.*"

I could swear that was the first time I ever heard Sister Sofia speak, with both her hands flying up in the air to emphasise her emotions. She really did believe that Catholic laws should last for evermore.

"Well, Reverend Sister - you are right. Even as a woman you understand these things." I shifted uncomfortably on my chair due to Father Sylvano's arrogance and the condescending manner in which he spoke.

"Yes," my uncle replied, "but the world is changing. Don't you think that the Catholic Church should perhaps adapt and change with it?"

"You disappoint me, Cardinal. What does your faithful nephew think about all this? He is young. Maybe he has a youthful perspective?"

At this point, the professor jumped to my defence.

"I don't necessarily think that we should involve the young priest in these discussions. He is still learning, and he might offend with his reply without meaning to."

"Well said, Alessandro." My uncle affectionately patted the hands of his dear friend in appreciation.

Dinner was tiring and lasted a couple of hours. I managed to smile and talk and laugh through it all, but not once did I look at Ciara. I could not bear it, and I could not afford to be the centre of gossip.

As we said our goodbyes, I was gentlemanly enough to shake the men's hands and kiss the women - even Ciara. I decided to return to my room for an early night, politely declining an offer from my uncle and the professor to join them in the drawing room for a tipple of brandy. Instead, I chose to take my presents and cards with me to the confines of my room.

It felt good to close the door behind me - to shut out all the arguments, discussions and naivety of the old. I revelled in the silence and comfort of my own space.

As always, when I started to prepare for bed, I emptied the contents of my pockets on the table. I found a little piece of notepaper which I did not remember putting there. It was pink with flower and white roses, and scented with a beautiful, feminine perfume - like sweet honey infused with jasmine.

How did you get into my pocket?

I slowly unfolded the paper and saw the inscription. It was neat and elegantly written.

Dear Romilly,

Thank you so much for inviting me to your dinner party. I would like to see you tomorrow night. 7pm at the Castel Sant'Angelo.

I presume you may get lonely sometimes?

I shall be waiting by the bank of the Tiber. Please come to me. I see the way you look at me when you think I'm not watching. I feel the same way about you too.

Tomorrow, I will show you.

Yours always, Ciara

My body sank into my bed. I didn't know if I would go and see her. One thing was for certain, however: I needed a very long, ice-cold shower.

Chapter 9

Iman

The wooden door of my bedroom squeaked a little as Sister Maria walked in.

"Isn't it all exciting, Iman?" She was beaming from ear to ear as if it was Christmas morning.

"What is?" I pretended not to know what she was talking about.

"Oh, do stop acting all ignorant. The pilgrimage to Lourdes."

"Well, I don't think that I can attend. I'm not really in a pilgrimage sort of mood. That is only for holy people. And I am not holy". Trust me to put a downer on things - Madam Miserable.

"So why do you think you're not? You've been moping around for weeks. What is the matter with you these days?"

She parked her bottom close to mine, forcing me to budge up on the bed. I was about to say my Rosary before this conversation started, but I was glad of the interruption.

"Oh, Maria, please do not delude yourself into thinking that I have any story to tell," I managed to smile at her.

"You might not have a story, but I think that you have a secret. Go on - excite me," she nudged.

"I cannot. I think that you might judge me, and also get all righteous with me. The truth is that I cannot bear to feel worse than I already do."

A slight knock on my door offered a welcome diversion, bringing with it the small frame of the mother superior looking quite unsure of herself, as was often the case when she entered my room. (Not that I ever gave her any reason to be – after all, *I* was the insecure, nervous wreck.)

"There you are, Sisters. We have all decided to go hiking this afternoon, as we know how nature is good for the soul, don't we?"

Maria and I both stood up in a hurry to acknowledge the presence of the reverend mother superior.

"Will you be joining us?"

"Yes, Reverend Mother," we replied in unison, like schools kids.

"It will be a good chance for us all to socialise - particularly good for the new priest, Father Vanderbelt. He is so quiet. Sometimes I think he is lonely. This will be good for him."

I could hear my heart at the sound of his name as Maria and I nodded together. Reverend Mother turned to take her leave and then, as if suddenly recalling something, stopped and faced our way.

"Oh yes - please do remember to wear suitable clothing and hiking boots. We will be walking from Broadway to Snowshill. It is a bit of a climb. Please make sure you take water bottles. I have prepared all the refreshments, so we can have a picnic at the top of the hill."

This excited Maria so much that she completely forgot about our conversation and promptly ran out of my room.

This was one of the rare days where we didn't have to look like nuns, or cover our heads. We would simply be *normal* women.

I suddenly became quite frightened and stood still to take it all in, as the reality of what was about to happen hit home.

First of all, I reminded myself that I had to wear a long-sleeved top to cover my scarred arms, despite the scorching hot weather. I also had to face seeing him again after managing to avoid him for a few weeks, when I seriously wondered if I could carry on much longer.

Only during the past few weeks had I realised how very good I was at hiding.

I positioned myself at the back of the church each time I attended Mass. I saw him look around, seeking me out. I kept busy. I had never been so busy before. I volunteered to work as a nurse's assistant in a hospital for battered women. I cleaned the garden and used up all my energy. Reverend Mother was understanding at dinner time and allowed me to eat in my own room when I was particularly tired.

On other occasions, I ate with the nurses. This way I escaped dinner in the parish house.

One thing remained clear though: I could not hide from Romilly forever.

I had managed for three weeks, but my day of reckoning finally arrived; the day I had to look at the face that tormented me (inducing lonely nights and haunted days). My feelings enslaved me and I was afraid that he would see right through me.

I picked out my light, vintage, white cotton shirt. It looked a lot bigger these days and my leggings felt loose too, so much so that I had to pin together the elastic waistband to stop them from sliding down. It was obvious that I had gone down more than one dress size - the gardening, walking and hospital work responsible for my slender frame; also the fact that I had skipped plenty of meals, choosing to feed myself with romantic thoughts. As I looked in my bedroom mirror, I couldn't help but frown at how skinny my legs had become, looking even slimmer and longer while in my walking boots. My neck had seemingly lengthened too, and my cheeks had sunk into my face yet ushered in a brighter skin tone highlighting the numerous freckles that dominated my complexion. I ran my hairbrush through my shorn locks so that the curls silently disappeared in a bounce of wavy rhythms. The darkness of my hair, I noticed, made my big, grey eyes shine in the mirror.

Could I be tempted? Why not? At this point I was going to Hell anyway.

I picked up my black, eyeliner pencil - which I had only used at Christmas - and gently made up my eyes. I also lightly applied a pink lipstick that was almost invisible. One had to look at me for a long time in order to notice its presence.

I was pleased with the transformation. Feast your eyes on me now, Romilly Kurt Vanderbelt!

I descended the stairs, slinging my rucksack behind my back. It felt light, containing as it did just sun cream, a flannel, a small umbrella, my phone and wallet. In my hand was my water bottle, which I intended to fill up in the kitchen. I turned towards the back of the house though as I heard voices in the living room. I didn't want to see him just yet, as my heart was beating louder than the sound of my boots on the stone tiles. I followed the narrow hallway towards the kitchen, bypassing the main part of the ground floor where the rest of the party had assembled, or planned to gather. A faint aroma of cold meats and freshly baked bread delighted my nose, making my stomach growl as I stepped into the kitchen.

The parish priest, Father McCormack, looked up from the gigantic water dispenser he was using to fill up his own bottle. I was surprised to see him there.

"Good morning, Sister Iman. Wow, how pretty you look, if I may say so."

"Thank you, Father. You mustn't embarrass a poor nun like myself." The sentence made me feel like a con artist.

"Nonsense - you look beautiful and ready to climb those hills. I must admit, I'd rather relax in my armchair in the garden."

"Me too," I whispered, and we both laughed at our little secret.

"I think I'll go out and remind the others to come and fill up their water bottles, lest they forget."

"Is everyone here then?" I couldn't resist asking.

"Yes, we've been waiting for a couple of you to come down and join us before setting off, as we'd all rather go together."

"Yes, of course - very sensible to all stay together. Who is coming exactly, Father, if you don't mind me asking?"

A different voice answered my question – a voice that emanated from the kitchen door positioned behind me.

"It will only be five of us, Iman - Maria, Father McCormack, Reverend Mother and me. Oh, and you, of course. Not everyone could afford to take the afternoon off."

I felt my back stiffen at the sound of his voice. I couldn't face him. I just couldn't.

I turned around and smiled nonetheless.

"Father Vanderbelt - good morning." My big eyes met his grassy, green ones. I felt a familiar sensation in my stomach, as if it had just been twisted, but then released a second later.

"I had better join the others," Father McCormack intervened. "We need to plan the route. Hope you're ready for the long hike, Romilly. I don't think I am. And I'm not the only one." He winked at me and stumbled out of the kitchen, unaware of the situation he was leaving me in.

Romilly's next words took me completely by surprise. I was at least expecting him to compliment how I looked. He had never before seen me in normal clothes. Nor had my hair shined so brightly as it did today.

"Where the hell have you been?" he whispered. Green eyes that spoke louder than his voice resolutely held my gaze, rendering me helpless. Unable to withstand the connection, I swiftly lowered my eyes, for I did not have sufficient strength to control the heat that suddenly began to rise up from my feet into the very pit of my stomach, spiralling uncontrollably through my cheeks....and lingering. Thank goodness for my darker skin! But there was no escaping his questions. I felt compelled to respond, to say *anything* - to stop him looking at me with those fiery eyes.

"I've been working - busy with the nurses. I've...I've..."

"Been avoiding me." I swear he was now slowly smiling, endearingly, teasingly. "No?"

"Yes."

A full-blown smile enveloped his charming, unforgettable face.

I said nothing more. I didn't wish to argue as such a state clashed with our tentative longing for each other.

"Why? If your plan was to drive me crazy, you definitely succeeded."

"I'm sorry. I have no words."

"I do." A beat, then: "Can I see you tonight, in your room, when everyone else has gone to sleep? Stay awake and wait for my call. Can you do that?"

I gave him nothing. I didn't know how to reply to this quickening of events.

"There is much to say," his voice pleaded, nay petitioned.

It was unlike a request – more a *command*, daring me to refuse. I simply nodded in response.

I wasn't sure why he bothered with someone as inconsequential as me. I wasn't sure why the sound of his voice made my heart sing. One thing I *was* sure of: He played the drums astutely and I danced to the tune.

I finally summoned up the strength to look at him, only to realise that he was already leaving the room.

"Did you want me to fill up your bottle?" I asked awkwardly, more out of panic because he was walking away again; my heart silently hoping he'd stay.

"It's already filled," he murmured with his back to me - his words vanishing from the kitchen along with him, as effortlessly as he'd appeared.

The hike up Snowshill wasn't as bad as I envisaged. It was both surprisingly refreshing and a little arduous - a heady, exhilarating combination for mind and body.

Life scuttled around us as we walked: green leaves dominating our sight line through the heat wave, birds flitting nearby (hopping and flying about), butterflies fluttering freely in the air (dancing to music that we could not hear, but still somehow felt). Up ahead, two green woodpeckers settled on the dry turf, immediately beginning to feed, each in their own allotted space yet bouncing off each other; greedily, but perhaps affectionately and protectively too. Maybe they were in love - soul mates intertwined in spirit, destined to stay together eternally. Perhaps I was mad or maybe, just maybe, an unrealistic and incurable romantic.

As we hiked up the slippery incline into the lonely, narrow road that would lead us to Snowshill, a group of hunting hounds approached us - at a guess, about fifty in the pack. A couple of men were guiding them quietly, and the dogs shifted forward in an orderly, pointed fashion.

Some of them surrounded us enquiringly, however, and one pottered up close to me.

I couldn't help but bend down to caress its lovely neck. Reverend Mother joined me, for she too couldn't resist, and so did Maria. Both men just smiled down at us, and when I looked up Romilly had his eyes fixed on me.

There is much to say.

We bid farewell to the hounds and their masters and carried on walking in silence, taking in all that nature offered – focusing on feelings and remembering to smile when we walked past a stranger.

Amidst the green bushes, foliage and tall trees stood large mansions on each side of the road. The charming, unspoilt village of Snowshill gradually revealed itself to us through the corner of Buckle Street, past the beautiful manor and old church; the sun suddenly bowing down to us and the clouds close enough to protect our faces. It was as if all we had to do was reach out our arms in order to touch the sky.

The light from the sun settled like a silvery glow on the beautiful stone church that dominated the centre of the green; the cottages surrounding it its little, loyal angels.

A heavy breeze suddenly filled my nostrils with the scent of lavender, and yet I saw none.

"There is a lavender field nearby," my *Michiel* said, as he watched me, read me, sensed what I was looking for. "I come up here a lot when I want to be alone. That's when I stumbled upon the lavender field. I had heard about it, but to experience it is a different matter altogether."

In that instant I didn't think it possible to love him any more than I already did.

I didn't know it was love. Oh, come on, Iman - don't be silly. You couldn't possibly be in love with him. He is a god and you, well, a mad time bomb ticking away slowly until its final psychological explosion. Tick..tick..tick.

"Now, I definitely want to visit the lavender field," Maria screamed in delight, which made the rest of us jump in laughter.

"Perhaps some other time, Sister. I think we might all need a drink urgently." The parish priest knew how to turn people down gently. Father McCormack was a most admirable man - equally full of goodness and charm.

The village made an ineradicable impression on my mind - one I would not forget for many years to come. I knew why Romilly came here - there was something heavenly about it; an aura that calmed troubled souls; a soul like my own; a soul that needed love, that craved patience, that wanted a loving arm and a little peace; a soul desperately looking for something to live for.

I knew Romilly was troubled, but by what I could not tell. Didn't Aristotle tell us that everyone was struggling in their own little way?

There is much to say.

We found a spot on the green and emptied Reverend Mother's picnic basket with great enthusiasm. Cheese sandwiches, sausage rolls, cherries and strawberries gave us something to quieten the singing of our empty stomachs.

He didn't really look at me again, but rather spoke to all of us equally. It was impossible to guess that he intended to visit me that night. It took a great deal of effort *not* to look at him. I tried, but my eyes always seemed like magnets drawn to his. And each time he caught me looking, whereupon I held his gaze just for a second, just as he held mine. We were definitely communicating, but without words, and it wouldn't be the first time.

Oh, don't be such a fool. He must think you a miserable and desperate lovesick teenager.

The walk back was easy as it was downhill. Summer stretched out before us with unbounded promise regarding the future.

The thought of a future actually made me giggle inside. What future did we all have though, but to live and die as the brides of Christ, accepting each new assignment bestowed upon us by the church? Was it any wonder that Romilly and I sought some excitement in each other's arms? The problem was I feared that it was more than just excitement for me. I needed him so very desperately. I wanted him like my parched throat thirsting for water in the desert. And my body yearned for his - to smell his scent, to run my fingers over his skin, to feel his tongue caress my hungry lips.

By the time we arrived at the parish quarters we were all exhausted. We gathered together in the parlour for some tea, but I quickly excused myself.

"I'd love to, but I need to use the toilet, and I'm afraid I shall need to retire to my room afterwards. Thank you so much, Reverend Mother for inviting me on the walk. It was simply beautiful, Father McCormack, Father Vanderbelt, Sister De Leon."

I smiled at them all and began to leave the room, but Romilly's voice stopped me in my tracks: "Wait a minute, Iman. I shall walk with you a second to discuss a request from the hospital."

"Of course, Father."

The rest of the party ignored us and focused on the tea and cakes being laid out by Maria. I thought I saw a curious look on Reverend Mother's face, but I might have been mistaken.

Soon we were out of everyone's sight as we slowly walked along the corridor towards my room.

"I enjoyed myself immensely today," he said, breaking the growing silence between us.

"Yes - me too. I'm so glad we were able to enjoy it together."

Why did I say that? I must really think more carefully before I speak.

"Yes, I was overjoyed when Mother Thérése confirmed that you would be coming."

"Was this all your idea then?"

"It was. I suggested a hike to Father McCormack and asked whether you and Maria could come. I told him I wanted to get better acquainted with the two of you."

"If only he'd known how well acquainted we already are," I quipped. He chuckled as we both remembered the morning we'd spent in his office.

We kept on walking, in silence this time; each of us in our own head, afraid to interrupt the other's silence.

Then we both started talking at once: "I'm sorry. Please - you first."

"I'm concerned about tonight," I whispered.

"Do you not want to see me?" He mimicked my tone.

We both stopped and faced each other. I was very close to my room. I could literally see my door through the corner of my eye. Just a few more steps and I would be in my safe place.

"You know I do."

"Then what?"

"Someone might hear us."

"I'm only coming to talk. Don't get any ideas." He winked at me as the blood rushed to my cheeks.

"What about when you knock?"

"What time do the nuns go to sleep?"

"I think everyone on this corridor is asleep by ten."

"Okay. Can you leave your door slightly ajar at midnight? I'll be here then."

"Okay."

"Thank you. I'm looking forward to it. Are you?

"Yes."

He smiled at me then. "See you later, *mon coeur*."

He stood and watched me enter my room before walking away.

I wanted to dance, but I was too tired. I'd studied a little French in school and so understood that Romilly had just referred to me as his heart.

I locked the door behind me and settled down for a nap. Just before I drifted off, I picked up my clock and set the alarm for an hour later. I had two hours of hospital duties prior to dinner, and so I had to sleep now if I was to stay awake later.

The time was 15:15.

Chapter 10

Young Iman

My biggest fear as a child was my peers finding out that the life I had calculatingly presented to them was one, big, audacious lie. I learned that the trick was not to get caught out, and so I detached myself from everybody. It was imperative I was silent and avoided relationships of any kind.

I was afraid that if I made friends, then they would see right through me. And, ultimately, my deception would be found out. Since school was my only solace, it was vital I kept that part of my life separate from home.

Ever since that horrendous night on my fourteenth birthday when Mother had made me parade my body for the benefit of her lecherous male friends, things had changed drastically for me. And, to think, I could never have imagined my life becoming any worse than it already was.

Because of this, I found it impossible to see any good in myself. And such a nadir was fuelled by a feeling of worthlessness that had grown in my mind like a cancer.

There were also other changes to my life.

I wasn't allowed to return to school. How could I after what had happened? Mother was very clever in that respect. She walked me to school and informed the headmistress that due to my deteriorating grades she had decided to educate me at home. The head teacher was naturally worried about this new development and enquired as to how my mother was going to achieve this.

"I love my daughter more than life itself and I fear what her future might be like. She is obviously struggling in school, so I will try home-schooling for a while. If this doesn't work out, then of course I will look at other options."

My dear mother knew how to turn the charm on whenever it was required in order to achieve the results she desired.

The head teacher tried to persuade Mother to allow me to remain in school, but her pleas fell on deaf ears. My mother, of course, had her own agenda, and if the head teacher had been aware of this she would not have wasted her breath pleading on my behalf. There were no social services for children in Nigeria and so there was simply no advocate for me.

I could neither say nor do anything to change my situation. She was my mother. And I lived in fear of her.

School had been my only escape, and now that that small window of serenity had been ruthlessly blacked out, my life was about to get uglier.

The other kids had been kind to me despite my constant, awkward demeanour. I'd done my best to keep a good distance from them because I didn't want anybody to know my secret. If I had made friends, then they would have invited me to their homes and my mother would have been inclined to do likewise. The mere thought of that was frightful. How could I reveal myself in that way? Them seeing the sparseness, them seeing the bareness of my room.

My mother bought me a Scandinavian dollhouse for Christmas.

My room has a lovely cream coloured tepee with fitted lace curtains.

My new teddy is called Fred.

We are going to Jo'berg for the summer.

We will be visiting our relatives in the country this Christmas.

I have a bunny rabbit called Nia.

The truth was that I didn't really mean to tell all those lies. I wanted, so badly, to feel like a normal kid. I had dreams of possessing those things. And I *did* have them - in my own, little, imaginary world. How was that a lie therefore?

After Mother emptied my school locker and picked up my items from the headmistress, she asked me if I wanted to go and say goodbye to my friends.

"No, I'm okay," I whispered.

I walked out of the school grounds with my mother without looking back. As we passed the school gate, I heard the bell ring. I looked up at the clock located outside the school walls. The time was 12:02.

Mother's negative feelings for me intensified as time passed. She scolded me given the slightest opportunity. She was very disappointed, she said, at my behaviour the other night. Everything was suddenly my fault.

When we didn't have enough milk, she took it out on me.

"If only you had lied about your age to those men, they would have paid us some money and we wouldn't be so broke."

Mother, alas, was fast on her feet and thought of another solution; a solution that might not bring us as much money, but a solution to our problems nevertheless.

After being hostile towards me for weeks, she suddenly came into my bedroom in the early hours of the morning - her demeanour pleasant, charming, accompanied by a smile for her only daughter.

"Hey, Iman, I have thought of a lovely way that you could help me make some money until you get older."

Unlike before, I was no longer the naïve, little girl eager to please Mummy. I knew that her plans would be anything but honourable. She was all that I had though and there was really nowhere for me to go. As my mother reminded me regularly, if I didn't want to end up homeless, living on the streets, then I would have to pull my weight to help her financially.

"How?" I asked, eager to get the conversation over and done with.

"Have you ever thought about modelling? I've looked into it for you. You have all the right features - the height, the skinny legs, the grey eyes."

"I don't understand." My head was reeling. "I have no idea how to do that."

"Well, I do. I have spoken to a wonderful agency. They took one look at your pictures and fell in love with you."

I couldn't quite believe it. Every ounce of sleep I had left suddenly vanished. I became as bright as a fox. Here I was thinking that my mother did not love me and all the while she planned to turn me into a star. Perhaps she had been crude sometimes and even unkind, but I was sure she had her reasons.

"Me? A model?" I screamed. I was certainly skinny enough. Isn't that what was usually required? I was also tall for my age. Mother had always said that I grew like a tree - skinny and lanky.

"But how, Mum? This is amazing." Without thinking, I flung myself at her in a warm embrace. And even though I felt her body stiffen, I didn't care. I needed this moment and I was going to have it.

"Well, let's not get too carried away, my dear. This is only the beginning. I'll let you know when we can go. I need you to carry on doing the jobs around the house. When you become a star we will be able to move away from here and have other people clean our house for us."

I didn't really mind cleaning, but I said nothing. I was in a good place with my mother and I certainly did not want her to change her mind about my new modelling career.

"You can have a few more minutes in bed as you don't have to go to school anymore. You'll need your beauty sleep now more than ever. Your wake up time can be 7am."

I was grateful to stay in bed for an extra two hours. Maybe it wasn't going to be so bad after all, this new way of living.

Daydreaming came to me easily, so it was no surprise that I had already begun to see myself on the catwalk alongside the beautiful models I saw in Mummy's magazine. My life would be so exciting and I would want for nothing. I should have known when my mother took me out of school that it was because she had great plans for me. Who needed an education when one could model for the great designers? I let out a loud laugh in my room - banging my head against the pillow in excitement and kicking my long, lanky legs.

Granted, my mother had not always been the best of parents when it came to showering me with affection or helping me with my homework. Perhaps, all along, she simply had better plans, bolder plans, ambitious plans for my future and so did not see the need to waste time with education.

A few days later, and without any warning, she told me that the photographer would be arriving at ten that morning. It was important that I had a shower and brushed my teeth. She said she would help me with the makeup as I wasn't experienced in using eyeshadow and lipstick.

I was stunned. Everything was happening so fast. I was excited too. This was the beginning of my stardom, after all.

He turned up at ten on the dot. He said he would have to take me with him as our apartment was not conducive for the photo shoot. He smelt like an old fish tank, and tattoos covered his neck. He spoke with a strong, Yoruba accent and it looked like he spent most of his time in the gym.

My mother asked to come along, but he insisted that it would be best if she didn't.

"Mothers do not usually attend. It's easier for the kids that way." He never took his eyes off me, even as he spoke with my mother.

I did not want to go with him. I didn't like the way he looked at me. He looked frightening, and the thought of stardom slowly began to dissipate. None of it seemed to matter now. I wanted my old life back. I wanted to go to school. I didn't want to go anywhere with this man.

My mother looked scared too and I think she suddenly realised what she had gotten us into.

"Look, Yemi," she said, "this was a mistake. I do not wish to go ahead with the whole thing any longer."

"Sorry, lady - too late to back out now. I don't show my face to people unless I'm doing business with them. Now that you've seen me, there's no going back. It's collateral, you see."

He took out a bundle of money and threw it at my mother.

"You'll get the rest when I drop her back home."

"What time will that be?"

"Maybe six."

He grabbed me by the hand and walked me to his car. I didn't argue with him or scream. I didn't say anything.

We drove in silence for what seemed like an eternity. I looked for a clock in his car, but couldn't find one. Instead, I noticed how dusty the car was. Spread everywhere were cassette tapes. There could easily have been forty. And empty coke cans spilled out of waste paper bags. No wonder he was in such a bad mood, considering his diet, I thought.

He also smoked a lot. He'd lit up a cigarette when he started driving and didn't stop smoking until we finally came to a halt in front of a large mansion in the middle of nowhere.

"I want to go back home," was all I could muster. I didn't want to get out of the car. I was petrified.

"I do not have the time to argue with you. I have paid your mother, so out, *now*." He got out of the car and banged the door behind him.

I thought that maybe my beating heart would explode and give birth to the blessing that was death. But there was no such luck. I followed him meekly into the mansion.

As soon as we walked in, he commanded me to take my clothes off and lie on the bed.

I had never seen a big, queen-size bed in the middle of a living room before. But then I had not been to many other homes. It looked strange - a golden bed with cream fur decorating a living room as it did here.

"Why?" I asked.

He looked at me and laughed out loud, revealing more nicotine-stained teeth than I could count and a few missing ones.

"Because this is where we take your pictures."

"Why do I have to take my clothes off? I can't be naked in front of other people."

"Look, it will only be me and another camera man. But don't worry, I'll make you a nice drink and you won't feel awkward anymore."

He walked over to a bar and mixed together some cocktails.

"I'm fourteen," I insisted. "I'm not allowed to drink."

"Look here..." His voice suddenly became sharper and more aggressive. "...Drink this and be quiet. I haven't got all day. If you're allowed to be here then *trust me*, my dear, you're most definitely allowed to drink."

I drank it more out of fear.

When I woke up, I was back at home with my mother. We never spoke of what happened. I didn't *know* what happened.

Yemi came back once a month, and each time he gave my mother a roll of money. I did not let it bother me so much as I grew older because all I had to do was drink his cocktail. But then I slowly became curious as to what happened to me after having the drink, so on one of my visits I decided not to drink the cocktail and instead pretend. I poured the drink on the carpet underneath the bed when he wasn't looking and handed him back the empty cup. He didn't notice my actions as he was busy setting up the camera like it was a very important job. One would think he was a surgeon with a sharp scalpel.

Perplexed, with my eyes mostly closed and my breathing running wild, I felt wary and frantic as Yemi's fast-moving hands undressed me, parted my legs and took pictures. Clearly he was an expert at this. He photographed my breasts, my thighs and everywhere else. He also played with my body, had sex with me...raped me. I wanted to scream. I wanted to cry. I wanted to shout for help. But I did nothing, as I remembered the harsh way he had spoken to me when I first came here. I did not want to be beaten - not by him and not by my mother.

My mother's friends also wanted me. I slept with them all. It made her happy and it gave me peace. My mother was an expert on contraceptives. She knew how they worked and fed them to me in large quantities. She also took me to the hospital regularly for general check-ups. It was something that Yemi demanded and he was, after all, her main financier.

I thought about my life and my future. I wanted more than this life I was currently living with my mother. I knew that if I carried on living under her roof, I would never be more than who I was now.

I wanted to talk to other people, but I had no friends. I also had no formal education, so I couldn't apply for a job.

I was beginning to sink into a certain kind of oblivion and depression, until I stumbled upon a piece of paper that was bound to change my life.

It happened while I was tidying up my mother's bedroom. She had specifically instructed me to clean every corner of her room, but to leave the bed exactly as it was. Her excuse was that she needed clean sheets, but the only clean sheets left were not quite dry.

I left the bed exactly as she instructed me to, but then she didn't return home on time. Being bored, I decided to see if the sheets were dry. I was in luck, so proceeded to change them.

Out of habit, I changed the pillow cases first, and today was no different. As I picked up the first pillow, I noticed a piece of paper. It looked unusual to me, and it had a red seal. The seal was broken, so I decided to take a peek.

The letter looked foreign and the handwriting was so beautiful that I couldn't resist reading it.

Dear Hadiza,

How are you? And how is my lovely Iman doing?

Thank you so much for looking after her and, although I'm a bit sad that you haven't managed to send me any pictures of her, I am still grateful for all that you have done, and are still doing.

I have not been in England for a while as I was sent to Uganda and then to Peru. I shall be settling back in England soon and I wanted to remind you about the deal we made when Iman turns eighteen.

I am making provisions for her to come over and join me here and, please, I want you to know that she wouldn't have to be a nun - she can be whatever she wants to be.

You will be greatly rewarded financially and I hope all the money I have been sending to you for her education has been enough.

Please let me know if you need any more.

I do not want to give Iman any high hopes so I would prefer it if you continue to keep me a secret from her until I can definitely come for her. And if I can't immediately, then I can start conversing with her directly when she turns eighteen.

Thank you once again for all that you have been doing.

God bless you, my child.

Mother Mary Thérése

Reverend Mother Superior

I must have re-read the letter about a dozen times. My head was spinning with excitement and fear. Who was this Mother Thérése and why was she helping me? Who was I to her? I returned the letter to where it had been and took the clean sheets back to the line. I did not want Mother to know that I had read the letter, but I knew what I had to do. All this time, all these years, she had made me work for her while taking payment from this Mother Thérése. My mother truly was the devil in human form.

I began to work towards my plan - a life that would take me out of this hell.

I snuck out to the local, public library whenever my mother disappeared. It was time I started thinking about my future. I educated myself about life in the Catholic Church. I started attending Mass to learn, to pray, to understand what God was all about. The more I prayed, the more I slowly began to feel alive. I felt love from what I could not see. I felt peace from what I could not hear. But then I *could* feel, see and hear. It was a different kind of feeling, seeing and hearing. I slowly emerged into a different kind of me - not fully, but at least partially.

I remember what Mother said when she initially saw me going to church.

"All the trips to that church will not put food on this table. You must not forget your duties here."

I joined a course in catechism and took my first Holy Communion.

I remember my very first confession.

"Bless me, Father, for I have sinned. This will be my first confession."

"Tell me, dear child - what are those sins? For all have sinned and come short of His glory."

I had planned it all perfectly. I couldn't possibly tell the priest of my true sins. I couldn't bear to see his face if I actually confessed to bedding all of my mother's male friends, plus the knowledge that my naked pictures were used for an adult magazine. No, Father, I think I will spare you the pain and discomfort.

"I lied to my mother and I got angry with her. I shouted at her and told her that I hated her. Sometimes I want to run away. Forgive me, Father."

"Please say five Our Fathers and ten Hail Marys. Go, my child - your sins are forgiven."

Wow, I thought - that was easy. Perhaps it wouldn't be so bad being a nun after all. That is what I wanted to be. I would be free from the world, binding myself to Christ only.

Surely I could wait a few more years. I was patient, but all I had to do was turn eighteen.

Turning eighteen did, eventually, come. Not soon enough, but come it did.

I told my mother that I needed her to take me to the sisters' convent as I was to become a nun. This was my back-up plan in case my benefactor failed to show.

She laughed so hard that tears poured down her face. "You?! After sleeping with all the men in Nigeria?"

"Dear Mother, if you don't, then I will go to the police and inform them about my life with you. Which do you prefer?"

Suddenly she stopped laughing and said that she had a better plan - a plan she had been putting off. There was a nun who wanted to come for me, but Mother had been giving her excuses as she didn't want to let go of me so easily.

"We can milk her into the ground, Iman. We can take her money. You do not need to go with her."

Perhaps I would have fallen for her tactics if I hadn't stumbled upon the letter two years ago, but I was too wise now. And if anybody cared about me at all, it was clearly my benefactor.

"I will do no such thing. I am trying to follow in the footsteps of Christ." The defeated look on her face did not bring me as much joy as I expected. "Who is this nun by the way?" I asked, feigning surprise.

"She is English. She will be coming to take you back there. But I will only do this if you promise to send me money when you get there. Otherwise, you can rot here."

I tried to hide my joy at the knowledge that my benefactor would be coming for me; that she had been making arrangements and obviously *cared*.

Just as the patient dog eats the fattest bone, so my patience was finally being rewarded and perhaps the perseverance of Mother Thérése as well.

When I left my past behind, that fateful day at Muhammadu Buhari International Airport, it was with a mixture of joy and sadness. I knew I was free, but I also knew I had scars that might never heal. If they were to heal, the process might take me a whole lifetime, or even many lifetimes.

Oh, well - one mustn't wallow in self-pity. There was still a lot to be grateful for.

Chapter 11

Romilly

We cycle through Kurfürstendamm without any care in the world. My mother's basket is filled with groceries. I sit behind her on the tandem, enjoying the breeze on my face.

Mama is a good cyclist and she always takes care to wear a helmet. Today, however, she said we ought to be free - we should fly with the wind. Her hair dances in the air, flowing and wavy, long enough to capture the space between us, but not quite blinding me. I can smell her hair. It has a somewhat different scent to it today. It reminds me of the rain forest, infused with a trace of the earth.

"Life is for the living, mon fils. Enjoy every moment. Live and then live some more."

Her voice is like a thunderous wave amidst the speed of the bicycle. She is flying with it and I'm delighted. I have missed her so much. It's so nice to be doing this with her. We are having fun. She races past the mall and all of a sudden I sense that we are not in Berlin anymore. We are ascending a hill. We go up, up and into a winding road that never seems to end.

Although I feel safe with her, there is a fear that suddenly envelops me. What if we fall? What if we die? This is too dangerous and Mama is going really fast.

I am scared and so I wrap my arms around her waist. She is very tiny, so my long arms coil around her like a beanstalk.

"You need to slow down. We are going to fall," I scream.

"When that happens, remember to get back up," she screams right back at me - smiling as she always does, even as she races faster than any car on the road.

Then she begins to fall.

Only her.

The groceries remain in the basket, defying the law of gravity.

I look down. I want to save her.

And then I begin to fall.

I opened my eyes as the dream faded into my subconscious, leaving a familiar heartache.

Oh, Mama, thank you for the crazy ride.

I tried to make sense of the dream, but I couldn't piece it together. Maybe it didn't mean anything. Mama had taught me that there was more to dreams than we were led to believe, because life was always communicating to us in one form or another. I made a note to speak to Alessandro about it later. He was the philosopher, the deep thinker. Perhaps he would be able to make sense of it all.

For now, I decided to dismiss any thoughts of dreams and chose, instead, to focus on the morning ahead. I climbed out of bed and grabbed the first t-shirt that my hands could find in my wardrobe, along with a pair of jogging bottoms. Outside, the sun was blazing, promising to bathe my skin in its glorious heat as soon as I left the building. I needed to hurry, for I had only two hours for my run before saying morning Mass. I picked up my earpiece and connected it to my iPod. As the sound of Sébastien

Tellier's *La Ritournelle* furnished my ears, I headed downstairs, opened the front door and started running.

My legs pounded the walkway as if running from an impending storm. I think I was fleeing something inside of me - the memory of the dream perhaps. These days, I ran faster and I felt the urgent need to advance further with each passing moment. I made a mental note to wake up earlier in order to complete a longer route.

This morning, however, I was consumed by the wonderful smell of the earth – this vestige of nature that accompanied me from my dreams into the land of the living. I did not need my mother's watchful eyes over me. Right now, I could accomplish anything on my own.

Thoughts of Ciara interrupted my consciousness though.

I could not see this woman. I *had* to see this woman. The mere contemplation of spending time with her tonight awakened a desire in me so strong that I suddenly felt alive. I felt happy, in an odd, tumultuous way, mingled with a sharp sense of culpability. Was it because the all-seeing and all-knowing could hear my thoughts? Or was it because I knew I would burn in Hell for all my sins? It didn't matter anymore, as I believe I had decided my future path.

I struggled with the realisation of my life as it currently was - a life I did not think was meant for me. Most of what I knew about the ethics and implications of religion were taught to me by a father I hated, yet also by an uncle I adored. How could both men believe in the same thing so arduously and yet be so different? Was religion missing a piece of the puzzle -

the part about Oneness and us all being manifestations of the *same* consciousness?

Tonight, I would see Ciara and hide my heart from the fear of shame, and maybe find a way to hide my face from the eyes of God.

The day did not pass as quickly as I had hoped. I couldn't wait for 7pm. The Castel Sant'Angelo would shut at 7.30.

"I will show you."

This was crazy.

"I can't wait for you to show me. I think I might have been waiting all my life for someone like you to show me."

I had lunch with my uncle and asked him if I could take the evening off.

"You mean not serve Mass at six?" he asked, with a look of total surprise.

"If that's okay with you, Uncle. I feel slightly ill. Perhaps it was all the rich food from last night," I lied. Sin number one.

"Yes, of course, Romilly. Will you be in your room?"

"Actually, I might go for a walk." I smiled innocently at him. I was afraid that he would see into my soul and thus the secret that I carried in my heart.

My uncle nodded, yet gazed at me puzzlingly. His confusion was understandable as I had never made a request like this before.

"How is Alessandro?" I asked, changing the topic, but also hoping for an interpretation of my dream.

"Ah, yes - my dear friend will be coming round for tea this afternoon. Would you care to join us?"

We agreed to meet at 3pm in my uncle's garden.

The conversation with Alessandro was lavish as always, yet took an even deeper turn prompting a myriad of unanswered questions; equivocal searching into what was actually true, and what it was that I *wanted* to be true - producing in my mind two very different, conflicting interpretations.

"I do not claim to be an interpreter of dreams, Romilly, but from what I can gather there might be a strong desire in you to live and fulfil your true destiny. And, in chasing that destiny, you might encounter many failures. However, failure is not really failure. Failure is simply a message that you should stop and think and maybe change direction. It's part of the journey, so long as you don't give up. This destiny, I am guessing, might be different from your present path."

"Different from the *life of a priest*? Please, friend, do not put ideas into my nephew's head." Cardinal Hugo was not a dreamer like Alessandro. "What could be better than this life? Working for God. Saving souls from eternal damnation."

"Well, I do not believe in all of that, as you know," Alessandro replied, winking at me.

"Please do not blaspheme, dear friend. We have walked this road before."

It baffled me how the cardinal and professor could argue about such delicate matters, yet repeatedly maintain a state of calmness.

"What if religion is just something that someone made up to instil discipline in the world? Can you at least open your mind to the possibility that something greater lives within you? Your own power…connected to a magnificent source of light?"

"Then, my friend, we must be saying the same thing. Because, to me, this source of light is God. And to you, well…"

"*I* am part of the great source?" This time Alessandro looked at both my uncle and I.

"Then you're saying you are God? Such modesty, Alessandro," the cardinal replied, looking at me for support.

"Well, Uncle - I think scientists try to explain why we experience *déjà vu*, why we feel and sense things so strongly - the ability to connect our minds to others telepathically, if you will; something that might allow us to believe that we are greater than we imagine."

Alessandro smiled at my reply - the cardinal not so much.

"This is all mumbo jumbo. You call yourself a man of God, a servant of the church of St. Peter," my uncle teased.

"Does having a mind of my own disqualify me from that service?" I dipped a piece of warm ciabatta into the bowl of fresh olive oil - at the same time admiring my uncle's garden. It was obvious that he spent a lot of time in here. Everything looked tranquil, and the palm and olive trees with their silvery, green leaves, provided a lustre shade over our heads. I had spent the spring painting the walls white for the cardinal, just like he'd wanted. The furniture had a rustic feel to it - the Indian, wooden dining table and chairs donated to him as a gift from one of his parishioners who happened to restore old furniture. The garden had a relaxed feel to it, but was simultaneously formal and very Italian. My eyes wandered past terracotta pots scattered between large urns that stood commandingly in every corner of the garden, to exuberant climbers tumbling over walls. Rosemary and lavender decorated the bottom halves of fences, bringing with them heavenly aromas which suffused our nostrils.

"It's important to believe passionately in what you preach." My uncle's voice brought me back to the discussion at hand. He picked up the jug of Bellini and refreshed our glasses.

"Perhaps he has a lot more to learn. Maybe he shouldn't be preaching just yet." Alessandro was testing my uncle's patience, and he knew it as he winked at me again indecorously. "There's more to life than allowing oneself to be enslaved by other people's need for control. Feeding that control is the *real* sin, I think."

"That's enough, dear friend," my uncle interjected mildly - his eyes pleading with Alessandro to be more sensitive.

Enough had been said to stir my mind with further questions, but I didn't wish to break my uncle's heart. He had, after all, taken me in when I first came to Naples all those years ago - a teenager, confused and unsure about the world.

That day now seemed like a distant memory.

My *grandmaman* had packed as much as I could carry, as I wasn't mentally fit to do much at the time. My papa was also there - ready to transport me to Rome. It was the first time I had set eyes on him since that fateful day when he took my mother's life.

"You know we would move much, much faster if you helped me." He was in such a hurry. Perhaps he felt uncomfortable in the home of his in-laws.

I remained silent. I did not wish to speak to him. I was seventeen years old - tall, strong and no longer the frightened little boy that he'd swung from one corner of the room to another. *Grandmaman*, on the other hand, could not stifle her tears. To her, I had replaced the daughter that she'd lost. For my part, however, I had learnt not to give my heart to anyone in case they were suddenly taken away from me. And so, although *Grandmaman* was like a mother to me, I was not quite the son that she craved - for I said nothing to her most of the time, although I did help around the house. I think she wished it was the other way around, but I could not give what I no longer had inside me.

It took us a whole day by train to get to Naples and I remained quiet the entire journey. Not once did I say a word to my father.

The cardinal received me wholeheartedly, with love and patience. He took upon himself the role of parent, and he selflessly looked after me without question. In addition to my six years of formal education into priesthood, everything I learnt about *being* a priest I learnt from him. The precision over sacrifices, the Liturgy of the Hours, the celebration of the Eucharist, the Canon law that stressed my role as a priest was not a mere profession, but a sacred and perpetual vocation symbolised by my state of celibacy.

It was only recently that I had begun to question all of that. *Why* did I do what I did? *Who* did I do it for? My family? My uncle? Myself? Something told me that

I already knew the answers to the questions that tormented me. I somehow knew I was living a lie. I didn't think I was brave enough, however, to change my direction.

I had been moulded into ascending one of the three holy orders of the church - graduating with Honours in a Masters of Divinity degree, in addition to my human, social, spiritual and pastoral formation. One would think it should take the scaling of a mountain to align my thinking with Alessandro's.

The realisation hit me, right there and then, as I savoured the warm bread in my mouth: I must have taken up the space of someone who had really wanted it. All that education and money spent on my behalf made me quake. Could I genuinely throw it all away? Wouldn't that be the most selfish option? After all, my position as priest of the Latin Church meant that all my actions were in *persona Christi capitis* - a representation of the person of Christ; a priest ordained by the Bishop of Rome himself.

It bothered me that it had all meant nothing, compared to what I could or *should* really be.

I had made promises to the church though which haunted my current thinking and kept me grounded.

The memory of my ordination unexpectedly passed before my eyes. Did I not pledge to diligently perform my duties of priesthood and respect and obey His Ordinary? Did I not prostrate myself before the altar, to be prayed for by the assembled congregation, with the bishop invoking the power of God the Father, the Son and the Holy Spirit upon me? Was I not presented with the chalice and paten which I would use in precision over the Eucharist?

The more I questioned myself, the more all doors and windows to my exit remained closed. I could not possibly disappoint so many people in order to claim my own *flimsy* happiness.

I swiftly made my mind up whilst sitting there in my uncle's garden. I would not see her. I would not go to the Castel Sant'Angelo.

"I actually feel much better, Uncle. I'll be happy to celebrate Mass at six, if that's okay with you."

"Well, I am glad that you haven't given up your vocation so easily under the persuasion of my friend here."

We all smiled at the thought.

"Mizu No Kokoro," Alessandro whispered under his breath.

"What? What did you say?" I was intrigued. Alessandro fascinated me in so many ways.

"I'm currently reading a book by Mark Rasheed called *Whole Heart, Whole Horse.* Mizu No Kokoro means a mind like still water. Your mind, dear Romilly, should be like still water."

"What does that mean?" I remained confused and perplexed. My uncle stayed silent, but his eyes looked at his friend rather uncomfortably, afraid of his next blasphemy.

"It means that when you look out into a completely still pond where there are no ripples or waves on its surface, the water takes on a certain kind of clarity. Mirror-like, so everything reflects quite clearly on the surface. Yet, if we do something to disturb the water, like drop a stone into it, ripples emerge and create a distorted picture that becomes a far cry from the stillness and clarity it once was. This type of stillness is what is used in martial arts. When you keep your mind still, everything that is presented to you is a lot clearer. By having a clear image of any and *every* situation, we can make informed decisions about our life's journey. However, if you're busy seeking excuses of why things should or shouldn't be, things become increasingly difficult to handle. Training your mind to be still and quiet, whilst blocking out the voices of others, will enable you to process true information in a way that is suited to every situation. Think about it."

It was as if he could read my mind - and I sat there, looking at him, too stunned to speak. My uncle, too, examined the professor, probably wondering what mumbo jumbo his friend would say next.

A mind like still water. I did not understand it, and so - like many things I did not understand - I threw the beautiful monologue to the back of my mind.

I excused myself and retired to my room to get ready for Mass. A cold shower was definitely in order to wash away the heat of my emotions.

The whole time I was in church, all I could focus on were thoughts of her. How I managed to preach about love and forgiveness I do not know.

I finished serving Mass at seven thirty. I couldn't help but feel sorry for Ciara who had gone to wait by the River Tiber for a man that would never show up. I should have gone to see her, if only to explain that I could not be with her in the way that she wanted. I suppose it was too late now. It was almost eight in the evening and there was not a chance in hell that a woman like that would still be waiting.

I went back to my room, unsure of how I was feeling. It was for the best, I kept telling myself. Such feelings had a way of diminishing when one occupied one's thoughts with more practical or pragmatic events.

I usually went to bed wearing only my boxer shorts in the summer. It was hard for me to fall asleep otherwise, even with the air conditioning.

Tonight was no different.

I was looking forward to spending my evening with *The Haj*. The more I read the book, the more I realised how difficult it was for me to put it down. My eyes navigated towards the part where Ishmael, the young lad, slept in his mother's arms while she caressed his member; a culture, I presumed, that existed in ancient Palestine. But an ancient practice that left me baffled. I loved my own mother immensely, yet such a notion left a positively revolting taste in my mouth.

I carried on reading about the Arabs, their culture and traditions, and how the historical situation in the Middle East developed. I must have read my book for a good three hours as the church bells rang eleven times. I decided to put my tome aside and drift into my inevitable nightmares.

A soft knock on my door meant I had to sit up and do the opposite. I hardly had any visitors at this time of night. Perhaps my uncle wanted to talk some more. No one else came to *my side* of the house, as they knew I would be asleep by now.

I threw on a laundered t-shirt and allowed my legs to slide into my black jeans. My hands twisted the knob on my door and yanked it open.

I stared for what seemed like an eternity - my brain needing a little time to process my surroundings.

Nothing in the world could have prepared me for that moment. I tried, however, not to dwell too much on what I considered to be an impossible situation. The corridor was dark, yet there was a hint of light from my reading lamp forcing its way out, illuminating the passage and conquering the shadows; assisting me so that I could look into the eyes of...

Ciara.

I let her in and closed the door gently behind her, immediately turning the key. It was important that no one heard us. It was important that her seductive voice did not permeate the house.

"I'm sorry. I had to see you. Please forgive me for coming here..."

I didn't let her finish.

In a moment of weakness, I took hold of her and pulled her body close to mine. My mouth descended on hers, coaxing her lips open with my tongue. With my inexperience came little patience. I simply wanted her, and so easily lost control. She should never have come...

Responding to my every touch, my every stroke of her face, neck and body, her tongue caressed mine with the same frantic fervour. It was evident that she wanted this as badly as I did. I felt myself harden, desperate to be free from my jeans. This was madness. I had to stop. I had to stop *now*.

My hands reacted before my body was able to, as I gently pushed her away from me.

There was a line - albeit invisible. And once I crossed it, there would be no going back.

Willingness, temptation - they both flittered with my mind and carnal needs, but I had to stay strong.

Chapter 12

Iman

It had just gone midnight and my door was slightly ajar, with only the sound of my heart for company. I didn't know what to expect. I wasn't sure what he wanted to talk about. So many thoughts rummaged around in my mind.

Perhaps he was going to tell me that we could not carry on this charade. Or maybe that he wanted us to run away together. Wouldn't that be the most delicious of ideas? I laughed at the absurdity of it. He was soon to become a cardinal in Rome. No man in their right senses would turn down such a great position of wealth and opulence, not even for love. And I didn't think it was possible for *anyone* to love me, let alone that much.

I got up and paced around the small space in my bedroom, as sitting still was draining the life out of me. I wasn't sure whether my white, cotton nightgown was appropriate. I was naked underneath, but it was hard to deduce such a thing as the cotton was thick enough to hide the intricacy of my contours. I felt that I should change - at least into a pair of leggings and top - but it was very late and he would be here soon. Now was not the time to be indecisive about my looks.

I stood beside the window, barefoot, enjoying the cold evening's summer breeze - too excited to think, to wish, to hope, to want.

I had taken the time to have a lovely shower earlier. It was important to smell nice. So, just before the clock struck midnight, a tiny spray of *Indian Summer* was all I needed.

My eyes danced around the door.

"What if he doesn't come?"

"Then life carries on as normal, Iman. Pull yourself together - he's only a man."

"No, he is not - he is a god."

"He is no god. He eats and breathes, just like you."

"He's a lot better than me. I bet he doesn't cut himself to draw blood. He doesn't have cold and dark nightmares. He doesn't feel the urgent need to end his life. I do."

I looked down at my arms. They were covered nicely. He wouldn't see the scars.

I looked down at my single bed in the corner. It was such a shame that my room was so bare. He would think me extremely boring. Not a single picture on the walls - not even a photograph of any family members.

The thought made me smile. Me? What family? Now, why would I have something so special? It was as if I had just dropped down from Heaven into this place.

The movement of the door caught my attention and I felt my stomach churn and twirl. He walked in and closed the door rather too gently behind him, locking it. Clearly, he was not one to take unnecessary chances.

He had on a white t-shirt and a pair of black jeans. Through his top, I could see the firmness of his chest, the lean muscles that shaped his arms, and - if one was to scan him entirely - his long, toned legs. Adorning his feet were a pair of leather sandals that made no sound as he walked towards me.

I let out a tiny gasp as I took in and fully absorbed his appearance.

My heart began to beat faster, causing a dryness across my lips, so much so that I had to swallow rapidly.

Stay calm please.

I don't know what exactly it was about him that I found so irresistibly attractive. Perhaps it was the way he moved with complete confidence, or the way his eyes pierced into mine, draining my very soul. Or maybe it was the way he spoke to everyone, with kindness in his eyes. He made me feel that I was the only person that mattered when it was *our time* though. His eyes expressed happiness, respect, love and adoration; a glow that I had not seen before. Perhaps that is why I found him so alluring.

Slowly, he approached me - smiling and teasing, knowing that I was his before even *I* knew it; my body and mind unknowingly submissive.

Tonight, nothing else mattered. Tonight, it was just him...and me.

He stopped...half an inch from my face. I had no choice but to breathe him in. Soap and aftershave engulfed my senses, overpowering me, overwhelming me.

"Did you think I would not come?" Green eyes suddenly held mine to ransom.

"I didn't know what to think," I whispered back.

His hands moved directly to my hair and, within a second, undid my bun allowing my curls to fall uncontrollably over my neck and face. A habit of his!

"Perfect," he beamed - his eyes still holding mine.

Not trusting my legs to keep me upright, I asked if he would like to sit down.

"No," was his reply. "Why should we sit, when we can stand just like this?"

"I thought you said not to get any ideas. It's hard to think normal thoughts standing this close to you." My, was I bold. Where did such courage come from?

"Is that why you are naked underneath that dress? Did you not think to wear something more decent knowing I was coming?"

Blood rushed to my face, and I was once again thankful that it did not show. If anything, my skin became darker when I blushed and so he would not be able to tell.

"I was *trying* to be normal, but I didn't know *who* might pop into my room. I just wanted...."

"Yes - I know what you wanted."

His lips gently touched mine - slowly, one kiss and then another; just the tip of his lips over and over, but like a feather. He was teasing me and I was playing along, wanting to be teased, luxuriating in the attention, enjoying the moment with him.

He stopped, without warning - even though my eyes remained closed and I felt like I was floating, soaring.

"We can sit now...and talk."

I staggered, ashamed at my lack of poise. I now knew the way he was though - that he would only do what he said and not what *I* said. The impossibility of him!

I sat down swiftly at the head of my bed, making space for him beside me, but he opted not to sit next to me and chose instead the chair by my desk, positioning himself rather comfortably. This way, he was directly opposite me, facing me. There was no escape.

"Would you like some tea?" I asked, gesturing my hand towards the little, pink Wedgewood tea set and tiny electric kettle on my desk. It was the only china I owned and the single, earthly possession I loved dearly.

He smiled at the tea set, shook his head and focused on my face.

"No, thank you. Tell me about *you* - everything. I want to know everything, and I really mean *everything*."

I was slightly taken aback at his request. I thought he was coming here tonight to talk to me, and not to ask delicate questions about my life. I knew one thing though - that if I failed to tell him something, *anything*, then I would risk breaking our connection. I had spent my whole life putting on a mask. Perhaps it was time to take off that mask? Perhaps it was time to show my vulnerable side? But what if the truth disgusted him? What if it all backfired? What if he looked at me with revulsion and reported me to the church? Could I trust this...stranger?

"Well, there is nothing much to tell. I had a pretty normal and happy childhood. All my life I wanted to be a nun, and here I am."

"You just kissed me rather passionately. I don't see that as the action of a committed nun." He was mocking me surely, watching my every move, assessing the situation. It was obvious he was trying to read me. I had spent the whole of my life fooling people, yet I was certain that I had finally met my match. He would not be fooled. He *could not* be fooled. My suspicions were confirmed in his next sentence.

"Thank you for that lovely story. Now, the truth, or we could play this game all night. Trust me - I really have nothing else to do. And now that I know this will take a little bit longer, I think I'll have that tea."

He was clearly not taking any prisoners. I knew, with him, there would be no pretence. He had come here for a reason and wouldn't leave until such importunity was rewarded.

"How do you know I'm not telling the truth?" I persisted, turning on the kettle and laying out the cups and saucers.

He said nothing, but gave a smirk which implied 'Don't go there, lady'.

"I don't know how to start or where to start."

"When you think no one is watching, you always seem to drift into this place." He tapped the side of his head. "I don't know where that place is, but my goodness, if I could take away the pain that I see in your eyes, I would. All I'm asking is that you trust me and let me in. I can't move forward with you if you don't let me in."

"You make me laugh, Romilly. Move forward from what? To where? We are stuck here. We are stuck in this life that we chose."

"Speak for yourself. I'm not stuck. No one is stuck in anything unless they wish to be stuck."

"What do you mean? What are you saying?"

"Let me in. Tell me about your past. Please, Iman - I wish to know."

The hissing of the kettle was a welcome interlude.

"How do you like your tea?"

"Very strong. No sugar and no milk." His eyes never left mine. He knew I was stalling.

After I handed him his cup, I started talking. It was about time I spoke to someone. It might be good for me to share my story. He wanted to know. I think I, too, wanted to talk.

And so I did.

I told him my mother had died giving birth to me. I told him my father had rejected me. I spoke about my fake mother and the way she had treated me. I told him I felt unclean and unloved most of the time. I told him I suffered from depression when I was alone and that I regularly cut myself. I told him everything…about the darkness that I carried around. I also told him that it was the first time I had ever discussed my innermost pain with anyone. I explained to him why I hadn't committed suicide - because I was scared of committing a mortal sin, scared of the teachings of the church and what they said about suicide and Hell. I was also scared living inside this body which had been abused so many times. I told him that I did not want to be a nun, but within the convent walls I could at least hide away from the world and, sometimes, my problems.

When I finished talking, I heard the church bell ring for the second time that night. It told me that I'd been talking for more than an hour and that he'd not interrupted once. He'd just sat there, looking at me, taking it all in.

My eyes drifted down to my hands as I suddenly realised that I might have lost him. He wouldn't want me now. *I* wouldn't want me now.

I sat there squirming uncomfortably under his penetrating gaze.

"I'm sorry for all of that. I guess it was therapeutic for me to talk about everything all at once. Please forgive me. I understand that you might feel inclined to do the moral thing and report my past to the church. I am a fraud, after all, and I'm sick and tired of deceiving everyone, especially Maria and Reverend Mother Thérése."

"Forgive you for what?" He gave nothing away in his expression, so it was hard to guess what he might have been thinking. I couldn't believe how easily I was managing to push away the only person that meant something to me.

"For talking too much."

He gave a non-committal shrug.

"I asked you. I wanted to know. I'm grateful for how you opened up - for trusting me with your innermost secrets. Thank you."

I certainly wasn't expecting that.

"Thank you for listening," I whispered, still undeniably ashamed of my past.

"What about you?" I asked. "What's your story?"

"Not tonight." He furrowed his brow, then got up and walked over to the space I had saved for him.

"I think you should sleep now, and I'll visit you again tomorrow."

"Really?" I couldn't contain my excitement. My face lit up and all my worries faded into the darkness in an instant.

"Oh, Romilly. I was scared that now that you know, you might find me repulsive."

"My darling, Iman - nothing you do could ever repulse me, but I do have a feeling that you have a lot of self-loving to do." He drew me close to his chest and held me there for a minute, stroking my hair, absorbed in the moment.

His words struck a chord in me – an awareness so strong and so true.

"I don't know *how* to love myself, Romilly. I really don't." By now, the tears had begun to flow uncontrollably down my cheeks. For the first time in my life, I cried for *me*. Self-hate, regret, my past, my lies, self-harm - it all became too much for me to bear. But in his arms, I found the strength to cry.

He gently lifted my head and looked into my eyes. Only then did he see the effect of his words - draining my eyes and smearing my face. Slowly, he kissed away my tears and then tucked me into bed.

"Tomorrow, wear a dress and don't have dinner. Perhaps we can eat together. I know it will be late, but it is all we have for now." He suddenly remembered his manners, for he added: "That is, if you'd like to?" His gaze was intense, daring me to turn down his request.

"With all my heart," I replied. How could I refuse him anything?

"Good. See you tomorrow." He planted a kiss on my forehead and left as silently as he had come in.

Tomorrow came quicker than I thought. I felt as light as a feather - in my head and in my heart. I was happy - *really* happy. Not because of the sunshine, or a lovely dinner. Not because of praise or laughter, or flowers or long walks.

I was happy because of *love*.

The excitement within me was too much to contain, but I knew I could tell no one. We were going against every law in the Catholic Church, in opposition to all that we believed in. The sin was great, but it was also irresistible and worth all the joy I was feeling.

I watched the parish priest celebrate Mass in the morning with a new pair of eyes. I could not help but look around the church in search of Romilly, yet he was nowhere to be seen. It was frustrating not seeing him. I refused to go for Holy Communion out of fear that the body and blood of Christ would burn me to ashes for my carnal thoughts.

It was my turn again to clean the church and I did it with absentmindedness and vigour. Maria was very amused indeed.

"Iman - what is the matter with you today? You left the mop right next to the altar. Can you imagine the look on Father Vanderbelt's face if he walked in later to say noon Mass with that dirty mop staring up at him?"

We both found the image hilarious.

"Will he be saying Mass at twelve?" I asked.

"I think so, but I will be busy and so will you, so we won't be able to attend."

"Oh, but I do very much want to attend. Why can't we? What are we doing this afternoon?"

She frowned at me somewhat suspiciously.

"I know something is definitely wrong with your memory, Sister." She shook her head with pity and affection which brought a smile to my face.

"Well, go on then - tell me. What are we doing?" My mind could think of nothing else - just Romilly. I kept recollecting his stern looks, his unmasked smiles, his kindness, his voice.

His face - so striking and well-formed. His kiss. Oh, my God - his kiss. His lips and touch that kept me yearning for more, that kept me wanting *so much more*. I was hungry for him and he knew it, yet he made me wait longingly.

"We'll be organising the list for the journey to Lourdes. It's in October. We've only got two months. However, we might be able to make afternoon Mass if we hurry up in here and get cracking."

I hugged her out of pure delight.

I worked so efficiently and a little too fast for Maria's taste, but I was sure she suspected nothing. After all, as a nun, Mass was supposed to be a most enjoyable experience.

That was certainly what I thought as we scrambled through the list of booked hotel rooms and chased people for payment.

Finally, I stumbled into the church at 12:55. Of course, Mass was almost over, but it didn't matter. Maria had suggested going in the evening as there was no point catching the peroration. I insisted that I wanted to light a candle and say a prayer though.

She had looked at me with admiration and whispered: "You are so committed. There is definitely a place for you in Heaven."

"Or Hell," I muttered under my breath, as I turned around to leave.

"What?" Her voice stopped me in my tracks.

"What?" I replied.

She looked confused as she walked back to her room.

Lunchtime Mass was usually served for the homeless and the elderly by committed Catholics who happened to be on their breaks. It brought peace and calm to an otherwise busy and hectic work schedule.

The parish priest resided over Mass again. Romilly was nowhere to be seen. I tried to hide my disappointment, but was at least glad that people were leaving, meaning my sadness was barely noticeable.

I missed him even more.

My phone beeped.

"We are having jacket potatoes for dinner. Reverend Mother would like to know what sort of filling you'd like."

I quickly texted Maria back.

"Not having dinner tonight, but thank you. I will be fasting from 6pm 'til 6pm tomorrow evening. I intend to pray all night, so forgive me if I choose to remain in my room alone."

"Like I said - you are special. Reverend Mother will be so proud of you. Don't forget to involve your Rosary."

"I won't. Thank you." I dismissed the guilt that had begun to creep into my feelings, as swiftly as I told my first lie of the day.

"Are you saying any novenas? Would you like me to join you?"

"No novenas this time. Thank you, Maria. I love you. See you tomorrow."

"See you tomorrow, darling. Xxx"

He dominated my thoughts. Even as I started to walk back to my room.

I always marvelled at how big our accommodation was. Perhaps it was to keep the priests and sisters apart. The priests resided in the north wing, while the sisters resided in the west. I worried for Romilly, coming to my part of the house at night. I just hoped he would never get caught. Affairs were dangerous. I didn't, however, want to spoil things by agonizing.

I walked through the side corridor so that no one would see me. I didn't want to explain myself and therefore ghosted my way through the hall, past the paintings on my left. The first one was *Moses with the Ten Commandments* by Philippe de Champaigne, then, in turn, *The Last Supper* by Leonardo Da Vinci, a mosaic of Jesus Christ in Byzantine style (copied from the Cefalù Cathedral in Sicily) and, on my right, *The Madonna in Sorrow* by Giovanni Battista Salvi da Sassoferrato - a classic, 17th century painting.

In the past I would never walk by without acknowledging the beauty of such wonderful paintings, even making a sign of the cross in front of Christ's mosaic.

Their eyes all accused me of a great betrayal now though. And so I ignored them. How could I not? I was in love with a man, or better still, a god.

I scurried on, knowing that there were more saints ahead to dodge and elude.

St. Luke's painting by Jean Bourdichon, *Saint Joseph with the Infant Jesus* by Guido Reni and the *Apostle Peter Holding the Keys of Heaven* by Marco Zoppo.

I walked faster, afraid of being judged, terrified of the punishment that I was sure would follow, either in this life or the next.

The truth was that deep in my heart I would serve any retribution, if I could have just one night in his arms. I would die a happy woman then. I would dance in Hell for him.

The day went fast, aligning fortune with my plans.

I changed and went to the hospital to help the nurses. My duties this evening consisted of washing dishes in the kitchen, which was a good thing – perfect, as I could daydream to the sound of the dishwasher and not appear rude to the patients (not trusting myself to be a good communicator at this time).

I was back in my room for 9pm.

This was intentional, as I didn't want to engage in conversation with Maria or my beloved reverend mother; both of whom – along with the other two sisters - occupied this wing of the house and would be in their rooms sleeping or just enjoying their quiet time, having no inkling as to what I might be up to. I didn't blame them for always going to bed so early. The sisters were very likely in their late forties and Reverend Mother was definitely in her sixties but refused to retire from God's work. And Maria simply liked to phone her family in the Philippines each evening before she retired.

We were all lucky to have en suite bedrooms, so no one really had to leave their room. Although we lived humbly, we were rewarded with the basics: a tiny fridge, bottled water, toiletries, and a radio or small television.

We were allowed to choose between having a television or a digital radio. I chose the radio.

Romilly had not specified the time he would be arriving, but I assumed it would be late again. It was important to be together when the rest of the world was asleep. This was the only way we could ensure our secret was just that.

My door was left slightly ajar for the second night in a row. I didn't want him knocking and inviting any unwanted attention.

The uniform I wore was swiftly removed from my body along with the head veil. They were placed neatly in my tartan laundry basket. My panties and brassiere were next to go. The plan was to visit the laundry in the morning.

My tummy growled with hunger, but the desire in my heart was stronger than my stomach's need for food.

In my relaxed state, I wandered into the shower and loosened my messy bun. I wanted every part of my body to smell delectable to him.

A few minutes later, I stepped out of the shower scented with a mixture of citrus and mango. It felt good to be refreshed and clean. I massaged some coconut balm into my wet hair and watched as the wavy curls danced around my face from the gust of the hairdryer. I also gently applied some coconut oil onto my skin, to keep me moisturised, and because I absolutely loved the smell. A tiny spray of *Indian Summer* was all I needed to feel heavenly. It had a hint of vanilla and raspberry infused in rose water. I didn't wish to overwhelm him with a strong scent.

Bouncy ringlets of hair formed around my forehead and down my back - a reckless and disobedient addition to my body. Wrapped around my torso was my grey, Egyptian towel - a gift from Reverend Mother the previous Christmas.

I scanned through the clothes in my wardrobe. He had asked me to wear a dress. No, he had *ordered* it. The thought made me smile; a man who knew exactly what he wanted from a woman and wasn't afraid to demand it. Perhaps I ought to have been upset, but I was frightfully impressed and completely turned on by his behaviour.

My door opened earlier than I had expected it to. He walked in and immediately glanced at me in my towel. After locking the door behind him, just as he'd done the previous night, he carried the food he'd brought with him to the table.

I was suddenly reminded of how hungry I was and was glad that he'd come early. I had completely forgotten about the dress. All I did was stand and stare as he placed the food on the table.

There was a large spinach and mushroom pizza, freshly baked and piping hot. On the side sat two small, opened boxes of green salad and olives. A bottle of dry white wine adorned the table along with two wine glasses and some cutlery.

"I brought Italy to you for dinner. Hope you like it."

He walked towards me and planted a tiny kiss on my lips.

His green eyes swept up my legs, lingered on my towel and landed on my face. His right hand moved to the knot in my towel just above my cleavage and undid it effortlessly. Before I could prevent the inevitable, giddy humiliation, my towel fell to the floor, revealing my full nakedness.

My heart pulsated in a way I didn't think possible.

"I thought I asked you to wear a dress." His stern voice didn't fit with the smile that cascaded across his face. His eyes drew me in, leaving me hanging on his every word. "Unless, of course, you didn't want to - in which case, the only other option is to be naked."

Chapter 13

Romilly

"Did I do something wrong?" The pain in her voice was unbearably stimulating.

Ciara's frustration was slightly louder than a whisper. She was frantic. She was upset. And I think she might have been slightly embarrassed. Oh, hell - she was going to get us caught!

"Please be quiet," I muttered, more harshly than I intended.

She walked to my bed and sat down.

"What are you doing here?" The question was a way of breaking the silence between us. I wasn't sure how to behave with her. I wasn't sure how to behave with *any* woman given my inexperience.

"You should have asked me that before you stuck your tongue down my throat."

"I'm sorry. I acted without caution. I lost control. I mean, you are here. Why? This is so risky." I was shaking. I was nervous. I was a fool.

"The same reason you lost control. I will be going back to Venice tomorrow. I needed to see you. I'm sorry. I should not have come." She looked uncertain - a pronounced change from the initial confidence that accompanied the Ciara I first saw.

I walked towards her and knelt in front of her. I couldn't bear to see her so upset, nor any woman. It reminded me too much of Marie-Ange.

"Hey, I'm glad you're here. I'm just scared that we might get caught. How about I come to visit you in Venice?"

Her face broke into a tiny smile.

"You don't have to lie to get me to leave."

"I wouldn't make empty promises. I think I might go crazy if I don't see you again." I was maybe already crazy for indulging her.

"Then why wait for Venice when we can have tonight, Romilly?"

"What if...."

"For how long will you spend your life thinking about fear and what ifs? What is wrong with simply living in the moment? Would it be so bad to enjoy tonight with me?"

"I will never be made a cardinal if I get caught. That is the reason why I'm in Rome - to train under my uncle."

"The man that kissed me earlier was no Cardinal," she hissed.

To say I was shocked at her bluntness would be an understatement. The woman had seen right through my façade - a pretence that even I mostly refused to acknowledge.

"Let me look after you tonight, Romilly." She moved her bosom especially close to me, leaving me no choice but to drink in her femininity. I could not control myself. The woman was sex on legs. "And after I'm done, you can be whatever you choose."

Her lips grazed mine, "A priest," she kissed my neck, "a cardinal," she kissed the base of my throat, "or my mere mortal man. The choice will be completely yours."

I was entirely taken by her. Hypnotised to a point of bewilderment, my mind alternated between succumbing to her whims and concealing my involuntary state.

"I..."

"Shhhh - don't say anything. Just be. Stay calm. Let me please and pleasure you. Just. Stay. Calm."

Her voice was relaxingly reassuring to my confused and disorientated self.

"I take it I will be your first, no?"

"Yes," I whispered.

"Then let me guide you, my handsome priest."

I liked to assert my physical and mental prowess in everything that I did. Perhaps because of this I was truly like my father. I didn't feel completely comfortable relinquishing control to another human being. It didn't feel quite right to me, but rather out of sync. However, there was curiously no arguing with Ciara. She was in command and I was completely and inexorably under her spell; her plaything in many ways.

There, on my bed, not far from the Pope's residential building, she took my hands and planted little kisses on them. She then got up and poured herself a drink from my cellar table.

"Tonight I will ravish you, and then you will ravish me." Her Italian accent had suddenly thickened amidst the passion that suffused the room. I could hardly think. It was as if she had hung me upside down over a cliff and I would be dead in a matter of seconds.

There was no doubt that I had already, somehow, become her lover, her toy. There in that room right in the middle of St. Peters Square, merely a day after the *La Festa Di San Pietro e Paolo*, I was to lose my virginity.

She returned from the table and sank her knees in the montage tiled floor, burying her face in my hairy chest. We were slightly uncertain, both of us, before we unlocked our hunger. My hands, in undiluted desperation and youthful ignorance, hurried to squeeze and touch her large breasts, tiny waist and hard nipples.

We tried to remain as quiet as we could, yet stifling our emotions induced an extra layer of desire within us. Her fingernails combed through my thick hair, sliding down the back of my neck and spine, creating a feathery feel as she buried her head deep inside my shorts.

My body surrendered to her expertise as her hands took control of my member; never before touched by anyone but me. I felt a fire building inside my loins, burning through every cell, navigating from the heat in my brain down to my trembling feet. Just when I thought I would explode everywhere, she captured the whole of me in her mouth.

Yes, she knew how to build my inferno in a way I could never have done myself.

I let go, conceded control and sank into my mattress with a blissful sigh.

We both lay there motionless and mute, each in our own thoughts. Later that evening, I stepped onto my minuscule balcony and inhaled the moist earth and remains of last night's bonfire.

We made love later - again and again. She was the teacher and I, very much the eager student. I was a fast learner. It didn't take me long to initiate control, and she enjoyed her descent into weakness.

She left for Venice the following day, but that did not deter us from making plans and seeing each other frequently.

I spent all my holidays in Venice and she visited her family more often than she used to; each night, when in Rome, spent with me.

She claimed to be in love with me. I wasn't sure that I was in love with her.

I was, however, addicted to her and would have been very sad if she had ended things.

For me, it was the perfect arrangement.

Ciara was a lot older than I originally thought - almost eighteen years my senior, and so it would have been impossible for her to bear me any children. She was also too mature to ask for more commitment than I could give.

She sometimes spoke of running away with me though. She often hinted that I should give up the Catholic faith and my dream of becoming a cardinal.

I told her that I had no dreams - that I was merely doing what was expected of me.

The likely truth was that I didn't feel a deep, irresistible need to spend the rest of my life with her. I was happy and content with the way things were. She had taught me so much about romance, however, that I genuinely didn't think I would want to love any other woman but her.

Years passed – seven, to be precise - and she remained faithful; no matter where I was, no matter what I was doing. During that time I stopped being a boy and became a man – a man who was to become Cardinal.

I was supposed to be preparing to take on the mantle and my uncle was becoming impatient. I explained to him that I wasn't ready, that there was still something missing in my soul and I needed to find it. The professor suggested charity work and I jumped at the idea. I decided to visit places afflicted by poverty; devote my services to the needy. This was perhaps selfish, as it enabled me to escape from my troubles, but it could also be considered penance for my sinful acts with Ciara.

At the age of thirty four I embarked on my journey. I was given two years to travel, before my expected return to Rome in order to carry the mantle for my family's honour.

My first stop was Nigeria, West Africa. I had initially been offered a place in one of the richer, more developed towns like Lagos or Abuja, but I declined this and insisted to my uncle that I preferred somewhere my help would be desperately needed. I ended up in one of the villages in the Niger Delta – a place without electricity or technology; a village so remote that one could hardly find a car.

The village was known as *Nsit-Ubium*. I was to stay at the church residence with the parish priest. He seemed grateful to have me say Mass with him, for he was very old and could hardly walk.

All the villagers moved around either on foot or on bicycles. They fed from their little vegetable and poultry farms, and they fished from the sea that surrounded them. They washed their clothes in the rivulet and they had baths in the stream – unsurprisingly, as the weather was so tropical. It reminded me of a little island surrounded by rivers and natural resources. It was simply *enough* – enough for the people and definitely enough for me.

Their initial reaction to me was one of wonder and awe. They touched my white skin and played with my hair. They also had a name for me: *Mmakara Afia owo*. It meant the white one.

When I wasn't saying Mass in the local church, I worked in the combined primary/secondary school, teaching the children how to count and how to read. I also taught them how to pray the Rosary, say novenas and properly recite the Lord's Prayer with dedication and commitment.

I introduced African literature to the older children. It was important to me to show them how wonderful writers had emerged from Africa and that they too could follow in such footsteps. A discussion on *Things Fall Apart* by Chinua Achebe tugged at my heartstrings. It happened to be with the brightest girl in the class, Imo. She couldn't have been more than fifteen.

"Father - it would be nice if you adopted me like Okonkwo did with Ikemefuna."

"I would like nothing better, but I'm not allowed to have children. Also, you have your mum and dad."

That seemed to do the trick. I couldn't stop the children comparing works of literature to what had happened in their own lives. It was the same with Ngũgĩ wa Thiong'o's *Weep Not Child* and Mariama Ba's *So Long A Letter.*

They took joy in composing their own stories and poems, which I relished reading in my bed at night with the help of a church candle; almost always laughing myself to sleep.

I taught the children how to draw and paint too. I had not picked up a brush since Marie-Ange passed away. My fingers worked tirelessly and magically, creating pictures that existed in my subconscious - bringing out all the pain that tormented me in my dreams; slowly freeing me from my past.

I ate with the children and played football with them - both the girls and the boys.

In the evenings, I joined their fathers for palm wine and the local delicacy, goat's head. I also liked snacking on bitter cola nuts. They tasted astringent and acidic initially, but had a way of losing this intensity in the mouth. The meals were often spicy, and I ended up emptying my bowels somewhat regularly. After a couple of months, however, my stomach acclimatised and I ate everything without hesitation - from delicious, afang vegetable soup, prepared with big, fat snails, to fufu and pounded yam. We had to use our hands to eat the fufu and yam, dipping it in delicious sauces consisting of vegetables, chickpeas, seafood stew or whatever was being cooked for the day. Never in my life had I tasted such mouth-watering dishes. The tomato stew they prepared with rice reminded me of meatballs in tomato sauce and the jollof rice was very similar to Spanish paella. They also ate lots of fresh vegetables and different varieties of seafood.

When I set off for Africa, it was to help children in the local schools, but when I left I realised that *I* was the one who had been helped. There was an almost heavenly peace that surrounded the place - a place with no money, technology or luxury, and yet, a place of boundless joy and wise counsel.

The people exuded warmth and generosity. They went to each other's houses without an invitation. They greeted each other on the street with humour and ardour. They laughed, ate and drank together. In the evenings, they nearly always put on a show with music, dancing, the beating of drums and a ukulele. They told stories to the children about their ancestors, along with folk tales concerning history and tradition.

The *malams*, who happened to come from the north, were mostly shepherds and animal herders. They were of the Hausa nomadic origin and they travelled and settled with their animals wherever they felt welcome. They roasted lamb, beef and whole chickens on barbecues with peanuts and ginger spices. They called this meat *suya*. People ate, drank, talked and danced to the drums. The flavoursome aroma of *suya*, infused with kerosene lanterns and pillar candles that lighted the dark nights, filled the air, teasing our nostrils and awakening our senses.

There was genuine happiness here - an authentic joy that found its way into my disorientated soul, erasing past worries and giving me hope.

I had learnt in Africa what true love really meant - how doing things for others was the most fulfilling emotion of all. It didn't matter what one's vocation was in life. What actually mattered was being happy. And the spreading of that happiness meant everything.

I stayed in Nigeria for a year, and during that time I somehow came to forgive my father and let go of my mother. It didn't matter anymore - it was the past, and it was important for me to look to the future.

As I walked towards the bus that would take me to the city to catch my flight, I tried really hard to put on a brave face. It didn't last long though. The tears suddenly flowed freely down my cheeks. But I didn't fight them - they were, after all, a reflection of my broken heart, knowing that I would never see my new brothers and sisters again.

The children made a leaving present for me, which I knew I would cherish for the rest of my life. It was a wooden painting of the face of Christ with the words "Uyo owo a do uyo Abasi" underneath. They were kind enough to translate it for me: "The voice of man is the voice of God."

I was humbled to realise that people with such minimal resources were more than willing to give and share what they had.

Cardinal Hugo had written to me asking me to come back to Rome. I had not seen him in a year, nor Ciara. I hadn't encouraged letters between myself and Ciara as I didn't wish to get caught, especially by my new, African countrymen who would have been very disappointed.

I hoped that Ciara had moved on with her life, as I felt no need to be in her arms again. I was slowly becoming the priest that I was supposed to be. Or so I thought.

I felt tempted to visit my uncle, but he was in a comfortable place and I needed to help *more* people and work for *longer*. My soul felt like a body that had gone running; a body that refused to stop until it could run no more due to exhaustion. If I had accepted my uncle's invitation, I would never have been able to carry on with my journey. And, right now, I was partly satisfied, but not fully and completely.

My next stop was India. It had taken the church only two weeks to agree to my request. It was evident that I was really needed in India. I was to live with the parish priest in Goa. I had read enough books in my lifetime though to know that most of the wealth in India managed to find its way to Goa. And so I declined.

I didn't want to live in luxury. I wanted to be amongst the ordinary people, as I was sure they needed my services more. It was my penance.

Africa had taught me how to be grateful for all that I had. And so I wanted the same feeling in India - perhaps selfishly!

After much deliberation, the city of Rishikesh was agreed. I would have preferred a more remote village, but I had to reach a compromise with my superiors in Rome, with my uncle acting as intermediary.

Rishikesh happened to be a holy city of pilgrimage and was said to be highly influenced by the Hindu religion, and so the number of Catholics present was small. Rishikesh was also the gateway to the Garhwal Himalayas where monks lived like spirits. The holy place housed the sacred river of the Ganges which flowed directly from the mountains into the city, purifying everyone and everything; a home for anyone interested in the practice of yoga and meditation, exhilaration and ascension, purity and wholesomeness, awakening and, of course, enlightenment.

To me, this place was foreign, beautiful, serene, spiritual and yet *somehow* the antithesis of the bulk of my beliefs.

It was in this place that I was taken ill. And it was in this place that I was sure I would die.

The illness, so intense and unlike anything I could ever have imagined, appeared from nowhere like a viper - eating me up slowly from the inside, tormenting me so severely that I begged for death each day and each night. But even death rejected me.

I had never experienced so much physical suffering in all my life. The doctor assigned to me informed me that I had contracted a combination of pneumonia and malaria – a diagnosis difficult to recover from as my condition was precarious.

The bouts of fever I experienced every evening were nothing compared to my loss of appetite or the fact that everything I ate was immediately rejected my body. I had a terrible pain in my stomach which kept me awake all night and throughout the day. My body quickly deteriorated into skin and bones enabling me to unhappily count my ribs if I chose to. The pain was genuinely one I thought I would never recover from and I was sure that I would die in India.

An old, but young-looking man by the name of Baba was assigned to look after me. He washed me and fed me. He also cleaned up after me, but never said a word. Whenever I mumbled my appreciation, he would simply nod his head kindly.

The cardinal had ordered me to go back to Italy at once, but I declined as it was impossible for me to travel in such a condition.

I kept seeing my mother each time I closed my eyes, and sometimes my father smiling silently at me – both of them begging me to join them.

I wanted to go with them, but I was not done yet. There was still so much to do. I needed to confess my sins to a priest - explain that I was a fraud, that I had *always* been a fraud.

I felt stronger in the mornings – sufficient enough to walk around the Himalayan foothills, and sometimes relax by the Ganges River. It was only a short walk from my accommodation. I was told by the natives that the river was considered holy, and so I would dip my feet into it and sometimes wash my face. The water looked so clean and pure that I even drank it sometimes - shamelessly so.

The Catholic Church looked after me when I couldn't look after myself. I was useless to them and yet they remained faithful. I grew weaker each day, knowing that I was dying. Yet, somehow, I refused to believe that the Lord would take my soul in a strange land.

Every night I saw my parents and I realised that it wouldn't be long now. I wasn't eating at this stage; a few sips of warm water was all that my body could take. Sometimes the water poured out of my system in the form of bile - the burning heat in my stomach a reminder that there was almost nothing left of me.

One particular night, I eventually lost my voice, and the villagers were sure that I would not see another sunrise. They took turns sitting with me so that I would not be alone during my final hours.

That was the night I thought I would leave the world. I waited for my parents to come for me, but they did not show. I waited for Christ Himself to come for me, but it was in vain. I did, however, mutter a silent prayer that only I could hear.

"Show your face, dear Jesus, and free me from my pain."

As surprising as it was to me and my caregivers, I woke up the following morning with a strong desire to visit the Ganges River again. My voice, too, miraculously found its way back into its box. I could still hardly walk though and so I begged Baba to take me in the wheelchair that had been provided for me.

There was something rather strange about him. He couldn't have been less than seventy years old and yet he moved as if he was twenty. On our journey to the river, I struck up a conversation with him.

"So tell me, dear sir - what is your secret to looking and being so young?"

"There is no secret, Father. I am whatever I believe myself to be."

"Yes, I've heard that a lot, but surely you must exercise. How else does one gain such eternal vigour?"

"I practise a little yoga. You should try it sometime."

His advice made me laugh as much as I could manage.

"I think it's too late for me now, sir," I replied, smiling. I knew I didn't have long. There was no point deceiving myself.

"Well, you have said it and it will be unto you just as you have said."

This statement of his made me angry. And I wasn't one to easily lose my temper.

"Please do not play games with my emotions. I say these things because of what I see and feel."

"Perhaps you should start believing in what you can *neither* see nor feel, but more importantly, what you want and the emotions that you feel when you want those things." He suddenly stopped in order to make sure that his words had sunk into the ears of this faithless priest.

We moved in silence by the river - each absorbed in his own thoughts. We passed some monks seated in the lotus position, clearly meditating. I could never understand such quietude and slumber.

"Why do they stay there all day meditating? Do they not have anything better to do with their time?" I asked, hoping to divert our attention away from the previous conversation. It was important for me to carry on talking, as I felt that I might lose my voice again and thus hang my head for the final time.

"The act you mock might be that which saves you."

We carried on in silence again. It was as if Baba only spoke to me in rebuke.

My nostrils suddenly absorbed the pleasant mix of soaked earth and cardamom spices which the wind transported from the nearby local market.

I stopped to catch my breath and welcomed a long since forgotten sensation in my tummy. I had not experienced a desire for food in almost three weeks and such a feeling ignited in me a hunger to carry on living, to be well again.

"What are you trying to say? If there is any hope for me, I need to know. Just don't tell me that I need yoga to survive. As you can see, I can hardly walk, let alone perform a downward-facing dog."

He suddenly stopped wheeling my chair. I wondered why, until he stood facing me with a broad grin on his face, revealing perfectly white, healthy teeth.

"That is the fire I wanted to see." He held out both hands in excited gratitude - his voice slightly elevated by a profound passion. "Right now, right here, we can begin your healing and maybe your transformation. You came to Rishikesh for a reason, and who knows, maybe it's time for you to come out of the darkness and into the light."

I wasn't convinced, but what did I have to lose? Absolutely nothing.

Chapter 14

Iman

We both felt the towel hit the floor. I looked down and tried to grab it impulsively.

"Stop. Please don't do that," he whispered. "It's okay - you are beautiful. I want to be naked with you."

His hands cupped my chin as his lips attacked mine, rather slowly at first, exploring, teasing, making me crave all of him. My lips begged for more, pouting and taking from him what he offered. My hands suddenly found their way to his neck - my fingers digging deep into his wavy, brown curls. For a moment, I forgot that I was standing naked and vulnerable.

Slowly, I began to unbutton his shirt, completely aware that his eyes were on me. I was measured and unhurried – ponderous almost - not because I wanted to be, but because my hands were unsteady.

He was looking at my scars, and I suddenly became conscious of my body's imperfection.

"I'm sorry." I stopped and picked up the towel to hide my body, even though I knew it would not assist in covering my arms. That was not the point, however. I simply needed modesty once more.

He carefully unwrapped me yet again though, kissing my neck as my nakedness resurfaced. His lips worked their way to my arms, my scars, my very being, and I watched – mesmerised - as he kissed each mark with tenderness.

In that moment, that precise moment, I knew how it felt to be in love with another human being. I understood how easily one chooses to die for another, give up everything for another and be completely enslaved by another. It was then that my soul became one with his.

He returned my hands to the buttons on his shirt.

"It's okay. Breathe. Take your time." His voice was a hushed whisper - his respiration, his exhalements, surprisingly calm in comparison to mine.

He radiated a faint scent of cedarwood and manly sweat, combined with fresh soap and shampoo. His hairy skin felt both strong and soft underneath my palms - like touching clouds in a still sky. I was on my knees now, sliding down his pants, revealing his underwear beneath, trembling at what I was yet to discover. I avoided eye contact with him, knowing that if I looked at him I would immediately stop and run away.

He helped me remove his pants as if he could no longer bear the waiting. He then yanked down the material underneath them revealing his very hard member.

His strong arms lifted me up as his lips joined mine like a hungry predator, devouring its prey after a long pursuit; his hot tongue penetrating my mouth, soaking up my desire which was slowly spiralling out of control. I did not believe that I was prepared for such intensity, but now I very much welcomed it.

The new-found dampness between my thighs was proof that if he did not take me and make me his *right away*, I would perhaps die from longing and want.

He must have read my mind, for quite suddenly I felt my body lifted up into his arms and transported to the soft sheets on my bed; lying flat in all my vulnerability and yearning for him desperately. He paused as his eyes assimilated the shivers of my trembling body which shamelessly revealed my fervour for him.

He draped his head over my neck and slowly touched my tremulous skin with his lips, moving down my voluptuous chest so that all I wanted to do was scream. The feelings within me began as lightly as the flutter of butterfly wings - the white ones I frequently saw glide past me in the Cotswold hills. My breath suddenly tightened in my throat, suspending itself almost as my hands dug deep into his hair - feeling the strands on every fingertip as he, simultaneously, kissed and played with my thighs, tummy and breasts.

His lips slowly surfaced once more, skimming across my cheek to my earlobe, nibbling it slowly and then moving down to the tip of my nose before hovering close to my mouth. I felt my body shiver as I uncontrollably, yet exuberantly wrapped my legs around his waist, arching my derriere to the rhythm of his body, wanting him to desperately make me his.

I was burning for him, and I think he was burning for me too. The sensation of pain and pleasure was driving me crazy. Just when I thought I could take no more of this torture, this heavenly abuse, I felt his fingers caress my wetness. I wanted to explode, but he wouldn't let me. Each time I bordered on an excited crescendo, he moved his fingers away - quite suddenly and intentionally. And then, without warning, his lips coerced my wetness, tasting me, thrilling me, driving me to insanity.

"Please, Romilly," I whimpered.

"Please what?" he whispered back.

"Please make love to me. I cannot bear it any longer."

My voice was barely audible, for I was shivering and trembling out of desire for him. He heard me though. He heard me well enough.

Slowly, he parted – nay, *spread* - my legs and gently eased his way inside me, instigating a fiery, but controlled and rhythmic pace; a cadence that took me from earth to every planet in every star system - stimulating my senses, merging my soul with his, so that our bodies not only bonded and amalgamated together, but our spirits roamed everywhere side by side and would do so for eternity.

We made love in every corner of the bedroom. He was tender. Then he was rough. And when I thought we had reached a conclusion or culmination in some sense, he would take me all over again.

It was the most enjoyable experience of my whole life and I knew then that I was overpoweringly and permanently in love with him. I knew then that I would give everything up for him if he asked me to.

It was gone midnight when we stopped to catch our breath. We entered the bathroom and showered in silence, each in our own thoughts - his eyes never leaving mine. It felt comfortable, natural, good. How could something so beautiful be seen or perceived as a sin, I wondered.

I wore the flowery dress that I had never put on before. It had cost me a mere two pounds at the charity shop. It did nothing for my curves, but then again, I was a nun. Today, I was a nun who loved sex though. I was also a nun who loved a man. I was a nun who loved to have sex with the man that I adored. As that simple, yet evocative thought entered my senses, I realised that not only was I irrevocably in love with him, I was also profoundly and undeniably fucked up.

"The pizza is cold, but I hope you're hungry."

"Starving," I muttered, still avoiding his eyes. I took the seat opposite him by the window, with only the small, round dining table dividing us.

"I hope you will look at me sometime soon."

I smiled, rather coyly and tilted my head upwards, pleased to see him beaming at me.

"That was beautiful. Don't you think?" He dug into the pizza.

"The pizza or me?"

"I'd say you, but the pizza also."

I became silent again. I didn't want our evening to end.

"Will you be staying the night?" I asked.

"Only if you want me to."

"I do want."

That night, after dinner, he told me everything.

He told me about his mother, Marie-Ange. He told me about his father, Hansen. He told me how his father had killed his mother. He told me about his siblings that he had lost touch with. He told me about Cardinal Hugo and his philosopher friend, Alessandro. He told me how he wanted to be an artist - how he loved to paint. He told me that he did not want to be a priest. He told me about Ciara. He told me that she had taught him a lot about life, about women, about sex. I felt jealous when he mentioned Ciara; thinking of another woman in his arms felt wrong and unnatural, but I let the feeling pass as quickly as it had arrived. He told me about Africa. And he told me about India. He said he experienced an awakening in India. He said he would tell me about it someday.

He told me something that bothered me. He said he had a feeling he was being watched, but didn't know how or why. There might have been coincidences, a hint of paranoia, but it concerned him all the same.

After talking close to two hours, he was suddenly very tired and wanted to sleep.

We somehow managed to fit our bodies together in the single bed. It was uncomfortable, but we didn't care. We would have been happy on the bare, cool, summer floor.

We quickly realised that we didn't want to sleep after all though, despite our exhaustion. We made love throughout the night and during those celestial hours the world seemed perfect.

He left in the morning. It must have been as early as 4am.

"Try to get some sleep. I will see you again tonight. There is much to plan."

"Tell me now, please. I cannot wait for tonight."

"Oh yes you can, *mon coeur*. Same time. And I will bring dinner."

We kissed briefly, but passionately, and then he was gone - just like the night before.

I was surprised that I did not feel tired. I guess I was too excited. I hurriedly performed all my chores, somewhat haphazardly – a fragment of guilt floating over me, but that was all. I *wanted* to do things properly - tend to the garden, clean up the church, say my Rosary and complete my shift at the local hospice - but I did everything dreamily; my head in the clouds, my heart pulsating.

I wanted to scream - tell the world the intimate details of what I had done, what I had been illuminated by. I wanted to yell to the universe how hopelessly in love I was. I wanted to confide in someone. But I couldn't. I had to hide it all inside.

That night I excused myself from dinner with the sisters. I told them I was tired and needed to pray. I lied, saying I was fasting. I was slowly becoming a great sinner indeed. I pushed this thought to the back of my mind, however, hoping it would stay there for all eternity.

On entering my room, I closed the door behind me. I made sure not to lock it, for it would be a disaster if Romilly was unable to get in.

I emptied my little purse's contents onto the table, delighted by the lipstick I had bought today. I showered in a hurry, taking care to wash my delicate parts. I then suddenly stopped what I was doing, preferring to gaze into thin air - while under the hot water - with a playful smile on my face.

I dressed slowly, taking care to choose a more delectable and delicate dress. This one was beige. I had never worn it before. It had been given to me a couple of years ago by a member of the congregation on my birthday. I had never allowed myself to even *think* of wearing it. Tonight, however, I would wear it for him. It hung to my skin as if perfectly designed for me - accentuating all my curves, making me feel attractive and sexy at the same time; a feeling I never thought was possible.

It was only eight in the evening. He wouldn't be here 'til eleven, once everyone had retired for bed. I therefore had three hours to kill.

The hours went slowly. I read a book I had picked up earlier from the charity shop for just ten pence. It was titled *The Borgia Bride* - the terrorist reign by Pope Alexander VI and his possible incestuous relationship with his daughter, Lucrezia Borgia. A familiar guilt was piqued and awakened in my head, bidding me to discard such a book, unfaithful as it was to the Catholic Church, even if it contained historical truths.

I must have got carried away, for when I looked at the time it was almost eleven thirty and he still wasn't here. I waited and waited. I waited for him all night, but he didn't show.

It was one of the great mysteries of life that a person could be very happy one day and exceedingly sad the next. I hoped that he might show the following night, full of apologies and remorse. He didn't. I waited for him a third night. Still - nothing. I would see him at Mass the following morning, I thought. But he wasn't there either. I was confused. He always celebrated Thursday's early morning Mass.

I couldn't help myself. I walked up to the priest after Mass and asked the question that had tormented my soul these last few days. He was a new priest that I had never met before. I would have to be subtle.

"Hello, Father. I just thought I'd introduce myself. I'm Sister Iman Williamson."

"Hello, I'm Father Dominic. I got posted here as an emergency replacement from Bury St. Edmunds." He had an African accent that I couldn't quite place. I did, however, recall that he kept apologising for his poor Latin during Mass. I almost felt sorry for him. God, of course, did not care about such things, but man did.

I began to feel different forms of panic rising within me. Why was he here? What sort of emergency had occurred? What had happened to Romilly? Surely, I would have overheard something - unless it was being kept a secret for now.

"Yes, I was a tad surprised to see you, as Father Vanderbelt always says Mass on Thursdays."

"Oh, didn't you hear what happened to him?"

The blood in my face must have drained completely. I knew then that my fears would be confirmed. Romilly must have been hit by a drunk driver whilst out running. He loved to run. Or maybe, worse, mistakenly hit by a stray bullet given the villagers penchant for shooting at wildlife in the community. Or maybe he had been right about being followed. Or perhaps he had suffered a heart attack, doled out by God due to his sins and involvement with me. Oh, God, please take *me* instead - punish me and not him. I beg you: *Not him.*

"Well - not him exactly." Father Dominic interrupted my thoughts. "Sadly, his uncle passed away in Rome three days ago, so Romilly was flown there straight away. We do not think that he will be coming back, as he might be made a cardinal now - lucky man." He laughed at his own stupidity.

I just looked at him, wondering what was so lucky about Romilly losing his uncle. Father Dominic quickly composed himself - returning my gaze as if he was going to command me to stand to attention.

I walked away - my head bowed. This news ought to have torn my heart into little pieces, but it didn't. I was relieved that he was okay and not hurt. I was also thankful for our magical night together, knowing that I would cherish it for as long as I lived.

Being thankful and optimistic eventually failed me dreadfully though. I tried to forget. I tried to move on. But each night I went to sleep, my pillow was soaked in tears.

Something good *did* come out of all this. I carried out my chores more diligently. I worked really hard without taking a break. I tried to keep busy throughout the day. But one thing I couldn't escape was the pain that crept up on me at night - slowly taking over my whole existence and reducing me to an emotional wreck.

Something else was happening to me though. And I was too emotionally drained by thoughts of Romilly to notice. I was too busy or blind to observe how my body was changing; too busy to notice that I had missed my monthly cycle three times; too busy to realise that I was carrying his baby inside of me; a *life* growing inside me. Too busy to see that everything was about to collapse and that I would no longer be a nun.

Too busy to laugh.

Too busy to stop.

Too busy to breathe.

Too busy to run.

Chapter 15

Romilly

I looked at the old man who was sure that he held the secret to saving my life and I realised I didn't even know his name. Nor did I understand the darkness and light that he spoke of. Surely he meant Heaven and Hell. Even as a Catholic priest, I always wondered how true that fable was.

"What may I call you?" I asked him.

"Everyone calls me Baba Aarush." He carried on pushing my wheelchair with the agility and strength of a teenager.

The German Catholic priest led by the Indian monk! Rome would snobbishly laugh out loud.

We ended up on a little patch of land by a flowing stream. Baba Aarush then guided us into a cave nearby. It was like a tiny temple and not completely without light as sunbeams illuminated inscriptions on the wall. They were written in Hindi, which meant I could not understand the lettering.

Baba sat down on the floor to rest. Perhaps he wasn't a god after all, I mused. I suddenly felt my blood's warmth return together with an elevated peace that I had never experienced ever. I could hear the water from the stream, flowing quietly from the hills to lower ground. I knew then that I could gladly die in this cave and be happy. My body, however, fought on through a moderate degree of pain.

I noticed that the cave had tiny, window glass pockets - about six or seven - and on the shelves of the pockets stood large, church candles. They started burning only when Baba Aarush arose from the ground and lit them with matches that seemed to appear from nowhere. Perhaps he had brought me to this cave so that I could die in peace - to the sound of the stream singing sweet, gentle music to my soul.

"We can sit here a while, Father. There is a lot of work to be done." His voice echoed all around us.

"Please call me Romilly. I have no need to be addressed so formally, especially not by friends." My voice echoed like his. It reminded me of my childhood when visiting caves with Mama. How I longed for her today.

He smiled warmly at me and I knew he regarded me as a friend too.

"It is important, Romilly, that you trust my teaching implicitly. You are very weak and so we will focus on fast lessons. If you require more in-depth lessons, then you can always return once you are healed. For now, we will focus on the healing itself." He took a deep breath and looked at me, possibly to make sure that I was paying attention.

I nodded. I didn't have a choice. One thing was certain as my senses sharpened - I no longer wanted to die in an Indian cave. I didn't object to dying in the presence of Baba Aarush as my friend and companion, but my uncle in Rome would be devastated - if not heartbroken. I was like a son to him. Ciara, too, would be overcome with grief.

"Your first lesson started when we entered this cave. It was dark and yet we could still see. And when the candles lit the place up, not only did we see better, but we *felt* better too."

I was lost. I couldn't think as deeply as he wanted me to. I was too busy shivering like a baby. The cave was unexpectedly cold.

As if sensing what I was thinking, he walked across to the open chimney, placed and lit some of the logs that had been stacked neatly close by.

"We will have to replace those," I whispered through gritted teeth, feeling bad for using someone else's fire.

"It's okay, my dear friend. Now, we *must* focus on what I am trying to teach you." He stretched out his arms and pointed at the candles. "We have light." He stretched out his *hands* rather dramatically this time towards the now blazing flames that slowly began to heat my bones. "And we have warmth."

The Asians were quite dramatic in their approach to life and speech, and Baba Aarush was no exception.

"How can I feel better through the candle's light and warmth? Surely when I go back to sleep tonight, the fever will return." The pessimistic me knew that I was trying his patience, but I did not care.

"You are a being that includes all forms of physical reality, both good and bad. You experience the reality that you focus on. If you focus on your illness, worry about it, give it all your attention and see the negative, then that will be *your* reality. There is no other way. It is simply the way it is. You *become* what you worry or think about the most."

"I can't help it. Everything around me reminds me of how I'm feeling. My body is constantly in pain. How can I not think about my pain and the possibility of dying?" It all felt like a waste of time. At least the cave was now nice and warm though.

"Do you remember the old story of the empty cup? I cannot teach you anything if your cup is full." He went to stand up and I panicked. He wouldn't dare leave me here to die on my own, would he?

"No, no - sit down." Even I was surprised at the sudden force in my frail voice. "My cup is empty. In fact, I have no cup. I need a cup."

He smiled at me the way a mother would smile lovingly at the stupidity of her two-year-old child.

"Relax, friend. I'm only going to turn the fire."

I watched him in silence as he picked up an iron poker behind the fireplace and stoked the fire with it. When he sat down again, he cleared his throat briefly and asked me an unexpected, surprising question.

"How old do you think I am, friend?"

"I'd rather not go into that. I wouldn't want to offend..."

"I am not a pretty damsel who concerns herself with such things. Humour me, friend. How old would you say I am?"

I hesitated for a second and then blurted out a number. "Maybe sixty?" I replied, bracing myself. I did not like this game.

"Why, thank you. I feel really flattered. I am a lot older than that. I am actually a hundred and two."

I started to laugh, even though the laughter caused the muscles in my stomach to hurt, akin to someone turning a penknife. "Look, you don't have to lie about your age to get me to listen to you."

"People lie for their own benefit. Whether you believe me or not is of no consequence, but what you choose to believe today, and act upon, might just save your life."

I sat up properly for the first time and looked at my new friend. He walked around as if he still had fifty years left in him. His features were strong, his skin healthy, his teeth all in place - a distinct, pearly white. Yes, he was bald, but he didn't even wear spectacles.

"I'm listening," I whispered - this time with a purposeful resolve to learn from the man determined to save my life.

"All your pain is in your mind. You must therefore begin to tell your mind what to feel. Your illness is only an appearance. Your body's natural state is perfection. This form of perfection can only be acquired when one has mastered the act of controlling the mind."

"How can I do this?" I asked; intrigue and bewilderment overcoming my initial scepticism.

"Care for your mind. What your mind thinks, your body gets, your life gets. Your whole human experience is given to you through your thoughts. The mind thinks death, disease, physical and earthly calamities, and these thoughts begin to take form until they become your reality. But if the mind sees good, wealth, happiness and a world of love, then it doesn't matter what your current reality is. It doesn't matter that you are in pain. It doesn't matter what the naked eye cannot see. It only matters that the mind thinks it. Whatever the mind sees will become your reality. So, today, we control the mind."

I watched as he stood up yet again. I thought he was going back to the fire that did not require attention. Instead, he dipped his hand into his pocket and took out a marker pen, and proceeded to draw a tiny circle on the wall adjacent to us - a circle probably the same size as my little, pinky finger.

"Are you allowed to do that in here?" I asked. It was important to me that we left things the way we found them so that others could enjoy such simple beauty.

"You concern yourself too much with things that do not matter. Free your mind, my dear friend." Who was I to argue with the great, enlightened one?

Baba Aarush commanded me to stare at the circle on the wall for as long as possible without blinking. I was to let my mind wander and then keep returning to the circle. As I stared and stared, something began to happen. All I could see was the circle and nothing else, and it appeared to be moving. This alarmed me and I almost jumped out of my skin.

"What is the matter?" Baba asked.

"It's moving. I'm sorry - this is too deep for me."

"It's moving because everything is moving - even this cave. Everything is in motion. I thought you would know that - you're the educated one, the westerner. It is merely science. When we stop all that we are doing, and begin to focus on the little things, we can see everything clearly for what it really is."

Mizu No Kokoro. Oh, Alessandro - I wish you were here to see all that I am learning. You would be so proud of Baba Aarush.

I started all over again - this time focusing on the circle for about twenty minutes. And during that time, something happened to me - an experience that I never thought possible; an elated feeling so deep, so intense, that it took me away from my physical burden and into a place of tranquillity, a place of peace. For me, this was where life existed. And my current life, by contrast, was death.

In that river of light, I could draw upon all the good health that I needed, all the peace, the warmth, the joy, the love. I didn't need anyone to tell me this. I just simply knew. I just simply felt *everything* I could feel. And I needed no one to tell me that this was the way to be whole.

Baba caught my attention and informed me that the next lesson would enable me to become the creator that I was inside. He advised me to close my eyes and enter my imagination.

"You must visualise your healthy body. See this body in your mind's eye - running, laughing, doing whatever you used to enjoy in Rome. See yourself back with your uncle...serving Catholic Mass...in Latin, in English, just as you would do in Rome. Close your eyes and begin to create your future. There must be no room for illness - no thought of dying. *You* are the creator. You simply are. Guard your mind from things that you do not want in your physical reality. This is our greatest gift from God - the ability to create."

I did as he asked, yet found it so very hard to focus. Baba said that it *would* be difficult, but like everything that benefited man, practice was essential. He said the more I practised, the sharper my focus would become. The problem lay with my desire, he said. How badly did I want to get better? How badly did I wish to return home as the healthy priest that I once was?

The third lesson was then upon us: self-improvement – believing, with unwavering faith, that what I wanted would find its way to me. "Look at your belief system like you would do a race. He who believes more strongly *wins* the race. You must believe, Romilly, that you are already healed, no matter how weak you are feeling. You must tell your mind that you are healthy and, in turn, your mind will begin to do the necessary work in order to put your body back together again. The human body is designed to heal itself. Talk to your mind and believe every word. Remember that healing is a gradual process - it might be automatic, or it might be practical. Everything and everyone that can help you heal will find their way to you. That is why we have doctors and nurses and architects and preachers."

The fourth lesson, he said, was to be grateful for everything – for what my eyes could see in every moment and future creations that existed in my mind. I was to be thankful each moment of every day for my good health - the air that kept me alive, my organs, my brain, my hands and my feet. I was to show deep appreciation for every experience, both good and bad, for my journey was perfect and I needed *every* experience I encountered to make me whole.

"It is important that you put these four lessons into practice straight away. I cannot stress highly enough how they assist the medicines that the doctors are giving you. They all work together, so self-discipline is essential. And most importantly, *love all*. You are not just a part of the world - you *are* the world. So in loving the world, you are truly loving yourself."

I practised what I had been taught every day and, although I avoided death, I was still weak and ill. Then, about three weeks later, one of the nurses informed me that her aunt - a doctor in New York - had recently come to visit family in India.

"I told her about your illness and she said that she would like to visit you and see if she can help."

I simply nodded. Perhaps this was the miracle that I had been waiting for. I was still in a wheelchair and so felt sorry for the doctor who would have to work miracles in order to strengthen me.

Dr. Menas was half Greek and half Indian. She looked to be in her sixties, was very bossy, highly educated and actually scarier than whatever it was I was suffering from. She also evidently knew her stuff. She discovered in no time at all that I was allergic to the drugs I had been taking for malaria and she prescribed a strong dose of antibiotics and antihistamines.

I was running within a week. And I also started to practise yoga. It was as if I had never been ill.

I was a new man and it was not only my physical health that had undergone a healing process, but my mind. My spirit too experienced such a vigorous transformation that I struggled to comprehend it.

Some days I was happy and grateful for the new me. Other days I was depressed and worried – concerned that I was turning my back on the Catholic faith.

I mentioned this to Baba and he replied: "Who says you have to belong to any one institution? Why can't you be free to fly? Is it so wrong to follow your heart and not the wishes of someone else? Look to God, my friend - not to man. Man controls man with rules. God gives you the wings to fly freely, and He or She does this with great love."

On days when I was overwhelmed by an unusual sadness, Baba explained to me that my past pain was coming to the surface, forcing me to face it and get rid of it. "What is this pain that you carry around, my friend? Let go, as only one person gets burnt: you."

The practice of yoga was my deliverance. I joined the monks on days when I woke up to darkness, in a desperate bid to lift my spirits. They practised yoga at five in the morning, just as the sun was beginning to rise. They would wake, stretching their whole bodies towards the direction of the sun, taking in the light with gratitude and adoration. At six in the evening they would carry out winding down exercises, as the sun slipped away for its nightly sojourn; a calming energy gleaned from the retiring glow. It was marvellous to behold a discipline which exuded both strength and salutation.

"You can start with *Hatha* yoga, my friend. It is simple and easy to follow. So when you go back to Rome, you will not forget," Baba explained.

"What does *Hatha* mean?" There were so many words, directions and translations in yoga, that I could not possibly digest them all.

"*Ha* means the sun. And *tha* means the moon. This is yoga that enables us to feel and experience *the now* - to be in the present and not bother with the past or future. Now is all that matters. Now is all that exists. Now is all that makes sense. Now, right now, is your only truth. We must try and stay in the now."

There was something invisibly uplifting in my soul whenever I engaged in this activity. Not only did I feel a supernatural massage that calmed my bones and muscles - I felt no emotional pain. I therefore decided to not only wait for my darkest days to elapse in order to be healed, but take it upon myself to practise yoga *every single day*. Baba Aarush explained to me that

Hatha yoga would assist the harmony of my mind, body and environment.

Although I was appreciative of western medicine, there was no better drug for me than the act of yoga, followed by ritual meditation.

I practised every day what Baba had taught me. And as I improved, I applied the same technique towards other goals. Such focus did not come without a price. I realised, for example, that I no longer cared about Rome - its opulence, becoming a cardinal. None of these things gave my heart any pleasure. I did look forward to seeing my uncle again though, and the people that were like a family to me. And any lingering bitterness towards my father had gone, for I was learning to forgive, and learning to love all.

My former way of living, of wanting greatness for myself, was slowly replaced with the joy of simple things: the movement of trees (the way they bent towards the sun to get light in order to survive); the words from the wind as it passed by (kissing my skin with its coolness, reminding me of its presence and that it, too, was important); the birds flying in harmony (as if every flap, every beating wing, was sending a message, asking me to understand); sparkles in the air like tiny diamonds (trying hard to speak, yet knowing that I could not possibly hear them, but only feel).

I ceased to be in a hurry - stopping instead to ponder, wait, see, hear, feel, reflect and be thankful. The more aware I became, the more I stopped to sense what I never could have before: the sound of the waves (so gentle, yet so strong); the artistic nature of the clouds (how they presented to me an eighteenth-century ballroom dance, with one cloud turning into the shape of a heart or kiss between two lovers).

Perhaps I was going mad. Or perhaps I was finally sane.

The inner peace I encountered was something I had never felt before. For the very first time in my life, I felt like I was flying. I felt free. I felt whole. And most importantly, I felt loved by God. Gone was the guilt that haunted me if I told a white lie. And I had ceased to condemn myself for having sex with Ciara. The burden of my mother's death and the hatred I had for my father – they were suddenly like layers of an onion peeled away. And what was left was an empty mind, ready to refill itself with intense, loving energy.

This energy rippled from the soles of my feet to the crown of my head whenever I lay down to sleep. I was consumed by it, frightened by it, but eventually grew to welcome it and crave its presence when it was not there. For when I encountered it, it was as if my body was rooted, immovable, pinned to the mattress - an electrifying jolt heating me up, leaving me shaking; in my heart a sharp pain, and my lungs somehow drowning. I moved my hands, but felt nothing - those same hands (attached to my arms) unusually lifeless, prompting me to *believe* I was dead, but *knowing* - through intense awareness - that I could never have been more alive.

The sound of this great energy in my ears was a reminder of my mortality - splitting my head in two, breaking down every old, programmed cell and installing new, vibrational ones. It pierced through the pain of my past and supplanted in my heart new-found hope. This was a frequency so high that I thought I might die if it did not stop, but just as the oscillations rose, they swiftly reversed, descended, fell, brought me back to reality in a gentle, loving way; a wind-blown kiss on my cheeks reminding me that I was not alone and never had been.

The opulence of the universe overwhelmed me - the beauty of it all. What I had previously taken for granted, I was now grateful to see *every single day*.

Baba Aarush had become not only my teacher, but my closest friend. And it was a privilege to have him guide me through this journey of self-discovery.

"I do not want to go back to living the life that I led in Rome. And yet, I have not the courage to break my uncle's heart. Would that not be unkind?"

"How can you think of being kind to others, if you cannot be kind to yourself first?" Baba replied, in total bewilderment.

We remained silent for a while, as we often did in our discussions. His next question confirmed that he worried about me the way a father would a son.

"What will you do for money? You need to live and survive. Have you got any plans? You are welcome to stay here, but I'm not sure that is your destiny."

"I've had the same plan all my life. But I am a wealthy priest. I inherited my mother's estate in Burgundy. She left the family house to me. I never sold it. And I never rented it out. I have caretakers who live on the land for free and I visit when I'm on holiday. That way I can feel close to my mother again."

"So, what is the plan? You keep calling yourself a priest, even though in your heart you no longer are one. You must call yourself that which you wish to become."

"But wouldn't that be deceit? I'm not that yet."

"When you said you were healthy and yet you were almost dying, was that deceit? Or did your affirmations heal you? The same goes with everything in your life. You must be in your mind, and declare what you are with your lips, *before* it manifests in your physical reality. The world thinks that one must do things first in order to become. They do not understand that one must *become* in order to do."

I rang my uncle a week later to say I would be coming back to Rome. He pleaded with me to go first to a small country village in England where a priest was badly needed.

"It will be for no more than five months, Romilly. Then you can come back home."

I did not want to tell him over the phone that I had plans to retire and follow my own path. This was something that had to be discussed properly over dinner.

"Please help them, Romilly. They really need you."

How could I not? If I was to inevitably break my uncle's heart then perhaps I could at least be kind enough to grant him the small favour of spending five months in England; only five months and then I would be *free*…to do as I wished. Even my uncle would grant me that.

~~~

Everything fell into place during that English, summer garden party when I saw her.

Yes, she was a nun. But she would also be *mine*. Of that I was sure - as sure as the moon orbits the earth. And when I looked into her eyes, I knew that she was no more a nun than I was a priest.
~~~

Chapter 16

Iman

My stomach was getting bigger every day. And I waited, thinking that he would come back to me. I was growing tired of waiting though. Perhaps he was already a cardinal - his old life long forgotten, our night of fervour erased from his memory like it never happened.

I tried not to hate him, but I was filled with a mixture of emotions. Not only was I utterly and completely heartbroken, I was alone in a quandary with no one to tell or share my strife with. Everyone would judge me, and who could blame them.

I was definitely running out of time and not even Maria, my dearest friend, knew my secret. She would certainly be disappointed in me, but I knew I had to tell her first before I confessed to the reverend mother. I wasn't sure what would happen, except for the fact that I would be allowed to resign my position as a Catholic nun.

The opportunity came sooner rather than later. I saw Maria in the garden - her most favourite place in the world. And mine too.

"Hi - fancy having afternoon tea with me later? There is something I must tell you."

"Look who wants to talk now. You've been like a zombie for months. I was so worried about you. I'm glad that you want to talk."

"Yeah, I'm sorry about that." I tried to avoid her gaze, pretending that the sun was too strong, thus shielding my eyes with my palm.

"What's going on, Iman? You look in much distress. Always remember that there is no problem that Jesus cannot solve."

"I think even Jesus frowns on me at this moment, Maria. I have committed a grave sin and that is why we must have tea together later, as I might not be here for much longer."

"What do you mean? Are you dying?"

I shook my head in response, alarmed at the thought. This made her smile.

"Then it's all okay. I do not wish to wait for tea. Come walk with me. I'm due a break from all this gardening. Let's enjoy the sun and walk up Snowshill."

"That will take an hour. Mother Thérése will wonder where we've gone."

"Well, if you're not here for much longer, I don't think it matters. Do you?"

"Wise words."

She took my hand and led me down the footpath where the trees provided welcome shade and breeze - hovering over us and in doing so hiding the sky; scattered sunbeams breaching their leaves, creating a warm, jigsaw-like luminescence.

We walked, initially in silence, breathing in the early afternoon air which was infused with rich foliage fragrance and loam (somewhat damp, even in the sun). Although I was hot inside with anguish, out here everything was cool - giving us the illusion of twilight, even though it was just past noon.

I noticed some large rocks and two robins. I wanted to be near the robins. I had seen such birds a lot lately. And I had come to interpret their presence as the teller of my emotions. Who dared argue with me? One robin and I was alone in the world. Two and I was with my Michiel in spirit. Three and it was Romilly, me and our baby. Even now, as Maria held me by the arm so lovingly, it still seemed to be just me and Romilly.

"Let's sit by the robins please. I do not have it in me to walk. I must sit and get this over with."

Thankfully, she did not argue with me. The rock was dry and the robins, surprisingly, did not fly away from us. Instead, they both moved closer. I smiled with joy. These heavenly creatures had been sent to comfort me. God was with me and who could say otherwise.

"I'm pregnant," I announced to her, without any warning. I was growing tired of her suspicious frowns anyway. And I didn't care for any reprimand. My directness was out of respect.

I held my breath. What would she say? Oh, please say it quickly, Maria. I'm leaving anyway and you'll never have to see me again.

Maria's eyebrows came together in a confused expression. Then, sensing what I needed, she moved closer and pulled me into her arms in a warm embrace.

"Oh, you silly cow. What have you done?"

"That's the problem, Maria. I welcome it. I do not regret it at all. I *want* to leave, but I don't know where to go. I have no one."

"What about the father of the child?" Her voice was high-pitched.

"I cannot talk to you about him. I cannot. So please do not ask me."

"Do I know him?" she enquired.

"Please do not ask me anything about him."

"You must tell me. How could you not? You cannot carry this on your own. Please trust me. I will carry his name to my grave."

"I'm sorry - I cannot. I must protect him. I love him." It was the first time I had ever spoken to another human being about my feelings. It felt so good to share my secret though.

Then, I started to cry - initially like a whimper, before my voice began to shake and all my pain came bubbling out like an overdue volcano. I wasn't crying because I was pregnant or because my shame would soon be known to the world. No, I was crying thinking of him – how much I missed him, and how deeply my heart ached for him.

I was grateful to Maria for not judging me, for accepting my story without scolding me or reminding me of my vows.

"Thank you so much, Maria. Now that you know, I must go and tell Reverend Mother."

"I have some savings."

"Don't you dare think of giving me your savings."

"And don't you dare stop me. I am giving to the baby. And you have no right to refuse. I have no need for the money. I am a nun. Hold on! Do not say anything to Reverend Mother until we have found you a place to live."

"I don't want to stay in Broadway. I'd like to move away from here - to a village where no one knows me."

"Cheltenham?"

"No - too close. I want a city, but one like a village. I want to walk around and visit museums. I want to *live*. I have savings too from the hospital work, so I do not need your money, Maria."

"How much do you have?"

"I checked my account this morning. It was exactly nine thousand and ninety pounds."

"Hmmm - that will not be enough for a single mum who needs essentials. I have inheritance money and I will give you some of it."

"But..."

"Shhhh! No buts. You will not be able to rent a home without a job, so you might have to pay six months' rent before you move in and that will be most of your money gone. Then you will need things for the baby. Just how far do you think your almost ten thousand pounds will get you?" We both started to laugh, mostly at the way she had said 'almost ten thousand pounds'.

"I will give you five thousand. That will help you for a year if you're careful and then, in that time, you can figure out what you want to do."

"I will pay you back."

"You will do no such thing. It is my gift to the baby. I have no need for material things and money. It would only have gone to the poor anyway. And right now, my friend, *you* are the poor."

We both laughed again. If this was how God punished sinners, then perhaps God wasn't the God that people thought He was. I felt so low at this point in my life, but He had stepped in and lifted me up. He knew I would have nothing and had provided me with enough to live on for not only a year, but maybe two or more.

I was so overwhelmed with gratitude that I went down on my knees and looked into space in prayer; my voice, a soft whisper, cutting through the twirling of the trees and the chirping of the birds.

I stretched out my arms and prayed to my Father in gratitude, reciting Psalm 103 from the Holy Bible; the African in me praying with such willingness.

"Bless the Lord, oh my soul, and all that is within me. Bless His Holy name.

Bless the Lord, oh my soul.

And forget not all His benefits.

Who forgiveth all my iniquities.

Who healeth all my diseases.

Who redeemeth my life from destruction.

Who crowneth me with loving kindness and tender mercies.

Who satisfieth my mouth with good things.

So that my youth is renewed like the eagle's.

Thank you, Papa, for being merciful and gracious, slow to anger and plenteous in mercy.

Thank you for understanding my frame. Thank you for remembering that I am dust."

I closed my eyes and connected with my maker, knowing - at that moment - that He would always be with me. I was no longer afraid what the reverend mother would say. I was no longer anxious about my future, for I now had enough to keep me comfortable for a while. I still missed Romilly, but I knew that I had to move forward and be strong for our baby.

Over the next couple of weeks, I saw my friend Maria in a different light. She hunted for houses like a deer hunting for water.

If I liked a place she didn't approve of, she quickly reminded me to consider the baby and the possibility that its dad might return. We viewed three houses in Cambridgeshire. Each time we travelled, we gave a different, but similar excuse to Reverend Mother. We were either volunteering at a homeless shelter or an orphanage. They weren't exactly lies, but we *had* planned it carefully.

We volunteered from twelve noon 'til four in the afternoon and this freed up the mornings to look at houses. I don't know how I managed it through morning sickness, but our charade persisted for three weeks. I was about to give up when Maria excitedly told me about a pretty cottage in a lovely village which sat at the southern end of Cambridge.

"You need a garden. You need a home. You need three bedrooms, so that I can come and visit," was her justification for visiting this place. I couldn't refuse. I needed a home. And at this point, anything would do. My tummy was getting increasingly big and, although I could still just about hide my bump, it wouldn't be possible for much longer. One more month and I was sure Reverend Mother would call me into her office and announce that I had to leave, before I could mutter "I'm sorry".

We viewed the Cambridge cottage the next day. Mother Thérése, having no knowledge of our *real* morning activities, offered to give us travel and lunch money from the church's treasury. We insisted that we wanted to use our own money - the same response that we always gave.

"God bless you for saving the church some money," she replied.

I wanted to die of shame, and Maria - seeing the look on my face - proceeded to rush me out of the office, before I broke down and spilled the beans.

The village of Foxton, I discovered three hours later, was the ideal setting for my present situation. It had well-preserved old houses and cottages that must have dated back to the sixteenth century. We made our way from the station using the estate agent's map and embarked on a ten-minute walk to the cottage. The houses we saw along the way looked so grand and beautiful.

"This place looks expensive." I looked at my friend questioningly. "I can't afford this kind of life. I must be careful with money."

"The cottage is eight hundred pounds a month. That is almost ten thousand a year. You can always apply for help with your bills as a single parent." She saw the disapproving look on my face and carried on talking. "Would you rather your child grew up in a dump? Is that what you want for your baby? I've researched this place and all I ask is that you keep an open mind 'til you've seen it." She stopped and faced me. "Think schools, Iman. And nice, aspiring neighbours."

"I didn't know my friend was a snob." I smiled teasingly.

"*Me* - a snob? I don't know what you mean."

I twinkled inside, feeling proud and happy to have a friend who thought of everything and planned for my unborn baby when I often struggled, because I was too busy yearning for my baby's father.

We walked through open fields, past houses with barns and horses, and said hello to people working in their gardens. Then we found ourselves in open fields once more, but with no house in sight.

"We are here." Maria came to a stop, gazing intently at the map.

"What's the matter?" I asked her.

"Well, we are here, but I can't see the cottage."

I looked around, but there was indeed no dwelling nearby. I felt thirsty and tired, yet stayed quiet. She had done so much for me already and I certainly wasn't going to moan. We stood there for about ten minutes, contemplating and wondering where the house might be. Well, Maria mostly, as I could only think that I desperately needed rehydrating.

"Are you okay, my friend? You look so pale and tired." She dipped her hand in her bag and pulled out a bottle of water. "Come - let's look for a place for you to sit for a while."

"I'm okay, Maria. I'm not disabled. I just need the water." I grabbed the bottle from her so fast that she started to giggle.

"Seriously, Iman - you need to start looking after yourself better. You now have another life to focus on as well as yours. Oh, look, there is a little footpath here and..." She didn't finish her sentence, as her grin said it all.

"Oh, Iman, if it's what I think it is, then I might get knocked up myself and move in with you."

I walked over to where she stood, right in front of the footpath, and my heart skipped a beat or two.

It was a tiny forest, but in the midst of this vegetation stood three, maybe four, small cottages. We walked up the path closer to the houses, enticed rather than curious. Their togetherness was one of the most beautiful things I had ever seen. And yet, each cottage had its own stone path and group of trees, adding to its privacy. A sign read "Drive carefully. Children playing" and my heart instantly grew bigger as I realised that *this* was where I wanted to live.

A blonde woman walked towards us. She wore a black, skirt suit with very long heels and looked like she was ready for business.

"Maria De Leon?" She looked at us both, her eyes questioning which one of us was Maria.

"Hi." Maria stretched out her hand. "That would be me, but the house is actually for my friend here." Indicating that was me, she introduced me. "This is Iman Williamson. Iman, this is Jodie McManus, the estate agent renting out the property."

"Oh, apologies. Nice to meet you, Miss Williamson." Jodie turned to look at me. "I didn't mean to be rude. It's just that I've been dealing with Maria here, on your behalf."

"Please, don't apologise. It's okay." I smiled at her. She seemed very charming and pleasant, but I had heard about estate agents' reputations when trying to sell you something. I pushed such negative thoughts to the back of my mind though and concentrated on the beauty of the place.

I let the sound of Jodie's heels, as well as the aroma of her perfume, guide me rather than follow her with my eyes. I preferred, instead, to gaze at the overgrown vegetation around me, which reminded me of a miniature rain forest *without* the rain, but with the morning sun blazing down on us.

We passed the first few cottages, surrounded by shrubs and trees that looked like they might tumble against each other. We then came to a stop and I stared – entranced - at the end cottage, nestled as it was in a small, forest clearing; dusty and grey with beams of glorious sunlight showering down upon it. It looked like it had suddenly sprung forth from the ground - a part of nature, a natural, stone formation seemingly out of a story book.

We approached this heavenly piece of architecture by way of a white, wooden gate, hidden amongst the bushes. The path weaved its way around the trees, feeding our eyes with pleasurable surprises and sweet, flowery smells after each step. Pink peonies adorned the fringes of the garden and festoons of honeysuckle wrapped their perfumed arms around the hedges. Early summer roses bloomed wildly, confident in their beauty, concealing dusty, sash windows close to the ground. Free-flowing ivy cascaded over the path. Clematis curled all around this fairy-tale English cottage, nearly reaching the sky via the rustic, stone walls. A picket fence, covered with vines, decorated the pocket-handkerchief-sized garden which led to a flagstone path that ultimately brought us to the blue, wooden, front door; a door struggling to shine through the arch of wisteria that hung over the cottage like a protective umbrella.

Beside the entrance was an outdoor wall clock. Jodie informed us that it chimed at twelve noon and twelve midnight. I stared at the beautiful clock, taking it all in. The time was 10:10. My eyes then drifted once more to the unbridled trees and I realised that the other houses were partially hidden from view.

As Jodie turned the key in the lock, she explained to us that the owners had bought the place for their granddaughter, but she had suddenly married and moved to Australia to be with her husband. They had tried to sell it, but no buyer was willing to put in the work required and so they had cleaned it up and turned it into a rental property.

"What do you think?" she asked delightedly, as our legs glided over the flat, stony floor. I could hear Maria dancing in delight, but could not see her. My eyes were fixed on the low ceiling with its exposed beams, which suddenly made me thankful for my five foot seven inch frame. It was a good thing Romilly *wasn't* here. He would have to bow his head under the beams each time he moved around.

The wall containing the open, inglenook fireplace was covered in stone mosaic, while the other walls around the cottage were panelled in wood.

"The chimney will be swept before you move in."

"When can I move in?" I asked.

My question set her in full motion: "We *do* have other people who would like to view."

"Cancel them," was Maria's response.

"I can't. What if you fail the referencing process?" Jodie asked.

"What if we pay you six months' rent here and now, with character references?" Maria shot back.

I love you, Romilly. Please come back to me. We would be very happy here together.

"Done. I'll cancel," was Jodie's reply.

We filled out the forms there and then, paid the money via online transfer using Jodie's laptop and left with a moving-in date.

Now, I thought - one last battle. I would have to face Reverend Mother sooner rather than later as my moving-in date was just one week away.

You will soon cease to be a nun.

I have never been a nun.

A volunteer.

A church goer.

But never, ever a nun.

My arms fell onto my tummy, touching my unborn baby with love and unconcealed promise.

Chapter 17

Romilly

The direct flight from Birmingham Airport to Rome Ciampino was approximately three hours and ten minutes. I couldn't wait to get off the plane as soon as it landed. The pilot announced just before the plane touched the runway that the landing time was 19:09. There was no time to think or meander. I wanted to hold the cardinal's hand, and it didn't matter that he was dead.

To think - the last time I saw him was when I embarked on my journey to Africa. If I had known I would never see him again, I would have gone to Rome for a few days before arriving in England. But he had wanted me to go to England and there was no room for protest. Yes, England, and now I had messed everything up because I could not control myself.

I felt awful, but I didn't entirely know why. I searched within myself in order to discover what it was that tormented me. Initially, I thought it was because I could not see Iman tonight. That was definitely part of it, but there was something more. Could it be because for some time now I felt I was being followed by someone in a baseball cap? Maybe. I had only seen the man twice, however, so perhaps it was a coincidence. Was it due to the fact that I had not been given the chance to bid my uncle, the dear cardinal, goodbye? Or was it simply that I was to be a cardinal myself, yet did not want to be?

It wasn't the fact that I had decided to resign from the priesthood that haunted me. No, it was *everything else*. Would I now be punished by the Almighty? What if the monks in India were wrong and I had been foolish turning my back on the one true faith? But didn't Baba Aarush explain that there was no competition, that all was perfect? Even the Bible suggested that God was happy to be worshipped in a way comfortable to the individual. So why did I feel so uncertain, so confused, despite my new-found belief that I was on the only, *true* road to life? If this path was so wrong, then why the tingling feeling when I closed my eyes and meditated? What was this vibrational energy that encompassed my whole being, warming me from my feet to my brain? How was it possible that through my own visualisation and positive affirmations I was able to heal my body using the power of the mind? Even if it was a coincidence, how was I able to *let go* of my painful past courtesy of spiritual energy? What was this new-found love that I felt for every single creature? Man, animals of every kind and nature. Why had I suddenly lost the will to enjoy material pleasures and thus engage my thoughts in saving humanity only?

I felt an intense love for myself that I had never had before. It gave me the confidence and boldness to do as I wished – so long as such activities made me happy, but were a service of some kind, not just for my own, personal gain. Working on myself, being the best expression of myself, would enable me to shine my light over loved ones, and ultimately the world. This confidence was also what I needed to face the church in Rome, even though an internal battle remained, raged, lingered and tormented me. How could I explain to them that I did not believe they were wrong, but that I now preferred a more intense, spiritual path, rather than their religious one? A path that would allow me to be with the woman that I loved and maybe have children.

My true, real, genuine self was still to be discovered, yet I wanted to spend the rest of my days pursuing it, so that when I died, I would do so without regret. I would live my dream, and not somebody else's. Not my father's. Not my uncle's. Not Rome's.

The Ciampino Airport bus had been on the road for close to forty minutes and finally came to its last stop: the Vatican. A stress-free journey - six Euros well spent, I thought. And it would now take me twenty minutes to walk to the centre of the city to the home of the late cardinal. I was glad I had not bothered with any luggage, apart from a small rucksack which held my toiletries and private essentials. I still had clothes at my uncle's, so I wasn't too concerned.

Rome, in the evening, provided a welcome break from my confused thoughts. Not only were the gilded statues illuminated by the lights of the city, but the Basilica could be seen from the front of the Castel Sant'Angelo. The statues stood like ancient gods drifting along the Tiber. And such a simile brought the river alive - dazzling my eyes with warm, sparkling lights.

This road reminded me of Ciara. I remembered the long, romantic walks we once had. Oh, my God – Ciara; another person whose score I would have to settle. She had written countless times and I had, very rudely, not replied. I enjoyed her attention for a *long time*. I enjoyed her concern for me when I was almost dying in India. I also shared her enthusiasm about us, until that fateful day of the summer garden party, when all I wanted was to make Iman mine.

Every step, every museum, every café, reminded me of Ciara. I walked past the Caffe San Pietro and recalled our first date. It stood opposite the Leonardo Da Vinci museum. We had skipped across to the museum after our tea at the café, hiding behind the great inventor's paintings and woodwork - kissing like teenagers, afraid that we would be seen and thrown out of the Vatican. The thought made me smile as I walked towards the Basilica. To me, St. Paul's Basilica was home. Whenever I saw that building, it radiated a warm feeling within me. Sadly, tonight, that warmth had disappeared - replaced by a sense of detachment.

I let myself into my uncle's home with my key. I was hoping that I would be on my own, but I was disappointed. Pedro ran to me with the rest of his family in tow. I started to well up inside for the family I had missed. We hugged each other, laughed and cried together, and shared our grief for my uncle. Pedro's wife offered to make me one of her delicious lasagnes, but I declined. I was too overwhelmed with emotion to eat.

"I would like a cup of tea though, please."

This was brought to me, along with two small, chocolate *cannolis*.

They informed me that my uncle's body was in the mortuary and I was free to visit at any time. They said that he had died peacefully and had not been alone. His friend, the professor, had been by his side. They told me that my uncle had been well, and that it had happened rather suddenly.

"The professor was a dear friend to him to the last - never leaving his side."

That night in bed, I wept like a baby.

The funeral took place two days later.

Ten months on and I was still there. It was almost Christmas and so much had happened. My uncle's death had left me a wealthy man, as he had no living relatives apart from me and my siblings. His mortgage-free apartment in Rome had passed to me and all his savings. The legal representative who read out the will estimated the property to be worth around €1.2 if I were to sell. And his savings amounted to another €2m, not including the original paintings that adorned the walls of the property. After tax, €2.3m was deposited into my account, along with the keys to my uncle's apartment.

My uncle had also remembered Pedro and his family in the will, leaving them some money, but not quite enough, I thought. And to his dear friend, Alessandro, he left all his books, his grand piano and his holiday cottage in Naples.

After the reading of the will, I felt a strong need to be close to my uncle, so without thinking I wandered into his study.

I didn't expect what I saw. Sitting in my uncle's chair was Alessandro, weeping uncontrollably, holding my uncle's picture to his chest. The scene was one that I would remember for a very long time and which revealed so much to me. I stood there with a multitude of emotions overwhelming me. Yet he was so lost in grief that he did not even hear me come in.

And that was when I knew.

I walked over to him and placed my arms around the shoulders of the man who had taught me so much in the years that I had known him; the man who appeared to know it all - whose wisdom was seemingly beyond limits.

My presence, I think, brought him a tiny bit of comfort and we just sat there together in silence.

"Did he know?" I asked him.

He simply nodded. He was wise and clever enough to understand what I meant.

"Were you two...?" He nodded again, before I could finish my sentence.

"You must never speak of it," he whispered, looking into my eyes for the first time that evening. "The church will not forgive and this will taint his memory."

There was no more to be said, for at that moment I very clearly knew which road I had to take; and there were no further doubts in my mind whatsoever.

The Vanderbelt family was a rich one. But it was obvious that the money my uncle had inherited from his parents was never spent on himself. The cardinal was a man of good taste, had grown up in a home of fine things, had treated himself to a lovely place at the Vatican, yet had very evidently saved the rest and chosen a frugal existence. Even allowing for his generosity towards charitable organisations, he had died a humble, wealthy man, not a gluttonous man.

My father would be highly upset at this turn of events, as he had left me nothing when he passed away - not his manor house in Berlin, nor the Victorian holiday home in West London. Both properties, along with his company, had been divided equally between my elder brother and my sister. His dear, younger brother, however, had left me close to everything.

"A priest has no need for material wealth," his will had read. "Romilly is living a very good life in Rome with his uncle who has taken up the role of his papa now, as tradition permits."

My mama, on the other hand, had perhaps foreseen the future, for she left my brother and sister nothing in her will, knowing that they would be well looked after by my father. All her possessions were to be mine.

I visited Burgundy on my holidays in order to feel close to my mother. It was the only place that truly reminded me of her. Burgundy was rich with history, art and museums, and was the one place, I believe, where my mother felt at home and ultimately came alive. With its borders lying by the Loire River and the Rhone-Alpes region, Mama enjoyed hiking and so we would walk up the Morvan hills and the Saone valley in the summer. The mere thought of it still put a smile on my face.

It did not take long to sell my uncle's apartment. Five months and the money was in my account. I felt no further need for Rome. I informed my superiors that I would stay and see to the cardinal's affairs, tie up all the loose ends, but then resign. They tried to talk me out of it, but I stood my ground. My life was mine, and I was going to live it.

The late cardinal's dear friend had been my rock. The philosopher, Alessandro, had helped me see things more clearly and rise victoriously from my inner turmoil. He was someone very easy to talk to, mostly because he was so open-minded.

"I keep feeling guilty all the time, especially because of the cardinal's death," I explained to him. "But also, because he might be disappointed in me wanting to give up my priesthood."

"Trust me, where he is, he will not be thinking of such things. Rather, he will congratulate you on your swift awakening, albeit a complex one." The professor had wisely calmed my doubts, the way a new puppy would induce peace in its owner.

We both sat in silence, reminiscing in the joy that the cardinal had brought to our lives.

We never discussed the relationship he had had with my uncle - not because we couldn't, but because there was simply nothing to be said.

"He was the only father that I had."

"Yes, a father, an uncle - but you are your own man, and you must walk your own path. Everyone has a personal journey to be fulfilled. What is your journey, Romilly?"

That was the question I needed to answer. I knew my journey. I didn't know how it would end, but I knew where it would start and I was adamant that I wished to pursue such a path until I took my last breath. Walk my path and fulfil my purpose, I must. After all, what was it that Rumi said? Was it not 'Keep crawling if that was all one could do'? Well, I think I could do more than crawl, for I had been blessed with great wealth, good health and one true love.

The first thing I did was buy Pedro and his family a place of their own. They had been left without a home, and without the cardinal's support would not have any work. I asked them to search for a home that would accommodate their whole family and to send me the bill. They never did – Pedro, I suppose, unable to accept my endowment. I therefore found them a house myself - a lovely, four-bedroom cottage which cost €300,000 (nothing given my fortunate inheritance, set against their needs).

I put Pedro's name on the deeds and handed him the keys. Gloria, his wife, flung herself at me, crying and blessing me in Italian.

"I guess it's payback time for all the years you looked after me, and fed me and the cardinal."

As I said my goodbyes to the professor and Pedro, I knew in my heart that I would never return to Rome. It held so many good memories, but I was no longer that person. I was brand new. And this newness presented itself to me as a reflection – measured, intricate changes that slowly began to take hold of my authenticity.

The old me ate everything and indulged in the finest foods when I could. The new me ate only what was needed to nourish my body. The old me did not see any sadness in throwing away leftover food. The new me could not bring himself to waste *anything*. The old me ate other living creatures. The new me felt a strong connection to animals and so adapted to a vegetarian diet. The old me held on to the pain of the past and played the role of the victim. The new me was grateful for the past, for the past had helped shape me. The old me rose most mornings at 5am to run. The new me rose even earlier…to run, practise yoga and meditate. The old me saw me first and then other people. The new me allowed me to see myself in others - every culture, race and tradition.

The old me was part of the world. The new me *was* the world.

My next stop was Venice. I was a little apprehensive about the trip. I didn't know how she would react. She had always been the dominant one in our relationship, and I still partly feared her. I would have to explain why I hadn't replied to her letters. I would have to explain that I had been in Rome all this time and didn't feel like making contact.

As I took my seat by the window on the train, I realised that it would take over three hours to get to Venice. And the sun was not yet up. To distract my mind from turbulent thoughts, I read Coelho's *The Alchemist* – a goodbye gift from Alessandro.

Coelho wrote about an Andalusian boy, named Santiago, and his quest in following his dreams. It was a fable of hope, faith, patience and love, and an excellent morning companion.

At 10:10 my train came to its final stop: the Venezia Santa Lucia Station. Venice had a way of freeing my spirit and erasing fear or doubt inside of me. And, today, it made my heart leap like a butterfly with new-grown wings.

Venezia Santa Lucia Station sat in central Venice right on the Grand Canal. Anxious, but happy, my legs carried me swiftly across Platform 22 and onto the causeway over the lagoon, where I was greeted by *vaporettos* - water taxis and gondolas. I watched as Venice's cold lagoon crept slowly and silently into the heart of the city, through obscure channels, not too far from where I stood. The ancient palaces and churches were seemingly afloat above the water - never moving, still strong, withstanding all battles and floods.

A single breath escaped my lungs as I luxuriated in this floating city of grandeur, sex, aqueducts and exquisite, romantic bridges. It was a temple I'd like to hide in with Iman. Oh, my God...Iman.

I will see you soon, my love. Don't you worry. Perhaps we can enjoy La Serenissima someday, when I will get down on one knee and ask you to be mine forever; and then ask you to marry me again each year for as long as we shall live.

I hailed a gondola - the face of the *gondolieri* hidden behind a mask, like a bad omen at the start of a Hollywood movie.

"San Giorgio."

A few minutes later, I paid him €31 and stepped on to the platform right in front of the café owned by the woman who might have been my companion in another life. She wasn't expecting me. In a world full of technology, I chose not to own a mobile phone. I was perhaps the only human being who did not have one, or feel the need for such immediacy.

I was glad of the warmth in her café. It oozed fresh, hot cappuccino and balmy, delicious buns. I suddenly felt very hungry. Her café was empty, but for an old couple sat in the far right corner, ignoring each other – together, but very much apart. I pressed the tiny button of the bronze bell on the counter and she appeared before me within seconds.

I saw the blood rapidly drain from her face as if she had just seen a ghost.

"Oh, my God. Romilly!" was all I could hear. Then, in one quick step, she was in my arms - hugging me and crying.

"I've missed you so much, my dearest. I have been so worried about you. I didn't know what to think. Why did you ignore my letters for so long?"

"Ciara, it's lovely to see you. Could I beg for a coffee?" I couldn't help but smile at her - my heart ached though, knowing that this visit would be my last, for I could never give her what she wanted. If I had never met Iman, I would have stayed. But Ciara could not make my heart race the way Iman did.

She brought me a cup of delicious, hot cappuccino and a rum baba. I dug into the bun which tasted like heaven.

"So, you've come here to break my heart."

Her words tore straight into my soul - so much so that I almost choked.

"What makes you say that?" I asked, after swallowing my first piece of bun.

"I see it in your eyes, Romilly. I know you. Remember?"

"Well, I thought I broke your heart a long time ago," I joked, in an attempt to lighten things. I wasn't very good at intense discussions.

"Don't play with me, *il mio amore*."

I remained quiet and focused on my breakfast, not quite knowing what to say as her eyes dug into me.

"Well?" she asked.

"Well what?" I feigned ignorance.

"Spit it out. What have you come to say that troubles you so?"

I had forgotten how feisty she was.

"I've come to give you a present - something to help the café. And then I will have to go."

"Go where? I thought you were being made a cardinal?"

"After all my sins?" We both smiled. "I don't think so. I have resigned my priesthood." I could not hide it from her. She knew me too well.

"What?" She suddenly became very happy. Perhaps I should not have told her, for she might expect more from me knowing I was no longer a priest. But then, she became solemn again. "So why do you have to go? Where will you be going?"

"I can't go into all that. I just needed to give you this." I handed her a brown envelope. "And say that I'm sorry if I ever hurt you. It should be enough to pay off your mortgage on this place and maybe live a bit more comfortably."

"You're paying me off? You think I will go and shout from the rooftops that you are a fraud?"

I was lucky that there were only two people in the café, but they were now looking at us. I did not understand what had happened. I had come here wanting to make peace and to make her happy, but I had angered her.

"I'm sorry, Ciara. I did not mean to upset you."

"So I'm not good enough for you now? *Who is she*? You think I'm stupid? Yes, I know about the woman in England. I had you watched, you son of a bitch."

The old couple suddenly sprang to their feet to leave. This did not deter Ciara one bit. I, on the other hand, was still trying to make sense of the fact that she had had me followed and watched. Perhaps Ciara wasn't the woman I thought she was. It all made sense: the man in the baseball cap.

"You had no right to do that, Ciara. Why did you do such a thing?"

"Because I love you, you fool!" she screamed.

My eyes flitted about uncomfortably - unable to look into her pale blue eyes as they welled up with tears. She had not aged at all. If anything, she looked younger and more beautiful than she had ever been. It would have been endearing two years ago, but so much had happened since then.

"No, you do not. If you loved me, you would not have had me followed, watched...a complete violation of my privacy." My voice was surprisingly low and steady, while she screamed like an uncontrollable siren.

"And she's been sworn to Christ, you shameless fool. A nun. May you both rot in Hell."

For the first time since entering Venice, the sorrow which filled my heart completely dissipated like a magician's puff of smoke.

"Didn't you happily seduce me when I was sworn to Christ?" I asked, before I could stop myself, knowing that it would sting like a ferocious bee.

"Just get out and take your filthy money with you." She spat at me, tears now coursing freely - mascara soiling her beautiful face. I wanted to hold her and comfort her, but that would send the wrong message.

I stood up with a heavy sigh, filled with regret. This was not how I had hoped to leave her. I had come to make peace, not war.

"Are you sure this is the way you want things to end between us?" It was my final attempt to smooth things out.

Ciara took one hostile look at me and swiftly walked out of the room, leaving me standing there. I picked up the envelope, put it back in my rucksack and started to leave. Her voice, however, stopped me in my tracks.

"Hey, *you!*" I turned around to look at her, hoping that maybe she had thought things through. "*This* is how I want things to end."

It happened in one swift, rapid moment. She moved towards me so fast that I had nowhere to go; my reflexes slow, taken aback by the abrupt, unforeseen wildness of it all.

I felt a hot, sharp plunge tear into my flesh, heightening my awareness, so that at that exact moment the world stood still. The look on her eyes was one of regret. I could feel my insides in agony as the serrated blade sank deep enough to make me stiffen.

I wanted to scream in pain, but I could no longer hear my own voice. Maybe I did scream - I will never know. Instinctively, my hands moved to my left, lower ribcage where I felt the pain. My body was wet. I looked down and noticed the bloodied knife on the floor that she must have discarded in panic. I started to feel weak. Blood gushed out of me untamed. Everything looked indistinct - blurred. She started screaming for help, but even *I* knew it was too late.

God had come for His own. And I would always be a willing subject. My world, as I knew it, suddenly became silent.

Chapter 18

Romilly

"**M**ama *look, I brought you a rose from the garden. It looks just as beautiful as you."*

"Ha, mon fils – merci, my love. Where did you find it? I do not remember having roses in my garden." My mother looked happy, but bewildered.

"You planted them last month - remember?" I was slowly losing my patience with her. She had forgotten last month, I was sure.

My mother smiled at me and shook her head. "I do not think a rose like this exists, mon fils. The colour is different. I have never seen a colour like this before."

"It's from God's garden, Mama. God said I could give you the seed. And then you planted it, and this is what it produced. Everything exists in the garden of God."

"And where did you see God, mon fils? In your dreams?"

"No, Mama." I could not keep the disappointment out of my childish, boyish voice. "Do you not remember? You seem to forget everything these days."

"Romilly, my dear - is that the way to speak to your mama?" My mama pulled me into her lap and planted a kiss on my forehead.

"I told you to stop that. I am no longer a child." I was suddenly a man, taller than my mama. And she was no longer young, but still beautiful. In one, swift second, she became old and frail.

"No, mon fils. I see you are all grown up and very handsome too. Come closer - let me look at you."

I returned to her. All I wanted to do was protect her and look after her for the rest of our days. But first, I had to tidy her garden. Her cottage looked tired, but Mama looked radiant. Even though her skin was frail from old age, and her back bent, her eyes still sparkled like the young woman I had known.

I knelt down in front of her, enamoured by the radiance of her eyes - the same colour as mine; a deep, grassy green. Her warm palms covered my cold cheeks in tenderness.

"What are you doing here, mon fils?"

"Why, Mama, I came to look after you."

"Do I need looking after?" Her brows knitted together in gentle mockery.

"I couldn't look after you before, and bad things happened. Now I am a man, and he will never hurt you again."

"Do you know something, Romilly?"

I did not reply. I just kept looking at her.

"You have so much to live for, and you have been blessed with a very long life. I will be here when you are old, and we will work on the cottage together, my darling son, with your wife and, someday, your children too."

"What do you mean children, Mama? I am a priest."

Suddenly, she was back - the young Marie-Ange; sitting up straight, skin flawless. I was still a man, and it was strange - my mum being the same age.

"No, mon fils." She shook her head, smiling. *"You are a man who is not limited in his endeavours. You are a god."*

"But, Mama..."

"Look behind you - there is a lovely lady approaching. She'll keep me company 'til you get back."

I turned around and saw a woman walking towards us. She was smiling. At first her face was blurred by the bright sunshine. Then, as she approached, I took a closer look and my stomach churned.

Ciara.

Chapter 19

Reverend Mother Mary Thérése Williamson

I am too old for all this excitement.

I hear about things like this, but I could never have imagined it happening in my own order. And from the one I very much called my own daughter. Perhaps this is the way everyone thinks. People assume that certain things will never befall them, until of course they happen, and then the shock is often worse than the bite.

I always knew that there was something quite different about Iman. She never truly belonged - never truly looked happy. She always seemed to be in a daydream, doing her chores, working diligently, following rules and regulations, but never fully present.

There was a past there, but a past she refused to discuss. There was depression and sadness, but she refused to let anyone in.

Those marks on both arms - signs that told me she was cutting herself. Everyone knows that self-mutilation is a form of release, of escape. What was Iman escaping from?

And the day when she walked into my office and handed me her letter of resignation - I certainly did not see that coming.

Hadiza had taken money from me every month, but she was never to be trusted.

People like Iman, who carry a sad, dull look around with them, remain sisters for as long as they live. The convent walls are their solace.

I must admit to wondering why such walls did not stop her from being depressed and sad. But maybe she is the epitome of someone who had to live a lie to survive.

That fateful day in Jos when I went to interview her, yet knew that it was a mere formality. I fell in love with the child from the moment her confused father placed her in my arms as a baby. I knew then that I wanted her for myself. But I also knew that I could not take her back to England with me at such short notice. Being a nun, I could not adopt her, and so I hatched a plan of my own - well, with Hadiza's help.

The arrangement meant paying her some money each month to keep the baby safe - until Iman turned eighteen. But Hadiza had not kept her side of the bargain.

Dr. Mohna was an old man, but not so old he couldn't enlighten me as to what had been going on. The doctor was a friend of mine from Jos. I would have preferred *him* to look after Iman, but he informed me that he couldn't. He was having problems with his wife and a new child would have made things worse. And so I had no choice but to leave the baby with the only other willing party - Hadiza.

Dr. Mohna told me everything when I visited. The child was not fit to be a nun. There were rumours that she was ruined both inside and out. If I knew what was good for me, what was sensible, I would turn around and go back to England.

I was too curious to follow his guidance. I had to see the child and judge for myself. I had to know how I felt upon seeing her again.

And see her I did – the feelings that first enveloped me when I held her in my arms returning instantly.

She looked wise beyond her years, but was still a child. She looked keen to please me, but she was actually desperate. She lied through her teeth to escape that place. She pretended to be happy, but deep down she was broken.

I didn't care that she was no longer a virgin. I didn't care that she was a lost soul. I only cared that she was the daughter I never had and I would do everything in my power to take her back home.

Everything had worked out quite easily as if the stars had aligned and made my dreams come true.

I applied to the embassy for a new nun to join our order. We were short of nuns and I approved just two applications: one from the Philippines and another from Nigeria. The British government did not deny me or turn me down. (I don't know what I would have done if they had.) And the rest is history, harmony.

"Reverend Mother - I must speak with you."

Those were her words two weeks ago when she walked into my office. I thought it was probably connected to all the charity work she had been doing with Sister Maria in Cambridge. Had she finally come to her senses? Would she now be prepared to use some money from the church treasury for expenses?

"Can it wait, Iman? I have a few meetings to attend to. Perhaps after dinner?"

"No." She shook her head rather violently. I had never seen anything like it. The poor child looked desperate. "I must speak with you now. I will not be here after dinner."

"What do you mean, you will not be here? Where will you be?" I felt the need to sit back down for my head was suddenly faint. She looked so pale and tired. What could possibly be the matter?

"Please take a seat, Iman, and tell me all about it."

"I cannot give you all the details," she said, pulling up a chair and sinking her slim frame into it. "But first, I must tell you how terribly sorry I am that I have sinned against God, sinned against the church and sinned against you." As the words came out, her eyes showed no sign of remorse. She tried to look as solemn as she could, but there was a look of relief that made me uneasy.

"What sin do you speak of, my child?" Curiosity took hold of me as she deliberated in answering my question. I then noticed that she wasn't in her robe - her hair uncovered, tied up in a messy, afro bun; her blue dress short-sleeved, exposing marks which told the word that she suffered in secret - her beautiful, dark skin unable to hide them. Her eyes were red and swollen - the result of numerous, sleepless nights full of tears. And it was obvious that she had lost a few pounds - a sign of not eating well.

Even taking into account such observations though, there was something else, something different about her: a silent content; a vibrant glow; a hidden joy.

"I would like you to accept my resignation, for I no longer wish to be a nun." Her words took me back to the reason she was here, slicing through my heart and leaving my soul in tatters.

I tried to compose myself as best I could. "Would you like to elaborate on what's going on? Why now, Iman, after all this time?" I couldn't control the anger slowly rising in my voice. I watched as she shifted uncomfortably in her chair - her beautiful, grey eyes wandering everywhere but my face.

"Like I said before, I do not really want to go into detail. I'd rather just leave quietly." Her voice was unsteady. She was clearly nervous. I almost felt sorry for her, but shifted such empathy to the back of my heart - replacing it with common sense.

"And you think that I will let you leave without an explanation?" My eyes pierced into her face, willing her eyes to settle on mine, which they didn't.

We sat in silence for what seemed like five minutes. I knew I had to say something, for I was getting nothing from her.

"What was the sin that you talked about earlier?" I asked. "Surely I deserve to know. I think I have earned that right." My voice suddenly rose in frustration.

Finally, she looked me in the eye. What she said next changed my whole world.

"I'm pregnant, Reverend Mother. Please forgive me..."

For a moment, my mind went blank. Then I understood why she looked different. My emotions skyrocketed out of control, even as I sat there quietly absorbing the information laid at my door. Anger, empathy, anger again, frustration, panic, back to anger – they all tore at me. And then, finally - disappointment. I was disgusted at her behaviour. How could she do this? When did it happen? How long had it been going on? What did she think she was doing? She was in her thirties - not a silly teenager!

"I understand." I raised my right hand to silence her. "Who is the father?" I asked.

"You know I can't tell you that."

"How far gone are you?"

"Three months now. So I wish to leave today before I begin to show. I don't want to be here when they start talking about me."

"Will you be moving in with the dad?"

"No. He doesn't know."

"Great. What a way to begin your life in the outside world."

"Please don't make this harder than it is. Don't you think I'm scared enough already?"

"Where will you be staying?"

"I found a small place in Cambridge."

That better explains all the visits to Cambridge. I reached inside my desk drawer and took out my cheque book.

"What are you doing?" she asked.

"I am supporting you and the baby." The solitary feeling in me now was compassion, plus love towards the only daughter I had ever known.

"You don't have to. Maria has given me a lot of money."

"Well, then - God bless her. You can start counting your blessings." I wrote her a cheque for ten thousand pounds. "I hope this will help also." I handed the piece of paper to her. If only she was aware of inheriting all that I owned anyway, then the reluctance to accept my money wouldn't have occurred.

"Thank you." She reached out, took the paper from my hand and then began to cry. I swiftly got up, walked around the desk and pulled her to me, crying with her. "Just promise me one thing," I sniffled.

"Anything, Reverend Mother." She sounded like the child she always was.

"That this time you will be happy. You will try to forget the past - if not for you, then for your baby."

She simply nodded.

"Can I come and visit you?"

"I think I'd die if you didn't." We were both smiling now. "Will you tell everyone once I'm gone?"

"Not the details, but they should know you are no longer a nun."

"Thank you. I better be going now. My taxi is waiting."

As she reached out to twist the door knob and open the door, I spoke before I could think.

"It's Romilly, isn't it?" I saw her back stiffen and watched as she pushed the door to without leaving the room. She did not turn around and look at me. She just stood there. And that was all the confirmation I needed.

"How did you know about him?" Her voice was a painful, almost silent whisper.

I walked up to her and gently turned her around to face me. She smelled of Estée Lauder's *Beautiful*, entangled as it was with female perspiration. Coming to me must have been very difficult for her.

"I think everyone saw the chemistry between you two. It was very obvious that you liked each other. You couldn't keep your eyes off him. And neither could he, off you."

"Why didn't you say anything?"

"One must never interfere with matters of the heart. Even God himself is love."

"But our sin…"

"A sin is only a sin when you make it so. Your baby is a beautiful blessing from Heaven. Thank goodness God doesn't judge us the way we judge ourselves."

"I love Romilly so much, Mother."

"All will work out well in the end, my child. All you need to do is believe with all your might and soul that happiness will come to you." I drew her close and planted a kiss on her forehead.

I suddenly did not feel like attending the meeting with the church elders and so I sent a message advising them that I felt tired. It was to do with the trip to Lourdes which I didn't feel like going on now anyway. And they wouldn't begrudge an old lady such a prerogative. There was, however, a letter in my desk that I hadn't yet read which had arrived that morning. I intended to read it later, but realised it was from the Vatican and so felt its urgency; something telling me it had a lot to do with Romilly and nothing to do with the Pope.

My fingers tore through the white, velvety Vatican seal. I then unfolded the letter and began to read.

"Dear Reverend Mother Mary Thérése,

It is with sadness and disappointment that I must inform you that Father Romilly Vanderbelt will not be returning to your parish. Unfortunately, he was stabbed by an unknown criminal a few days ago, shortly after resigning from the priesthood. He is currently in critical care and we have been instructed by his doctors that he has very little chance of surviving.

We will keep you updated in due course.

Yours faithfully

Father Paul Dimitri,

Vatican City

Roma."

I read the letter again and again, until it felt wet in my hands, eventually realising that my own tears were the reason why. Poor Romilly - so handsome, so kind, so full of life. Poor Iman - eagerly awaiting her one true love, not knowing that his life hung by a thread. I would not tell her. I *could not* tell her.

I walked towards the roaring fire and threw the letter in. I then poured myself a large glass of sherry.

Chapter 20

Romilly

I woke up slowly, not to daylight as one would expect, but to the darkness of my own room; except, it didn't *look* like any room that I had been in before.

I tried to sit up, but the sharp feeling inside my left ribcage made me cry out in pain. It was only then that I realised there was someone else with me.

"Padre. Oh caro, Padre Padre, sei sveglio. Gloria a Dion el piu alto."

The voice of Pedro, at that exact moment, was like a homecoming. I wanted to embrace him with all the love in my heart, but I couldn't move and had no recollection of what had led me here.

My bedside lamp flickered and then came on, enabling me to see Pedro's face.

"Father, you are awake. We have been so worried, Gloria and I. I sent her home as she has barely left your side. We have been taking turns."

"Pedro - what is going on? Where am I?" I wasn't sure that my words reflected what I wanted to say clearly enough. My head felt impossibly heavy, and so did my legs and arms - not easily shifting under the covers. It was a weakness that I had never known.

"You don't remember *anything*?" His voice was hoarse as he looked at me intently, searching for signs on my face that I might recollect *something*.

"Don't speak too much, Father. I shall get the doctor. I am to call them in immediately when you wake up."

"Please, don't leave me just yet. I feel scared."

"Romilly, please do not be scared. Let me get the doctor." He tore himself from me and hurriedly left the room. It was only then that I heard the sound of the monitor bleeping near my ears, as my eyes were drawn to the polystyrene-tiled ceiling and nothing else.

My mind began to search for reasons and thought of the dream that I'd just woken up from. I felt a pull, redirecting me back to it. And I started to search like a computer until I found it, while lying in my hospital bed.

I then realised - I was supposed to be dead. But I wasn't. I had been spared once more.

Oh, my God - Mama. I had been with her. She was old and beautiful, and she asked me to leave. What happened to me? I tried to get up again, but my legs were too heavy.

I heard footsteps. A tall, black man walked in, followed by Pedro and a female nurse.

"Well, Father Vanderbelt - so glad to see you awake." His Italian was flawless.

"What happened to me?"

"Don't you recall anything? You were attacked in Venice."

"Attacked? By whom?"

Even before I finished asking the question, it was as if the word Venice triggered a single memory in my brain. And then it all started to come back.

Ciara.

The doctor explained what had happened, but all I could think of was Ciara, my mama, my death, my hospital bed and Iman; the amazing women in my life. One had given birth to me, one had tried to kill me, and the other was the love of my life. My darling Iman - she would surely have given up by now. Nobody could wait that long for another.

"How long have I been here?" I asked.

"A little over three months. We noticed that you were healing nicely, but just not waking up - so we decided to give you time. I am delighted to see we made the right decision."

So am I. I did the maths in my head. From the moment I left England for my uncle's funeral, to the endless months in Rome, and then onto Venice where I almost got killed, up until this very moment. It seemed like just over a year to me. She definitely would have forgotten all about me.

"How long will you keep me here? I feel fine."

"No you don't." He smiled kindly at me. "A few days. Maybe two or three weeks. Your wound has healed nicely, but you will need physiotherapy for the pain in your ribs. And you have been in bed for some time, so take it easy on yourself."

"My rucksack. Do you have it? It contained all my personal belongings."

"It's in the safe, Father. The nurse will bring you all your items now that you are awake."

"Thank you so much, Doctor, for helping me."

"You're very welcome. Now, you must rest."

I watched him leave, with the beautiful nurse in tow. The bleeping on the monitor was distracting. How was I supposed to sleep with such noise? And the smell of disinfectant in my room was so pungent that I wanted to run. Another two to three weeks, he said. God help me!

"Father - how are you feeling? Are you okay?" He looked genuinely concerned. Bless Pedro and his wonderful, kind heart.

"Yes. I'm actually fine. It's just that my arms and legs feel heavy. Is there something else wrong with me that the doctor forgot to mention?" I had missed most of what the doctor had told me. I was too busy thinking about Iman.

"No, Father. I think you are suffering from the side effects of the drugs. And you have been unconscious for a *long* time, so your muscles must be tight."

I nodded at what I believed to be true, but suddenly felt uneasy. I needed to ask Pedro about his sister-in-law, yet was scared what answer might come back.

"I need to ask you a question, Pedro. I had a dream about Ciara. Where is she? Have you heard from her?"

Pedro started to shake his head as he took the seat next to my bed. He then buried his head in his hands and began to moan. I had forgotten how dramatic and demonstrative the Italians could be, so I allowed him his histrionics.

"Father, it was very sad. That day was the worst day of my life. First we got a call at the Vatican about your unfortunate incident and then, later that afternoon, we received a message about a lady that had committed suicide. It was Ciara. She jumped into the Tiber and killed herself. How could she do that? *Why* would she do that? And you - what were you doing in her café?"

It was obvious that Pedro had no idea that Ciara had stabbed me. The news of her death drained the blood from me instantly. I lay there not knowing *how* to feel, *what* to think, or *how* to comfort my friend. I felt incredibly sorry for the woman who had fallen in love with me so helplessly, and whose love I had failed to return.

"It was all my fault, Pedro. I'm so sorry for your loss." I had to tell him. I could not live with myself otherwise.

"What do you mean, Father? How could it be your fault? You were on your death bed when Ciara threw herself in the river. It had nothing to do with you."

"I broke her heart, Pedro."

"You are a priest. What business do you have breaking hearts?" Pedro began to look at me suspiciously. "What happened to the young man that I have cared for all these years? What did you do?"

"I'm so sorry, Pedro." I could not hold back the tears of regret and pain that began to flow down my face as I confessed all my sins to him. I held nothing back. I told him the whole truth. How I had fallen for Ciara's charms, how we had been involved in a secret fantasy, and then - how I had fallen for another woman and resigned from the priesthood. I did not tell him I had been stabbed by Ciara. I did not want Ciara's family members to ever think of her that way.

"I need to know. Was it Ciara that stabbed you in her café? Because that is where you were found unconscious."

One beat.

"Is that why she killed herself? Because she thought you were dead?"

I started to shake my head in denial, as the tears continued to flow freely and shamefully down my face, subduing the pain in my ribs.

Pedro's skin was as white as a ghost. And I saw in his face a look of disappointment, anger and pain.

"I shall go home now and tell Gloria all that you have told me. I don't think I ever want to see you again. Goodbye, my friend."

He did not visit me again at the hospital. And I knew that I had lost a friend. I also knew that I deserved it.

Why did doing the right thing have to hurt so much? My heart bled for Ciara, and her death tormented me each night in that hospital room. When I closed my eyes, I saw her running towards me with the knife. I knew I needed therapy, but I think I needed Baba Aarush more.

He always said that whenever or *if ever* I felt that hope was lost, the only thing I needed to do was give love.

And so, I started by giving myself love, in order to be strong enough to give it to others. The will to give my love to others is what prompted me to start meditating again and practising yoga…in my hospital room as soon as I could move.

I began to focus on all that I wanted to do and the people I wanted to help. I thought about them ceaselessly. I planned it all in my mind. Then I wrote it all down. I then applied for an African visa. I was lucky - the visa arrived before I was discharged from the hospital.

After my discharge, I wanted to visit Pedro and Gloria, but decided against it. Ciara's death would still be fresh in everyone's mind and it was therefore best to let time pass. Maybe one day, they would forgive me. Maybe one day too, I would find a way to forgive myself.

On my last day at the hospital, I thanked the staff for looking after me, and handed them a cheque for €1,000. I wanted them to go out for dinner, on me. I then got the next flight to Nigeria.

My trip to Nigeria was to fulfil a need inside of me that had grown so large I thought it would explode my soul into little pieces if I did not indulge it.

I needed to see the little girl, Imo, again. I wanted to do everything in my power to help her, her family and her community. I didn't know what lay ahead for me. I didn't know how much longer I would be given. And so it was important that I fulfilled my soul's mission. I needed to contribute my finer side to humanity. In doing so, I could – perhaps - derive a tiny bit of peace and maybe balance things for all the people I had hurt during my lifetime.

Ciara especially.

They were surprised to see me again and had not been expecting me. They cooked and danced, and I sat under the moonlight like before, telling stories. I had almost forgotten what it was like to be with them. I was still suffering inside, yet tried to hold it in - choosing instead to devote all my energy into doing what I had come here for.

I stayed in Nigeria for seven months in the same rural village that had accepted me two years earlier. I helped build a school for the children with the finest materials. I opened an educational trust for Imo, so that she would be able to attend university, study and become all that she wanted to be. Each of us worked together, transforming hut after hut into little houses - upgrading them so that they resembled houses in the city. My reward was the look on their faces. The men wanted to adopt me. And the women wanted to feed me. They still called me Father, not knowing I was no longer a priest. I thought it best not to disappoint them. I only wanted them to be happy. And them being happy made me feel good inside.

Once more I had to leave them, this time fully aware I would likely never see them again. But life had taught me that one must never say never.

I had one more journey to fulfil before returning to *mon coeur* in England – a memorable trip back to India. I needed Baba Aarush more than ever. I needed his shoulder to cry on. I needed him to revitalise my soul. But alas, Baba Aarush was no longer alive. I was told that he had passed away just a week before I arrived. And so, I was left on my own. His death, though, was part of a beautiful story.

He had cooked a meal for the whole community, fed everyone and distributed all his goods to the poor; what little material things he had, for he was a spirit as far as I was concerned, floating amongst us in a body. Finally, he visited each home with greetings and well wishes, before retiring to his own abode just after midnight.

Legend or myth recalled him meditating all night in his bedroom, after asking his fellow monks not to disturb him. And when the sun came up, Baba left this world.

Nabhitha, one of the nuns that lived in his home and who had helped to look after me, came to see me in my room.

"Father."

"Romilly - please. I do not go by that title anymore."

"Oh, why not?"

I just looked at her and I guess my eyes said all that she needed to know.

"Baba always said that you would come back one last time."

"He did? How did he know?"

"The wise one always knew. He left something for you. Wait here - I shall get it." She floated out of the room, like a feather, leaving me bewildered.

Minutes later, she appeared with an easel, canvas and set of paint brushes, art pencils and watercolours.

"What is this?" My eyes began to well up. It occurred to me that I had cried more in the past few weeks than I had done in my entire life.

"He said it is time - the beginning of your becoming."

She watched as I sat back down on my bed - head buried in my palms, crying like a baby; all the emotions of art that I had suppressed now bowling over me. There was no greater kindness given to me than the one I experienced at that precise moment. I cried not only for me, but because I would not see Baba again in this life (the one who had altered my whole existence).

Returning to India had felt like a wasted effort initially, due to Baba's death. I now knew such thoughts to be mistaken though.

"He said you will know what to do. He said to begin at the cave." She brought both palms together, as if in the form of a prayer signalling her departure.

"Namaste," I replied to her, bringing my own palms together as well.

Baba Aarush had explained to me the reason behind that gesture. It was to recognise and acknowledge the god that existed in every human being, and in doing so, it was easy to obey the greatest Law of Christ: to love thy neighbour as thyself. How could one accomplish this, Baba asked, without understanding and remembering the god that existed in everyone? This way it would be easy to show respect, to give compassion, to be kind to every human being, striving to be the best that we possibly could.

I remembered a flash of words from my mama: "You are limitless. You are god."

Then the dream began to make sense.

My next stop was the cave by the sea - the place that had hosted my very first meditation lesson and where my healing had begun. This time, I needed a different type of healing. I needed to forgive myself for Ciara's death and move on from the past.

The cave was really no different from the last time I'd seen it. It was as if no one had been in it since then. I looked around, trying to remember the way I had felt - how fragile I had been upon first coming here. I was sure that I was going to die, but a new thought process had changed all that. I had been completely healed, and it had taken me only three weeks to reach such a state.

Now, I was here for a different kind of healing - like a man trapped in a house, held hostage for a very long time; unable to leave the house because being held hostage was all he knew. And then, he woke up one day and realised that there was a new world outside - one he desperately wanted to experience. But in order for him to leave that house, he would have to break down an iron door. And rupturing an iron door was no small task. In fact, it was close to impossible. Unless, of course, one came to realise that nothing in life is impossible. After accomplishing such a thing with 100% determination and unwavering belief, a new task presented itself before him. He now had to find a way to adapt - to live in the new world that he'd fought so hard to enter.

I was like that man - trying to break down the iron door.

I stayed in the cave for three days, eating nothing and drinking nothing. It was important for me to feel the pain I was carrying in my heart, for it was recent and inescapable. The stabbing, the suicide, the loss of my former life, the love that I was yet to see - I needed God to tell me that everything was okay, that He was still with me.

I had brought a few things with me to the cave: my Bible, my notebook from Baba's lessons and my painting kit. When I was not praying and meditating, I was practising yoga and painting. I painted the cave in all its glory and it surprised me how easily the brush sat between my fingers - how effortlessly my canvas came alive. Such an endeavour filled my heart with long-lost joy and I knew then, very clearly, that this was my destiny.

At the end of the three days, I had destroyed the iron door. And I knew what to do, what to *be*.

Chapter 21

Reverend Mother Mary Thérése Williamson

I secretly preferred this month to the other months of the year. And there were many reasons why. The leaves, although not blossoming like in spring time, bowed gracefully in preparation for the next season; their colours blending shyly with the early darkness that colonised daytime. The cold weather crept into my old bones, but did not hinder me while I walked in the Cotswold hills. And Halloween, I adored, but as a nun could not openly worship, unlike my dear Iman.

Seeing her yesterday was ample proof of how well she had adapted to life outside the church. And her little girl, I swear, was the prettiest baby in the world. It was undeniable that Romilly was the father, for she carried with her those beautiful, green eyes; the ones that Romilly had unknowingly tormented the congregation with. Thinking of the child filled my heart with sadness and joy. The poor child might never know her father. And yet, Iman hadn't stopped believing that he would return, even after raising their child alone for almost two years now.

It was over a year ago since I had thrown the letter from the Vatican into the fire. I had hoped that I would be able to tell Iman about it one day, but the more time passed the more difficult it became. And so, in the end, I did nothing - and said nothing. And as there was no further correspondence from Rome, I unquestioningly feared the worst. Sometimes it was better *not* knowing - especially if the truth was unpleasant.

Iman had surprisingly blossomed into a woman, which I never thought possible. She looked happier and radiant - so full of life, music and laughter. I made the effort of visiting her at least once a month - sometimes twice - as it was impossible to stay away for long, having met her child and fallen hopelessly in love with her.

Iman's scars now appeared old - not fresh as they were in the convent.

It had bothered and concerned me at first, upon her leaving, but there was now no doubt in my mind that Iman was living her true life's purpose. Her daughter I secretly called my grandchild, for Iman had been kind enough to make me the girl's godmother at the christening; a christening that was attended by just the three of us: Maria, Iman and myself. It was better that way, as church members could be unforgiving – thriving off gossip. Iman was strong though - always smiling, always showing love to everyone and everything. Her face radiated love so easily, and this was evident in her eyes, how she looked at people she was conversing with.

There was love for her garden - the way she looked after it, maintaining its beauty with dedication and hard work; love for her home - the beautiful, heart-shaped twigs that she adorned it with, plus pictures of her little, gorgeous girl. Iman took pictures of her girl everywhere they went and placed such memories all over the house.

"Not only for me, but for Romilly, so that when he comes home he won't have missed a thing," she lovingly expressed on one of my visits.

Her faith in him knew no bounds.

I remember once walking up to her as she tilled the soil in her garden - her little girl sat nearby on a picnic blanket, sucking on bright red strawberries. I could hear her talking, but couldn't make out the words. As I got closer, I heard the tail end of her sentence.

"Thank you, Father, for bringing Romilly back home to us."

"Is Romilly here?" I couldn't help but blurt out. I must have made her jump.

"Oh, Reverend Mother," she started to laugh, "I didn't see you there." She rushed towards me and adorned me with a warm embrace; the type she gave so generously to everyone. "No, he's not, but he will be. That's why I was giving thanks to God."

"I hope you're not disappointed, my dear."

"O ye, of little faith. Blessed are those who do not see and yet believe."

"A wise quote," I replied, for indeed our Lord Jesus said the exact same thing to His followers. Who was I to doubt the strong faith that Iman carried around with her like a visible halo.

Gone were the days when she walked around in solemn silence. Gone were the days when she looked lost and confused. This new person was slowly becoming who she was supposed to be. And the transformation had given her a brand new childhood; her stolen childhood suddenly replaced. This new woman was unlike other women. She didn't scowl. She never moaned. With her, everything was okay - the world was perfect.

I remember the conversation we once had in her garden, after Maria decided that she missed her friend too much. We therefore baked cakes and went over to Iman's for afternoon tea. Iman could never refuse a lovely piece of cake.

"I don't understand why people say no one is perfect, Reverend Mother. Of course we are all perfect. How can we not be, when perfection lies within us?"

"Would you say the same about murderers and paedophiles?" Maria boldly interjected.

I remained silent, waiting to hear how my beautiful daughter would reply.

"They have simply lost their way. This does not mean that they can't find their way back to the perfection that lies within them."

Iman managed to see the good in everyone. I was proud of her, and loved her with all my heart.

It was over two years now since she'd resigned from the convent - our life, our world – yet she had slowly transformed herself. Whilst still pregnant, she joined an art and craft club in Cambridge. There she learnt how to knit, crochet, make greeting cards and home decorations. She created each pretty, hanging decoration in her cottage with her own hands. And because she was afraid of running out of money, she started an online shop for her art creations, naming it *Romiman Products*. This way, she said, he would be part of everything.

I did not understand where she found the time to make all her creations. When she wasn't tending to her little girl, she was working in the garden or knitting a jumper. She had no real friends apart from Maria and myself. She made hanging love hearts, Christmas and Easter cards, and knitted me so many scarves that I ended up donating some to the nearby hospice, unwilling to indulge myself.

"Oh, Reverend Mother - I made them for *you*. I'll make some for the hospice too if you promise to keep yours."

Sometimes I felt she needed me to keep an eye on her finances, for I feared she would give all her money away and be left with nothing. When I asked how much she made from the online shop, I was surprised at her reply though.

"About £800 a month, after tax - enough for me to pay my bills and feed us."

"Well, thank God for Maria and myself," I chipped in teasingly.

"On a more serious note," she said, between giggles, "I hope to pay you both back someday…when my business takes off."

"I noticed that you didn't say if - you said *when*."

"I have faith in my abilities, Reverend Mother. There is no room for self-doubt."

~~~

Today, I felt so tired. I would not do any real walking. I simply wanted to read and so visited our local library. The library seemed full of books by new authors I hadn't heard of. Children pottered around
~~~

with their parents, but they were not the noisy ones; I think each mother strived to be the loudest. Did they not understand library etiquette? I reminded myself to be patient with people - not everywhere could be as quiet as the convent.

I left the library without having found what I wanted, and both endured and enjoyed the slow walk back to the convent, as the morning chill crept over my skin, making me shiver, giving me goosebumps.

I wanted the old classics: Thomas More; Chinua Achebe; Virginia Woolf; Rabindranath Tagore; Jane Austen; Alfred Lord Tennyson.

I took out *Utopia* from my collection. Today, I would settle in my office and read it all day. I had it all planned - lots and lots of tea as I luxuriated in my book. No disturbances, no lectures from Reverend Father, no complaints from the nuns. I was going to lock myself away.

Just after lunch I retreated, yet heard a knock on my office door, even though I had specifically discouraged such approaches today and hung out a 'Do Not Disturb' sign.

"It's my day off," I asserted jokingly. Usually, when I said something like this, the nuns would giggle and come in anyway. This time, however, I heard nothing.

The knock came again.

"Come in," I answered, putting on my professional, motherly voice, unsure who was behind the door. But before the door was opened, I suddenly sensed who it was. I recognised that knock. Only one person knocked like that. It was an unusual way of knocking which made it distinct.

It was a simple knock - just one rap. No volley of knocks followed. I could feel my heart racing. Was this really happening? Could it really be him? Or was my mind playing tricks on me? Maybe the person behind the door had knocked more than once, but I had simply not heard.

He walked in boldly, but quietly. He seemed a little unsure of himself and - if my eyes didn't betray me – a tad nervous.

I dropped *Utopia* on my desk and looked at the man standing in front of me - the one who had somehow managed to survive; the one who had a woman and child waiting for him; the one who was no longer a priest.

All at once, the world felt like a much better place.

And a smile broke out across my thin, worn-out face.

Chapter 22

Romilly

There are circles everywhere, and there are sparkling lights in my darkness that I choose to ignore.

The darkness of the room is blacker than the night sky, and it's like no other kind of darkness. There are people in here with me. I can sense them, hear them, feel them.

They are hiding and this induces a feeling in me to hide too. I am okay in my darkness until the people in the room begin to speak.

They say they are coming. I do not know who is coming.

"Don't let them see you," they say. "Hide away from them - they are coming."

I suddenly hear footsteps, so I hide behind what feels like a table.

The door opens and the sound of footsteps draw closer. I feel fearful and see a tiny light.

The light is emanating from my stomach. No, please stop - don't do that. They will see me if you shine too bright.

The light ignores me and shines even brighter. I do not think to cover the light. The thought never occurs to me. I do not speak. I cannot speak. I can only think. But because of the light, I see the one that has opened the door. I see the one that has seen me because of the light.

She is lovely, blonde, beautiful. She has the most angelic smile and she giggles like a school girl in love.

She also giggles like a mother to a newborn baby. She is not my mother. And she is not like any woman that I have ever seen.

I suddenly feel a chill. I am shivering all over. My body is shaking like a naked, charged-up, electric string dipped in cold water, but this is stronger than electricity. It is like a fever, but stronger than a fever. My body is vibrating so much that I wish to be electrocuted instead, as that would be more gentle.

She walks towards me and although she is still giggling, she is full of empathy for my condition.

"Awww, it's okay. It's okay, my darling." Her voice is different. It has a metallic tune. She sounds like the birds that wake me up in Rome at the beginning of spring. But her singing voice has words. She is like the sun, the moon, the stars, the birds, the lion, the sea, the sand, the clouds.....she is like everything good. She is like love on legs, with sunny golden hair. I am at her mercy. I think she has the power to make this stop.

My ears begin to chime. I have heard this sound before, but only when meditating. It is a high-frequency sound and is always mellow, always gentle. Right now, however, it is louder than my ears can take. It is too strong for me; it is too strong for my head. I know that in a few seconds the loud sound will cause my head to explode, for no human ear can withstand such noise.

The closer she moves towards me, the louder the noise in my ears. The closer she gets to me, the more intensely my body vibrates.

It is becoming uncontrollable and I think I must die to make it stop.

"It's okay, awww, it's okay. I'm here now. I'm here."

She touches my leg and I awake.

The vibration stops, along with the noise.

The train stops, at Foxton Station, and I leap out.

I am slightly overwhelmed by the dream. But something tells me now that I am not alone - that I have never been alone. And although I am scared of facing Iman, for I know not whether she will accept me, I do know - without any doubt - that she is the one for me, and I, the one for her.

I am not alone. I was never alone.

Chapter 23

Iman

Okay, I'm only human, right? I mean, I'm getting tired of waiting. But not during any moment in all my life have I felt so strongly about something, even when all the signs point in the opposite direction. How much faith can one have? I know God is fond of testing my patience, but this is too long. Will my little girl grow up without ever having the chance to meet her dad?

People think I'm creative and smart. They think I fill up my days with activities.

Today, for instance, I have already mapped out and planned what we will do. I do not care about the weather - come rain or shine, we play, run and walk. And my baby never complains. It's as if she was born to be British.

I made candles for my garden lanterns. Reverend Mother once told me about her trip to Japan. She spoke about a long walk that she had undertaken in Mount Takao, just outside of Tokyo. She said the thing that remained memorable to her had been the lanterns…in every path, of every garden, no matter what the weather. Well, I couldn't imagine the candles staying alight under heavy rain, but I supposed that's why lanterns were made.

I wanted my garden to look like that in the autumn, so that I could sit with my baby and tell her African folk stories - the ones I heard being told to other children when I was a child.

My fake mother thought I was washing up the dishes, or that I had gone to get some wood for the fire. Oh no, I would sneak behind the mango tree and listen to the old folks tell the most amazing stories; my favourite story of all being *Ali Baba and the Forty Thieves*. I had heard so many versions of that story that I couldn't wait to get the book for myself. But I had to wait, because my fake mother did not believe in girls filling up their heads with fiction. All she cared about was me finding a way to pay for the food we both ate (clothes being a bonus). The hand-me-down clothes from other children were just enough.

My little girl would never wear hand-me-down clothes. She would have the very best that I could afford. She would never have to endure child labour like her mother did. She would be allowed to remain a child for as long as she wanted, without an overzealous adult snatching such a gift away. She would not be introduced to men at an early age in order to put food on the table. Her studies and social activities would be her only concerns.

Amidst the luxury of my thoughts, I noticed that my baby girl had fallen asleep. Her pram provided a safe haven underneath the late morning, autumn sun. She would be secure there, napping cutely, while I raked the garden and cleaned up the beautiful, brown leaves.

I heard the sound of my little iron gate. I wasn't expecting anybody. Maria and Reverend Mother had a way of pleasantly surprising me, but today was Sunday, so it could not be them, for they would be busily engaged in church activities. It was the same routine each Sunday, depending on which Mass they attended; a routine which broke up the day.

After Mass would be the Legion of Mary meeting, then lunch preparation for students and the homeless. By the time it was over, it would almost be evening Mass. There was no way on earth that they could be with me on a Sunday.

I walked towards the gate - mobile phone in hand in case it was an intruder. I had no reason to be scared where I lived, but one must never be too comfortable or complacent.

The first thing I noticed was his shadow, so I was sure it was a man or a tall woman with a manly build. I stopped in my tracks, waiting for him to proceed further. My clock tower chose that exact moment to alert me that it was now twelve noon. My little girl – light sleeper that she was - would be awake soon for her lunch.

The soft, incessant voices and laughter of my neighbours failed to drown out the chiming clock. I strained my ears to try and listen to or gauge the person walking towards me, but the autumn leaves began rustling softly, adding to the cacophony of sound.

He then emerged into full view.

I must have stopped breathing for a second or more - my heartbeat so loud that I could hear it. His familiar cologne - how could I forget it; the wind dutifully carrying his scent my way.

His face broke into a smile. And at that moment, nothing in the world mattered - apart from him, apart from now.

My legs stopped moving just as his pace quickened. He looked slightly older, with a few lines around his eyes. His legs seemed leaner in his black, skinny jeans and his grey jumper was unable to hide the fact that he had lost a few pounds. He was always a healthy weight though. In fact, I don't recall him ever having excess weight on him. Somehow, he looked so svelte - his face longer and thinner, his cheek bones more visible, his eyes healthy and bright, so that the green around his pupils glittered under the sunshine.

He was standing in front of me now, looking at me - his hands on my face, caressing me slowly. I wanted to speak, to ask him where he'd been. I wanted to scream, jump and dance. I wanted to punch him, cry and ask him to leave.

But all I did was gently close my eyes at the feel of his skin on my face. His touch brought Heaven and butterflies. His presence brought an unwavering peace and happiness so true that all I could do was stay silent.

Suddenly, we were interrupted by crying and a child's voice shouting "Mama! Mama!"

"Oh, my God - where is she?" he asked.

He knew. How else could he have known where I lived? Mother Mary Thérése.

I had tears in my eyes. I could not trust myself to speak, and so I simply took his hand and walked us past the rose bushes to the willow tree where our little girl sat in her pram, looking confused without her mummy.

I ran to her and picked her up.

"Hey, baby, it's okay - I'm here," I cooed with my baby voice. "There's someone I'd like you to meet. Your papa. Say hello to Papa."

I could almost sense what he was feeling at that moment. He could not take his eyes off her.

"And what's your name, gorgeous girl?" he asked, as he scooped her off me into a warm embrace. She surprisingly fell into his arms, like she had been waiting for him all this time.

"Marie-Ange," the little girl replied.

His face was full of tender sadness. He looked at me with flowers in his eyes.

"Are you here to stay?" I asked. For me, that was the most important question. Everything else could wait, but I would not let Marie-Ange fall in love with a man who chose the priesthood over her.

"If you will both have me, for I have nowhere else to go. Can your home be my home?" His eyes pleaded with me not to turn him away.

"My home has always been your home, mon coeur," I replied.

"We'll talk about everything later, for there's much to discuss. For now, come you two - let's go and sit in the light."

All three of us held hands and walked in the direction of the sun's rays - eventually sitting in joyful silence watching Marie-Ange run in circles, chasing the pretty butterflies.

THE END